HOT PTERO-DACTYL BOY -FRIEND

HOT PTERO- DACTYL BOY -FRIEND

ALAN CUMYN

SIMON & SCHUSTER

First published in Great Britain in 2016 by Simon & Schuster UK Ltd
A CBS COMPANY

Originally published in the USA in 2016 by Atheneum BFYR
an imprint of Simon & Schuster Children's Publishing Division,
1230 Avenue of Americas, New York, NY 10020

3 5 7 9 10 8 6 4 2

Simon & Schuster UK Ltd
1st Floor, 222 Gray's Inn Road
London
WC1X 8HB

www.simonandschuster.co.uk

Simon & Schuster Australia, Sydney
Simon & Schuster India, New Delhi

A CIP catalogue record for this book is available from the British Library.

PB ISBN 978-1-4711-4467-7
eBook ISBN 978-1-4711-4468-4

Printed and bound by CPI Group (UK) Ltd, Croydon, CR0 4YY

MIX
Paper from
responsible sources
FSC® C020471

Simon & Schuster UK Ltd are committed to sourcing paper that is made from
wood grown in sustainable forests and support the Forest Stewardship Council,
the leading international forest certification organisation. Our books displaying
the FSC logo are printed on FSC certified paper.

For Gwen and Anna, who rock

Half the absurdities of life we don't even see, they are so on our own noses. The other half—that's your life, baby.

—Lorraine Miens

1

It started as a speck in the east, a hint of black that might easily have been a crow. The sky was full of crows in late September, crows by the thousands with their squawking, nervy calls, the way they would mass on a stand of leaf-losing trees, a fractured black cloud of them. It might've been a lone crow, and maybe that was why Shiels turned her head and looked up.

She was stepping out of Mr. Postlethwaite's portable classroom, his forgettable English class, already checking her text messages. Autumn Whirl was less than ten days away, and the band was not yet chosen. Rebecca Sterzl was never going to get a handle on that committee. Shiels would have to step in herself, but how to do it deftly, without setting off a bomb? She needed Rebecca to function still for lesser duties. And then . . . a speck. Maybe a crow? No reason to even look. But she did.

Was it before, or just after, that a worm in her gut bit her? It was such an odd feeling. An organ pain, almost, from something inside, sleeping somewhere—her plumbing perhaps—about which she had been completely unaware. It had never bitten her before. There was no reason to pay attention.

The speck got larger. Even from a great distance it seemed possible to tell that the wings were not usual. They arched and seemed, somehow, blacker than crows' wings, and became larger even though the speck was not heading directly her way but moving in a zigzag. Then the wings weren't actually black but a sort of metallic purple. Royal, maybe, or what a truly harsh band might wear at a three a.m. blast with spook lights and a lot of stage smoke.

That's one face-rake of a bird, she thought—"face-rake" being the term that Sheldon had invented, having stepped on a rake a few weeks before.

Zig, zag. North-south, north-south. How to explain this weirdness to Sheldon? For three years they had shared news of everything fractured. Like the parakeet impersonating a baby on the bus, the video of which he had texted her, with commentary. And Principal Manniberg's hair loss pills, which he had left out on his desk for Shiels to see, as plain as day, and which she had told Sheldon about later when they'd been hacking into the student newspaper blog because they'd lost the admin password and they were the only ones who knew it.

Or used to know it.

They shared everything.

Now Sheldon wasn't here, he was tutoring math lab in the south basement, so she had to be aware of every oddity for him, especially how the whole crowd of students simply seemed to know at the same time to cock their heads and gaze out over the sports field, the track. But the football players didn't look. They were all smashing into the tackle dummies and whatever else football players smashed into. The cross-country runners were on the track. They didn't look either, but kept running in little clumps of legginess. Shiels was only vaguely aware of them in the first few moments.

More than twenty kids were standing with their books and backpacks, and their skimpy blouses and short skirts, with bare legs or thin pants—everyone shivering. Probably five were standing exactly like Shiels, with phones out, supposedly checking the world. But the world was forgotten.

One freaking huge royal purple non-crow was cutting a path through the gray sky to their little patch of green.

"Holy crackers," someone said.

Zig to the north. Zag to the south. Not a bite, now, in Shiels's gut—if that was what it was. Something else. Something worse.

She wasn't feeling any part of the cold wind.

Her phone fell out of her hand and bonked onto the hard old pavement. As she bent to pick it up, she thought:

Martians could be landing, and I would still bend to pick up my phone.

The purple thing, "it"—*he*—was sharp in many places. That was becoming clear. Sharp in the cool angle of his wings—God, those wings!—and sharp in his gaze, in the way he looked them all over as he passed.

He stared right at her with huge, dark, ancient eyes. She flushed from the roots of her hair. It was as if a switch had been flicked to percolate.

He circled round—like a gymnast on iron rings, rippled purple muscles in a chest made for flying. Was that when she dropped her phone?

Did she drop her phone again?

A beast with wings circling, circling. And that spear of a nose. Shiels saw, like everyone else, exactly what he was going for—Jocelyne Legault, with her bouncing blond ponytail, oblivious to the danger. Those skinny, white, tireless legs in her yellow shoes with her pumping little stick arms, rail-like shoulders, boobless torso—her impossible body, really, kept impossible by her daily hours of leg-lung workouts around and around that dreary track.

"Jocelyne!" Shiels cried out. It was in her nature to act, as difficult as it was to shake off the stupefying sight of an ancient predator suddenly appearing high above the athletic complex. "Jocelyne!" Others, too, awakened, yelled to the cross-country champion. How many races had she won over the years? But she was modest to a fault. The only way she could possibly justify spending all those hours alone chugging around would be to win an Olympic gold medal in something. Was there even an Olympic event for cross-country running? Possibly not. She was a tiny, robotic, overachieving nobody—not Shiels's summation, but rather what was commonly understood in the information cloud of all things Vista View High. Jocelyne Legault could outrun a sweating, grunting, gasping pack of two hundred leggy girls racing through backcountry trails, but she would never get a date to Autumn Whirl—would never break training in the first place. Impossible!

Yet all those social distinctions fell away like mist when the monster circled above her. Her stride did not falter. She was, as ever, alone. Was she sprinting? No, it was just that her regular pace was crushingly quick, so no one could keep up with her, not even the senior boys, who were clumped behind her, possibly lapped already. Jocelyne Legault was in her own universe, as usual, when the dark-eyed, spear-beaked thing circled closer and closer. Obviously aiming for her.

Bob-swish, bob-swish went her tidy blond ponytail.

What was Shiels trying to do, running toward her schoolmate? Did she think she could personally beat back the monster, send him flying off like so many crows squawking around the roadside carcass of a struck raccoon? (Crows were squawking far above, a murder of them, in the old estimation. Shiels knew the word, thought of it briefly as she and the others—others were running now with her—raced to save Jocelyne.)

The gates of the sports field were chained shut, loose enough to let in those on foot, one by one, but tight enough to discourage a bike or motorcycle, and absolutely too narrow to allow a vehicle. As she pushed through the small opening, Shiels thought maybe she should order one of the football players to drive his truck through the locked gate and scare off the purple fiend. Any number of football players drove trucks. The parking lot was adjacent, and probably eight or twelve young jocks would have raced into action if she'd unleashed the order. But the football players were still oddly oblivious to the threat. *If they were an army*, Shiels thought, *we'd be lost in any sudden attack.*

"Hey! Hey! Get off her!" she yelled.

She was through the opening in the chain gate, on the track now, sprinting, her version of a sprint. Her pants were loose enough and her shoes were sensible—she could be fashionable, on a given day, but usually went for comfort, which Sheldon respected.

She was the last person anyone would have expected to lead the charge against an invading beast. A leader in most other ways, yes, of course. But this too? Yet there she was. Others were following, though the football players were only just starting to look around.

"Jocelyne!" Shiels screamed. Finally the runner glanced over her shoulder, as if some competitor might be about to overtake her. The shadow of those wings darkened her face; her eyes lifted, her arm shot up just as the creature crashed into her like a leathery bag of rocks falling from the sky.

Shiels stumbled then too, but over her own feet, and nearly wiped out. When she recovered, the thing—it, *he*—was standing on the track in the north end, near the sprint start line. He had risen up on his skinny reptile legs, and had his wings outstretched—he looked enormous—with beak raised as if about to spear poor fallen Jocelyne Legault.

Shiels glanced around desperately, her mind for a moment full of the possibility that someone on the track might have a javelin she could hurl at the beast. But there was no such thing, all she had was . . . her phone.

She saw the thing brandish its glistening beak, like something out of a hopeless Hollywood movie.

She kept running.

"Leave her alone! Get out of here! Scram!"

Down shrank the menacing beak. In folded the wings. The thing seemed to deflate before her as she approached; it folded up, batlike, until it looked more like a skinny umbrella, reached out improbable little three-fingered wing hands, and drew the crumpled body of Jocelyne Legault to its deeply muscled chest.

His deeply muscled chest.

"What do you think you're doing?" Shiels yelled, as if the thing could talk.

He opened his mouth, one might even say conversationally. She was within striking distance of him now—for him to strike her, run her through with that lance of a beak. But she did not feel afraid.

She was aware of everyone else having stopped many paces away. Even the football squad, decked out in armor practically, was keeping a prudent distance.

"Back off now," Shiels said. "She's just a girl." It was her student-body chair voice, her elected official persona, and in this unusual moment some small part of her actually felt like a "body chair," whatever that might be, a powerful piece of equipment (not furniture, although Sheldon often spun bad puns from the image)—a sturdy instrument of power.

And it—*he*—was somehow a boy too, Shiels thought, as well as a creature. A very odd three-fingered boy with chest muscles rippling up his . . . fascinating purple hide as he lifted the fallen runner, who seemed to have fainted. He held her wrapped in his wings. Shiels thought for a moment he would spring into the air carrying her somehow, yet she could see at once how impossible it would be in the current configuration. He was holding her in his winged arms, which he would need to fly anywhere. His legs had claws too, but he would have to transfer Jocelyne . . .

"Put her down!" Shiels yelled.

He looked at Shiels then, like someone terribly old . . . and improbably wearing, she just now noticed, a backpack. (It was purplish; it blended into his hide.)

The yawning open again of the terrible beak. The thing spoke. "Not zo . . . Engliz yet," he said.

Jocelyne Legault snuggled closer into his muscled chest (how hard does he have to work to fly, Shiels wondered?) like she had never snuggled into anything before in her life.

The crows were scatter-shrieking, thousands of them, it seemed, filling the air.

Shiels knew it, almost all of it, in a moment: that he hadn't come to eat them at all, or attack Jocelyne Legault. No, he was a student—a very strange student, the first of his kind ever to attend Vista View High.

Shiels knew it, yet still she said: "Who are you? What do you think you're doing here?"

Peeking out of his purple backpack was a little pink sheet, a cross-boundary transfer. Shiels recognized the form.

Jocelyne moaned further into the beast's arms.

"Mebbee . . . go nurz?" It was hard to reconcile. The thing standing there. Talking.

"What?" Shiels said.

"Nurz. Nurz!" His beak clicked when he spoke.

Nurse. He knew about school nurses. "Have you been a student before?" Shiels blurted.

Of course he had. The pink sheet was a cross-boundary transfer. Her brain was all gummed up with exactly the sort of thing her intellectual guide, Lorraine Miens, had written about in *Organic Misgivings*—what Miens called "practical/improbable absurdities," the way life constantly surprises us with what we feel at first should not be true, and then accept without question: the round Earth, flying men, text breakups. This thing looked as if it ought to be extinct, nonexistent, yet here it was swaying and unsteady in front of her, carrying documentation.

Probably Manniberg had forgotten to brief her, as usual.

"Follow me!" Shiels turned, and the entire football squad, still many paces back, gave way. She charged, chin down, fists clenched, arms pumping. At the chained gate she whirled again and saw that the thing was having trouble keeping up with her, that he seemed to be staggering to both hold Jocelyne aloft and move forward at the same time.

Her heart jagged, she realized, somehow, she needn't charge anymore; this wasn't about defending the school or anything like that. The beast was struggling, he couldn't actually hold Jocelyne up. She was bleeding at one knee, a nasty scrape. She wasn't unconscious, but she wasn't entirely present, either.

"You're going to have to put her down," Shiels said in as normal a tone of voice as she could find. And then — "Jocelyne, can you stand?"

The creature huddled forward and, with surprising gentleness, rested Jocelyne's feet on the ground. His beak looked razor-sharp, and he had a knifelike crest of sorts angled backward out of his head. And his body was covered in short, fine fur—it glistened. Jocelyne couldn't seem to keep herself from touching it. She leaned and hopped, still clutching him, and the beast hop-hipped—he wasn't entirely comfortable upright—and they all squeezed through the opening.

At the rear entrance of the school Shiels took the pink sheet from his backpack.

"I'm the student-body chair," she said evenly, and tried to look him in the eye, for reassurance. The form, neatly typed, listed a single name: *Pyke*. In the address line was written *Cross-Boundary Transfer* with no previous school listed. Under languages it said *English* and *Pterodactylus*.

"You're a pterodactyl? Your name is Pyke?" Shiels said.

Pyke made a barking sound—his own name? His beak dipped precariously close to Jocelyne's throat.

"How old are you?" she asked.

But Jocelyne was slumping again. Pyke caught her, and Shiels held open the door. As they passed through clumsily, she glanced again at the form. He was eighteen.

Really?

He was coming in practically overage. Another line on the form read *Explanation for lost time: Other commitments*.

The nurse was there. Someone must have told her something exceptional was happening. With only a short, frightened glance at Pyke, she pulled Jocelyne into her office and closed the door. Shiels was left standing alone with the pterodactyl—with Pyke—in the otherwise empty hallway. But a huge crowd was gathered at the doorway, staring in at them.

His torso was heaving.

Those pecs. That fur. It was as if he were a museum exhibit she needed to touch.

But she restrained herself. How to talk to him? "I'm afraid you've made a terrible mistake," she began. His head angle changed. "You've arrived at the end of the school day, not the beginning." His eyes narrowed. "You need to come back at nine o'clock tomorrow, understand?" She held the paper out to him. She hated her hand for shaking, but this was an unusual situation. "And our principal, Mr. Manniberg, can be a stickler for details. You're going to have to do a much better job with your personal information. All right?" As if the mighty Manniberg himself would be a far more terrible adversary.

Ha!

Pyke snatched the sheet in his beak, twisted backward gymnastically, and tucked it into his backpack.

"Where are you from, anyway? What are you doing here?"

When his beak was shut, his jaw naturally curved upward in a devious grin. The light glistened in his eyes.

He turned, and moving on all fours—his wings folded,

umbrella-like—he was at the doors and through in a liquid instant.

The crowd massed there—it looked like half the school—parted quickly enough, but his pink sheet fluttered. Did someone pluck it from his pack? Shiels wasn't sure what she saw. It took a moment to follow him through the doors. That sheet was being passed around while football players laughed and Pyke watched them all with quiet, still eyes.

Shiels's phone throbbed, but there wasn't time. "Give it back!" she yelled at Jeremy Jeffreys, the quarterback, who now held the pink sheet gleefully. "He's going to be a student here, just like you."

Jeffreys scoffed, though in his other hand he held his helmet as if he might need a weapon. "Hey, freshman!" he called to Pyke. "You're eighteen already! What'cha been doing all these years?"

As terrible as Pyke's beak and claws looked, Shiels saw that the crowd could tear him to shreds. If she allowed it.

"He had other commitments," she declared.

A howl of laughter engulfed the group.

"What?" the quarterback chortled. "Fighting off woolly mammoths?"

Shiels grabbed back the pink sheet. "Haven't you ever heard of personal privacy?" She stared down the quarterback until he glanced away. Then she tucked the sheet more securely into the pterodactyl's backpack, and raised her voice so others might hear. "I think you'll find a welcoming environment at Vista View. We're honored that you chose to come here."

Pyke was glancing backward at the doors to the school. He seemed to be worried—for Jocelyne?

But then he hunched forward again—he really seemed quite small when he was on all fours—and exploded upward. Shiels, Jeffreys, everyone staggered backward in the shock of the moment, as if they had been standing too close to a geyser.

Shiels's phone throbbed again. Manniberg. He never texted her, yet there it was. *New arrival soon, test case. Let's talk tomorrow a.m.*

She performed a sanity check. In the dirt in front of her—claw marks. The crowd around her—gaping. In the sky—Pyke, once again a speck in the distance, a sharp and zigzagging head followed by a riotously twisting tail of crows.

Eighteen? He didn't look a day less than sixty-five million.

Shiels met Sheldon by the mailbox on Ridgeway, on her route home, as usual. With their busy after-school schedules, they could not always depart the building together. He was wearing the secondhand tie she had found for him, with colorful garden gnomes set against a black velvet background.

"What were you thinking, running out into danger like that?" he said. He was fingering his phone. Vhub, the social site that was the whole collective cranium of Vista View—she and Sheldon had helped popularize it on her way to becoming chair—was erupting with news of Pyke's unusual arrival. The little purple vein (or was it an artery?) in Sheldon's left temple was pulsing.

Her parents, both doctors, would kill her (metaphorically) for not knowing the difference.

(They didn't know anything about Vhub, not really. But they certainly knew all about veins and arteries.)

"It looked like he was going to fly off with her or something," Shiels explained. "Hello to you, too." And she stepped right up and kissed him, in part because Sheldon—who could be urgent in private, in his parents' den in the dead of night after homework and organizing—was uncomfortable showing affection in public.

She also kissed him, though she could hardly admit it to herself, because she desperately needed to kiss someone then. Her body was surging with something—extra adrenaline, maybe, or pheromones or dopamine or something scientific she might've known about if she had paid better attention in biology (and to her parents' chatter), but maybe not. Maybe this sort of thing was not covered in biology or by parents at all.

She kissed him hard and deep on the mouth and wanted him to put his stupid phone away for one minute and wrap his arms around her and feel muscular for once. Like . . . an animal.

She felt like an animal.

But the kiss stayed mostly one-sided for too long, and then finally she backed off and pulled herself together.

"What was that for?" Sheldon asked.

He was not normally dim. Even emotionally he could be quite knowing. Like that first session three years ago over the *Leghorn* "Things That Rot My Mind" issue when he'd pulled back from his keyboard, when they had been alone in the same airless cubbyhole off the library for fourteen consecutive hours (or so it had felt), and he'd just looked at her—he'd looked the very same kiss she had just given him.

Most of the time, in private, he could drop anything to look a deep kiss at her and lean over to her so they could throb together.

But now he was asking: "What was that for?"

She didn't . . . didn't know. She took his hand (soon, with the cold winds building in the days ahead, they would need gloves), and they walked in uncharacteristic silence down Ridgeway and across to Thorniton Avenue. He had large, warm hands for an unathletic guy, the kind of hands that can instinctively find and knead out a knot under a shoulder blade or squeeze life into quietly exhausted feet propped on the sofa.

They felt strong and sure, those hands.

Finally, when they were close to her embarrassingly large house, he said, "So—what's he like?"

And those things she was going to say to him about the flying monster—mostly they stayed inside her.

"Everyone's going to hate him," she said instead. "I've seen it starting. Jeremy Jeffreys, the whole football squad, practically attacked him! He can barely talk. His beak looks weird. And those flapping wings—what's he supposed to do with them in class? He won't be able to sit without bonking someone. I don't know what he's thinking, coming here. He already injured poor Jocelyne. I don't know if she's going to be able to run anymore."

How injured was Jocelyne really? Shiels had no idea. She didn't know why she'd said it.

"Did he go straight for her?"

In this moment, disappointingly, Sheldon looked ordinary to her. His curly brown hair, so fine to run fingers through, just seemed limp. Had he even washed it today? Well, it was true, they had been up much of the night working through the details of the committee configuration for Autumn Whirl. And she didn't like a boy who was too fastidious about his appearance. Sheldon wasn't naturally interested in such things—appearances, or committee configurations. He was much more of a writer/observer type than a planner/doer/looker. But he did it—plan, organize, wear the ironic tie that she'd bought—for her. To be true to her.

She didn't like this feeling of hiding things from him. What was she hiding? That worm, whatever it was.

"Shiels?" He'd asked a question. What was it?

"It sure looked like he went straight for her," she said. "But he didn't mean it, not at all. He's actually pretty helpless, if you think about it, in a sort of adorable way. He seems to have no idea what he's doing. That beak—it'll be like someone carrying a sword around in the halls. Maybe he could get a sheath or something."

Sheldon was waiting for his kiss now that they were not on a main street. He was leaning in—listening to her, but waiting, too.

He almost never initiated a kiss. He just sort of . . . made himself approachable, and waited for her to bridge the gap. Why did he do that?

Shiels could never imagine the pterodactyl doing that.

And then she burst out laughing—poor, confused Sheldon, they almost always laughed together—but she couldn't help herself. Such an odd thought—kissing a pterodactyl!

"What—what is it?"

All right, the world was changing, a pterodactyl had more or less dropped out of the sky. But a real kiss, with Sheldon, at the end of the day . . . a real kiss, with eyes closed, and his boy breath, and the smell of him, his quiet urgency and the softness of his cheek and the little prickly bits he still needed to shave . . . could still make the whole rest of the world fall away.

IV

Jonathan came roaring down the stairs two, three at a time as soon as Shiels made it through the door. He had the feet of a man—*clump, clump, clump!*—but the gangly body of a boy. Too many limbs to know what to do with them all, that was the impression her brother made these days.

"*What was he like?*" Jonathan croaked, his voice breaking as it did when he was excited. (But when was he ever excited? Never. The boy usually had the cold sludge of adolescent attitude in his veins.)

"Who?" Shiels asked, just to be annoying.

"Pyke! Pyke! You were right there when he arrived. I saw the video and everything!"

So someone had caught and posted it after all, which made it far more real and important for Jonathan than, say, if he'd been there in person when his older sister had raced across the sports complex to confront a supposedly extinct monster.

"Nothing special," she said. "He's not very good at landing. Poor Jocelyne Legault. She must have been scared out of her skin."

"So . . . so . . . like, you saw him? Up close?"

"I had to," she said simply.

"And his wings—like, what are they, about thirty feet across?"

"Good God no. They're maybe, I don't know, six feet. Eight? And he's not very tall, really. Shorter than you. Unless he stands really straight. Which he seems to hate to do."

Jonathan was going to be tall, like their father. Shiels was patterned more after their mother, in the compact fireball mode. Even with exquisite posture she was still—

"But he looked enormous on Vhub!"

"Well, maybe somebody stretched the truth or something. I guess mostly his wings were folded up when I got to him. He was holding Jocelyne."

"So he's going to . . . He's coming to our school?"

This was the longest conversation Shiels had had with Jonathan in years, it seemed. Over the pterodactyl, naturally.

"Looks like it. He's probably in your class."

Jonathan did a funny little hop-flip motion with his feet, as if he were on his skateboard. His face was all flushed, and his pants, as usual, were nearly falling down. As she watched him, Shiels started to feel uneasy. "I didn't . . . I'm worried about how he'll be treated," she said. *Clump-flap, clump-flick* went her brother, from one imaginary trick to the next. He could not stay still . . . unless he was in front of a screen. Then he couldn't get up to save his life. "A lot of kids might be mean."

What more was she going to learn from Manniberg in the morning? Probably not much. When was Manniberg ever prepared for anything?

"Pyke looks like a scalded dude," Jonathan said.

"But he doesn't know anybody, and he can hardly string together two words."

"Sure got to know Jocelyne Legault pretty quick!" Jonathan said. *Clump-crash.* He wobbled on the carpet, as if about to lose his balance. He dropped to one knee, then bounced up and twisted nonchalantly. "The man's got wings," he said.

Wings indeed. It was almost too much to think about. The interlude with Sheldon was draining away, and other thoughts came rushing back. Shiels had reacted instinctively to what had seemed like a dangerous situation, but now it was something else. What was it? Her mind was churning over. She didn't know what to make of it, or how she felt, or what to do.

The PD—parental dynamo—were dining out, so Shiels fixed herself an arugula salad with almond slivers and then baked organic corn bread from a simple recipe she found online. Jonathan finished the corn bread but also ordered a pizza. He had a shocking disregard for his own health and for the PD's express wishes. Yet they had left a credit card on the busy tray in the kitchen island for so-called emergencies, and Jonathan knew—and Shiels knew that he knew—that they didn't look closely at the monthly bill. Better pizza than drugs.

Normally Shiels would conference in the evenings with Sheldon, if he wasn't physically with her in her room. They would go over the half dozen or so joint efforts they always seemed to have on the boil. She had an English project due in the morning—she was preparing to create a fan blog for the crippled poet Alden Eldon, whom she had personally discovered (along with about seven other "fans"). Weeks ago, when she had happened upon his work, she'd been struck by the evocative streak of lameness shading so many of his poems ("morning now, and I am just a cup of coffee"). But somehow, on the verge of creating the blog, she had trouble summoning her earlier convictions. She needed to feel more, to get back in the mood, but first . . .

. . . She just sat going over it all again: the dark speck in the sky getting larger, the way her feet had taken off when she'd seen that Jocelyne was in trouble, how the monster— Pyke—had stood semi-glowing with pterodactyl heat close enough to spear her through if he'd wanted.

The muscles in his rib cage trembling, rippling.

Those eyes.

(Was he afraid of her?)

The frail blond runner draped in his winged arms. (Why hadn't he landed on Shiels, knocked *her* down, picked *her* up like she was the most precious thing in the modern world?)

Sheldon vibrated her four times in the course of the evening, but she didn't pick up. She had the Alden Eldon blog to do. Which took a lot of thinking.

It took a lot of thinking to get around to thinking about Alden Eldon.

Finally she texted Sheldon back. He called immediately. "Where are you? I've been at you all night."

"We need an emergency assembly over Pyke," she blurted. "He's going to be a completely ostracized circus act. I mean, think about it—that beak! It'll be against the code of conduct for him to walk down the hall. Manniberg is going to have to address the school, and we're going to have to get briefing notes together for him to do it or people simply won't know how to act. I'm worried about the football team. I think I told you they would have torn his wings off if I hadn't been there. . . . I have a meeting with him in the morning, but don't tell me he's prepared. You know he isn't."

"You have a meeting with Pyke?"

"Manniberg! Don't be dense." He could follow her thoughts perfectly well, even when she was being scattered. If he was offended, he would've said something, but he didn't. She felt him pause for a breath.

All right, she could be brusque with him, especially in moments of intensity, but she was hard on everybody, including herself. And he knew that, didn't he? Didn't he love her exactly for who she was?

Being able to kiss the way they did meant they could say anything to each other.

"How is any of this your responsibility or concern?" he said finally.

"I'm student-body chair. Everything is my responsibility!"

"Even the pterodactyl?"

"He has a name! He has rights! All we need is one ugly incident, and Vista View is going to be tagged as anti- . . . as anti- . . ." As Shiels was talking, she could almost feel Pyke next to her again, surrounded by the hostile crowd. She wasn't tired anymore. It was a rush to be decisive. "Anti-diversity! Not on my watch, Sheldon. It's my reputation too. We need to do this."

"It's after two in the morning," Sheldon said, in that voice of his that, fundamentally, agreed with what she was doing. He always agreed, finally. He had no defense against her energy, Shiels knew. He just gave in.

"We need to hammer out a charter, a sort of code of

conduct, for dealing with pterodactyl-students," she said. She would frame it out loud, the way she was doing— letting the rush happen—and he'd start to take notes and then ask pertinent questions, and that was how it was going to get done. Like they were two brains connected by the grid—almost the same person.

"Are we really calling him a 'pterodactyl-student'?" Sheldon asked. Brilliant! To focus on the language from the get-go.

To get the language right.

"He's not a pterodactyl-student." She paused, breathed, waited for the rush to continue. "He's a . . . New Cultures Arrival."

"We could make a New Cultures Accommodation Protocol," Sheldon said.

"Not a protocol. That's so—"

"Okay. It's just a . . . New Cultures Accommodation."

"It's the NCA," she said. "We'll have it in place by nine a.m. for Manniberg to announce. It's all about . . ."

"Trusting the welcoming spirit," Sheldon said. His dear, dear voice in her earbuds (practically an implant!). If he were here beside her, she would pull him to her. They would . . .

Well, if he were here physically, they might not get the NCA done. And that was the most important thing right now.

• • •

Normally Shiels collapsed in a heap at the end of busy days, and slept, oblivious to the world, until her alarm jolted her back to her obligations, sometimes as early as five in the morning, if the project list of the particular day were snarly. Early-morning thoughts were clearer, bolder, more focused yet more likely to range toward fresh solutions. She counted on rising anew, strong and able in the head.

But now sleep was slow to come to her. She thought again and again of the play of those dark wings, and now, somehow, felt like she could smell him right next to her — an earthy, potent, wild aroma. And when she did finally drift off, she dreamed of Sheldon, of all people, who had improbably just bought new yellow running shoes like Jocelyne's and was eager to try them out. And so Shiels was running with him, but without shoes herself—her feet were slapping the grass as they might have ten thousand years ago, racing across some rocky meadow (but her feet were tough; nothing hurt). Sheldon appeared in the distance, then, naked except for his yellow shoes (free of any logo) and an old pair of underwear so battered and ripped, they looked more like a loincloth than anything else. His body was hard. He had changed. He was just as lean as ever, but she could see the movements of his back muscles, the lovely tight shape of his thighs . . . and his hair was longer, and he had shoulders (he looked good with shoulders). She wanted to be closer, to see for sure. So she sped up, her strong bare feet shaping themselves to the ground so that she hardly felt any hard stalk of grass, any shard, any little spiky shrub she happened to . . .

She happened to be able to jump over most things, quite easily in fact, effortlessly, her body was so . . . She jumped so well, she only had to touch the ground now and again, bouncing like a moon walker . . . flying.

She was flying. Not high, barely off the ground, but with just the power of her mind she was able to do it. Quietly. No need to tell anyone. What a fuss they would make! She looked down at the ground passing beneath her, how smoothly it all worked.

Power of mind. Anyone could do it. Keep the right pressure—no sudden thoughts or mental movements—and she would stay afloat.

Aloft.

Flying.

And here was Sheldon. Turning to her. With his new body. He was darker, harder, like he'd been carved from purplish ebony . . .

What was ebony? A hard, dark wood.

Piano keys.

Oh, those shoulders!

He didn't seem surprised to see her. He had to turn his

beak—such a long, sharp, dangerous weapon! And then she was breathless in his arms, soaking in his heat, his soft fur, his pungent . . .

Why was she breathless? This had all been so easy. Practically effortless.

V

It was silly, and she knew it was, yet just for a moment the dream changed the way she looked at Sheldon. There he was at the pickup spot, the corner of Roseview and Vine, in his slouchy pants and worn old faux-ironic trench coat and the faded black canvas running shoes he wore unthinkingly, even through the worst winter storms (which would surely be coming soon). His hair was rumpled, as usual. He was looking at her with those puppy-dog eyes.

He looked soft all over. Not a hard angle to be found.

"Do we have to have twelve points?" he said. "Ten was good enough for God and Moses."

He looked like a pillow you could mush into any shape and it would just lie there on the bed, inert. Shiels had woken forty minutes after her alarm, coverless, soaked in sweat, thinking of angles, hard edges, hot tangents a body might want to lean into.

"Hey, you look nice," Sheldon said, lifting his glasses. "What's the occasion?"

Without his glasses, his face had a washed-out vagueness to it. His eyes looked weak. They *were* weak—that was why he wore glasses. But to really see something, often he took his glasses off.

"I don't have to wear the same thing every day," she said.

They were walking now. They hadn't kissed. It would've been perfunctory anyway. Roseview and Vine was semi-public. She'd have smudged her lipstick if they'd kissed, and Sheldon would've said something—he was unused to the taste of it. Anything he said would have made her feel uncomfortable about wearing it.

Was this what it was like to be married? she wondered. To know exactly what your partner's reactions were going to be twenty chess moves later?

"Let me see the list." She took his phone out of his hands. Despite his strong fingers, she couldn't help noticing how easy it was to steal the thing.

"NCA—New Cultures Accommodation."

Was it good to lead with an acronym? Not everyone was in love with them.

"Vista View High is an open-atmosphere school welcoming to students from all cultures and backgrounds. Diversity

is our strength, and as representatives of new cultures arrive, we strive to foster the rich inclusiveness . . ."

Sheldon was walking with her as she read aloud, shambling in his way, as if exhausted somehow, old. She had noticed it before, but it had never bothered her.

"I'm falling asleep already," she said, "and this is just the preamble."

"Well, maybe we don't need the preamble." He was giving in, as he did so often. "It was your idea."

"It can't sound United Nations. It's got to be relevant, punchy. And we can't say things like, 'arrive, we strive.'"

"What?"

Shiels read him the passage again. "I can fix that," he said, and he took back his phone and happily thumbed in new text.

She wasn't used to walking in heels. She had to step carefully along the rough sidewalk to avoid ruts. She found herself scissoring her legs like fashion models do, and swinging her hips, just a bit. Sheldon paid no mind. His nose was in the phone. The coolish breeze made her legs feel more alive than they had felt in . . . forever.

She was wearing zebra-patterned leggings, and a short dress she'd bought months ago but had never actually worn before. Of course Sheldon didn't notice. *Hey, you look nice.*

Practically didn't see her.

She let him talk. He read the whole thing to her, but

as they neared the school, she felt her heart swelling until it seemed to engulf her chest. Sheldon hadn't noticed, but others would. People would comment. "Shiels, my God, look at you all of a sudden!" As if she'd been a librarian most of her life.

Nice. She didn't look *nice.* She looked something else. She felt something else.

She felt herself gazing at the sky, quite naturally, even while Sheldon was glued to the text as they walked along. She had brain compartments too. She could comment on point number five—*All students must recognize the fundamental rights and dignities of others, regardless of physical forms and differing species backgrounds*—while scanning the horizon for any sign of those angled, dark-reach wings.

She wanted to see them again.

She was twisting inside, like a wet towel, with the discomfort of the yearning.

And who should meet them on the way to Manniberg, but Rebecca Sterzl? The hall was its usual jostling cacophony— voices, smiles, bobbing backpacks, lockers clunking open and slamming shut, some girl cooing on the phone—"Oh my God, scissors?"—some guy muttering, "banana face." And Rebecca cut through it all. "Triumphant Agony!" she exulted outside the office. "We finally got to demo them last night, and they are . . . Shiels, are you listening?"

Shiels was listening, but the words weren't gelling. She was looking for a sign of him—for Pyke, for those hard-bent wings, for his hop-hip gait—in the hallway. He hadn't been in the sky outside. He must be in the building. She wanted to see him before she got to Manniberg, who naturally had not set a time for their meeting. He never did. He just waited for things to happen, for her to come to him.

"You have my full attention, Rebecca."

Sheldon was still fiddling with the text. It had to be ready to go in the next couple of minutes. But Sheldon was a rock under pressure. It freed up Shiels to deal with everything else.

Rebecca caught her breath. She was birdlike, vibrating with urgency even over small things.

"The band. For Autumn Whirl. We've found it. Triumphant Agony. They played a demo for us last night at Maggie's. . . . I mean, there's turbulence. And the bass player is gorgeous. I can share some files if you want. They fit our price range—"

"Is it danceable?" Shiels asked. A hesitation. "Did Maggie say she thought it was danceable?"

Shiels had a way of just waiting, standing still and looking unimpressed. Rebecca began to come apart. "They're absolutely in our price range," she said finally. "And they have a girl. She's a drummer. They'll show up on time."

"Did Maggie actually dance to the music?"

"It's just . . . we're almost out of time!" Rebecca's chin quivered.

"It's Autumn Whirl. The music has to coagulate. Yes?" Shiels wrapped the frail girl in her arms. "You're going to be great. I know you are. We've got plenty of time. Keep looking!"

Rebecca pulled herself together, but her eyes still seemed frightened. "Is there really . . . Do we really have a pterodactyl in the school now?" she asked in a low voice, as if afraid to be heard.

"He's a boy," Shiels said. "A pterodactyl-boy, and I've met him. He'll be fine. Believe me, I'm dealing with the issue!"

Shiels spied Manniberg heading around the corner to the south wing, away from his office, as if he'd seen Shiels and Sheldon yet instantly had found something else to do.

Shiels had learned so much from him already about worst possible management styles.

When Rebecca was gone, she said, "Who else have we got to find a steaming band?"

Sheldon put his phone away. "Morris is on it."

"Seriously? Morris?" Morris could barely crawl out of his parents' basement most days.

"Morris knows music," Sheldon said.

A quarter to nine, and Shiels felt herself growing calmer, felt time slow down in that familiar way when seconds, words, actions became important. Manniberg had headed into the south wing. She could practically smell him. He wouldn't elude her.

She was moving so fast that Sheldon could not keep up, but she felt it as slow—every dip of her body to miss someone else in the jammed hall, every footfall perfect, focused, right. It wasn't what she had felt the day before, racing after Pyke—that had been outside her usual realm of experience. But this—tracking down Manniberg, getting the NCA into his hands, into his brain, as the seconds drained before the bell—this was her arena.

She belonged here.

And there he was! Hiding in the science room with Ms. Glaskill, crowding her against her desk with a green sheet in his hand, engaged in phony conversation. He betrayed himself—he turned to see Shiels just as she sailed into the room—because he must have known at some cellular level that he could not escape.

Shiels Krane was about to change the course of yet another of his days.

Besides, he was the one who'd called this meeting.

"I need a minute of your time, sir," she said, dropping her voice the way she had figured out how to do years ago, when she'd been student-body chair of her elementary school and at first no one—*no one*—had taken her seriously.

Manniberg had a fattish face—portly, to use an old word—and his mouth twitched. On the bald stretch of his high forehead, tiny white hairs were growing, almost as fine as Pyke's fur. His eyes took her in, neck to toes and coming back to rest finally at chest level. So she remembered what she was wearing.

Good. She had stunned him as an opener.

"We have a situation developing that you need to address right away, before it gets out of hand. It's about the new student, Pyke. I don't know if you've met him yet. But we have real reason to fear—"

Where was Sheldon? He had the NCA text; she was going to need to quote from it in less than a minute. Had he really not been able to keep up?

"—a backlash against him, sir. I can't put it more plainly than that. He's new, he's foreign, he's a different species, and students here are not used to dealing with—"

"Ms. Krane," Manniberg said. He was trying to do nothing. It was in his nature. Principals avoid proactive decisions whenever possible. They—

Where was Sheldon?

Sheldon was not there, but his message arrived just as Shiels's hand touched her phone. In a blink she had the NCA text in front of her.

"It's my most urgent recommendation, sir, that you convene an immediate assembly. I happen to have a text of procedures we need to present to the Vista View community."

Manniberg squinted at her screen. Why did he not carry his glasses?

"Point number two is crucial," she said. *"Privacy and protection of students from all walks of life, including different eras of evolution, must be promoted and maintained so that a normal atmosphere conducive to learning and rich cultural exchange is safeguarded at all times. Photographs, video, and other digital records of private students, regardless of species, should be banned from social media unless express consent has been—"*

He squinted at her doubtfully. The science teacher, Glaskill, had not left, but she might as well have disappeared.

"He's a freak and he scares people!" Shiels blurted. "We attack what we don't know. It was my initial response, and I've seen it already with the football team. So we need a protocol"—wrong word! but she pushed on—"a code of understanding, coming right from the top, from you, today I believe—this morning, if possible—that will outline acceptable behaviors and help all of us deal with what is, I think you would have to admit—"

Sheldon, at last! There seemed to be a commotion in the hallway. He'd fought his way through the crowd.

"Are you talking about the pterodactyl-boy?" Manniberg said.

"Yes! He's going to get beat up. He looks different. People are not going to know how to behave around him. . . ."

"It's a school board initiative," he said. "We were lucky to get him. We're taking a low-key approach."

Naturally! If it was ever possible to do nothing . . .

"*I* pitched it, actually," he said, "and the board went for it precisely because of your whole campaign last year to build up Vhub, do you remember?"

Did she remember? What kind of absurd question was that? But Manniberg was an educator. He liked to hear himself talk.

"It was in response to the whole issue of bullying and online predators. You got the students doing all their socializing on the school network. Brilliant! What was it you said about Facebook?"

It was just a slogan. He was going to remember it himself in a—

"*Your parents are on Facebook!* Perfect. It's not reasonable to expect people to stop talking or to not take videos. But let's keep everything about Pyke on Vhub, which you and Sheldon can influence through your own posts. Don't tell people to do it directly. That never works. But you know what I'm saying?"

Shiels felt her jaw go slack. Really, Manniberg, principal of the dead, was coming up with this kind of approach?

"Nod your head, tell me yes," he said. "I think I have to look after this . . ."

Manniberg slid by her to investigate the commotion in

the hall. Shiels paused for a moment to give Sheldon her look—*What in the rotting compost bin were you doing when I needed you right beside me?*—then pushed past.

Was it a fight in the halls? Already?

"Break it up! Get to your classes!" Manniberg yelled. He had a thin voice for a heavy man, and none of the verbal heft that a good vice principal would normally bring to crowd control.

Where were the vice principals?

The hall was a squash of bodies, of people straining to see something hopelessly hidden within an ever-contracting mass somewhere in the middle of the crowd. Manniberg had to push people aside to get anywhere.

Was it too late? Had the football team, slow to action yesterday, decided to dismantle Pyke now, this morning, before anything could be announced, before the NCA could be put in place? Shiels had moved as swiftly as she could have.

She and Sheldon waited on the outside of the crowd. The situation was beyond them now. Whatever was developing was developing. Shiels had raced to the rescue yesterday, but this was the principal's turf. His solution? To try to finesse something through Vhub when already it was coming down to a lynch mob?

Manniberg was a big guy. He was pretty good at pushing kids this way and that.

What could she have done? She could've called him directly in the early morning, perhaps, roused him from bed, and pressed upon him the urgency of the situation.

A life was at stake.

An endangered life, a rare spirit, newly arrived from the great beyond. People couldn't deal with that, could they? They had to destroy what they couldn't understand.

(Shiels didn't understand it either, but at least she hadn't tried to destroy it. She had confronted it up close, when it had looked like Jocelyne Legault was in trouble. But she'd seen the wings fold up, how small the boy actually was. And what did Manniberg want to do? Just keep everything off Facebook?)

"Clear out! Break it up! Everyone to your classes now!" Manniberg roared. Shiels imagined the battered body, how scrawny it would look, like a mauled bat, a rat with wings . . .

"*I said move!*"

They moved. Reluctantly, like crowds gawking at guillotines in the French Revolution. How were people any different now? They weren't. They were just as depraved, just as base, just as . . . human.

Humans being human.

How we love to watch . . .

What?

Pyke emerged from the core of the seething mass . . . very much untouched. Sort of erect, and dignified, and shining almost (his hide had a luster even in the dull fluorescence of the high school corridor). He saw her—those magnificent, ancient eyes locked on Shiels in her short dress, her zebra leggings, her high-heeled shoes—and then he passed on. Hop-hip. Hop-hip.

His long curved mouth hung open just a little, relaxed, as cool as shade.

He was walking with Jocelyne Legault.

Together. They were leaning against each other.

The crowd in the hallway had nearly rioted, out of pure curiosity, just to see Pyke and his girl . . . together.

Pyke and his girl?

When they had a bit of space, the pterodactyl snapped open his wings in a sort of shoulder shrug—*whoosh!*—that caused a rush of wind, a palpable *oooohhh* swirling through the crowd. Anyone trailing too closely would have been hurled against the lockers, it was such a powerful movement, but over in a heartbeat, and then he was folded again, next to Jocelyne.

Shiels felt it as a kind of sinking inside, like when something you've been holding finally gives way and you never even knew, until suddenly it's difficult to stand where you are, and your stupid high-heeled shoes hurt your toes, and your knees don't want to work all of a sudden, like they have gone on strike, and your boyfriend has to clutch you. (Boyfriend? She felt his strong hands

43

suddenly supporting her elbows, and her instant thought was, *Who are you?*)

But if not for Sheldon she might've ended up sitting in the middle of the hall, a puddle of mush, while Vista View High's new royal couple passed by.

VI

Jocelyne Legault! Why was it so galling to see her, tiny, in her warm-ups and running shoes, her loose athletic top, walking beside Pyke, nestled under his wing— literally—demure and safe-looking and obviously besotted?

Why should Shiels have cared? It should have been a relief that Pyke was not battered and bruised, that the NCA would not, after all, be needed. Who could have anticipated such a reception for a flying beast now enrolled at the school?

Overnight the beast had followers.

Of course, suddenly Pyke was all over Vhub. All over! But when had it happened? When had Pyke and Jocelyne ever had time to get together? Since last night? Really? Twelve hundred and eighty-four students, and now countless conversations about the great running champion and the only boy in the school who could fly. Of course they were together! Hadn't Pyke been smitten ever since he'd seen her from high above the track—that bouncing blond ponytail, those tireless legs? And hadn't he cradled her in his arms, and hopped her over to the nurse after his bruising landing?

And wasn't he different in every way from every other boy? Those muscles. Those wings. His eyes. The things he must've seen.

Of course Jocelyne had fallen for him. No other boy could keep up with her. But Pyke—

Pyke had something extra. Everyone felt it. Yesterday Shiels had thought they were all making fun of him. Had she completely misread the situation? Clearly the whole school now pulsed in a new way. Crowds gathered around the door in Mr. Saint-Croix's math class, and not because of fractional polynomials. Pyke sat in the last chair in the far corner, his little tail tucked under, wings in check, his crest pointing backward like a shark fin. He was not taking notes but nodding his head, clicking his beak like he was paying attention.

Utterly different. Famous already. A star, a celebrity in the school on the day he'd arrived. The real danger was that news could not stay contained. The world was going to beat down the doors of the school to see the beast who clicked his jaws and hung around with a running champion. How to stop that feeding frenzy? How to contain it? How to—

Our business is our business, Shiels posted, hardly thinking of what she was doing. *Let's keep it on the Vhub.*

Sheldon reverbed it immediately with his own twist. *We know what we know*, he sent. *Our secret. Let's let it happen here.*

Between them they had more than nine hundred followers in the school. The reverbs started, slowly, then came in more quickly. Someone wrote in: *Let's not tell our parents.* Someone echoed: *No one else needs to know!*

Fifty reverbs, then sixty-five. Then Pyke wrote in. When did he get a Vhub account—just today?

Tezding. Tzting. Hllo u from me.

And the whole thing went crazy.

VII

All right, all right. It happened more or less as Manniberg had figured—a few careful posts from Shiels and Sheldon, a word or two in the hallways to the right people, and soon it was all over. Everyone knew. The New Cultures Accommodation was simplified to a single focused idea: just keep what we know about Pyke within the school, no need to open him up to public feasting. Who knew what the world would do to him when he was discovered?

He would be discovered eventually, of course, but Shiels had bought him some time and protection. Had it been her idea to rally the school this way? Not really, but some part of her knew to seize upon it. The most important thing was that she seemed to have acted in time. YouTube was not exploding with pterodactyl videos. Pyke was not trending anywhere but on the Vhub, safe inside the halls of Shiels's own high school.

Why didn't she feel any better?

(A damning confession: She didn't even spend much time on Vhub anymore, having more or less popularized it with the Vista View world last year. It was for everyone else's chatter, for her to use occasionally now when necessary. It was strange to see how robust it had grown, beyond anything she had expected.)

Meanwhile, almost unaccountably, life went on. Rebecca sent the music files during physics, and Shiels forced herself to listen to one and a half songs, surreptitiously, during a string theory presentation by Chandra Xu—really, who could understand any of this?—and it just felt like noise, like her whole life had crapulated into a slow-motion train crash with car after car plowing in.

Utterly undanceable.

And not just because she was still steamed over Pyke.

(Why was she steamed over Pyke? A new boy—a freshman. Almost beneath her notice.)

He had walked straight past her, student-body chair, in the hall. When she'd been wearing her zebra leggings. As provocative as she got. Yet he was with . . . a cross-country runner?

Really?

Train cars upon cars crumpling and screeching. That was what this music sounded like.

Rebecca and Maggie both wanted to hire them?

(She checked Vhub surreptitiously—they weren't supposed to use it during class, but of course everyone did—to see if Pyke had posted anything new. Nothing. One hundred and forty-one commentaries on his single post, but Shiels certainly was not going to read those).

Delegation. What a farce. The most important things you had to do yourself.

(Shiels imagined her Chesford University interview—months from now, if she got it. *When* she got it! Her mentor, who didn't even know yet that she was going to be her mentor, Lorraine Miens, professor of political anthropology, leaning in, lifting her glasses. The same Lorraine Miens who had ventured into war zones interviewing musicians and playwrights. Cutting through the bullshit. "I see a lot of busyness in this CV, Ms. Krane—an awful lot of personal, shotgun-blast effort. But how do you work with others? How do you bring out the strengths in those around you?")

"So," Chandra Xu said, "is the universe expanding or contracting? Or is it doing both at the same time? The further we get toward penetrating the mysteries of dark matter, the closer we come to the contention that pattern is paradoxically central to the nature of unfolding chaos—"

(And Shiels was struck in her imaginary interview, stammering in front of Lorraine Miens—with her tragic face, the heaviness in her eyes—speechless. A real leader would say something at this point, perhaps about the very nature of humanity? Something simple yet profound that Shiels would clearly have to prepare beforehand. That was what these goal-fulfillment imaginations were about—putting herself in front of Lorraine Miens now, time and again, in a sort of endless rehearsal. So she wouldn't simply blurt, "I've been wanting to go to Chesford ever since I read *The Soul's Wager* when I was only twelve. It was the first book I actually sweated over, alone in the library, just me and the dictionary, about a page an hour. I would read sentences aloud and let them soak in. I have never wanted anything else so much . . ." She could *not* blurt out such sophomoric nonsense to the woman who had walked across Iraq in the worst of it reading poetry to maimed children. She would need to rehearse.)

She would need to stop looking out the window, as if something might be there besides the storm of crows that had gathered suddenly, massing in the treetops near the green bulbous water tower, like a storm about to burst.

She had one more month to complete her Chesford application. Then sometime in the new year—the universe willing!—she would be summoned for a personal interview before the board. They took only six freshmen per year in political anthropology, from about two thousand applications.

But who else was going to be able to say that as student-body chair she had helped ensure a safe and nurturing educational environment for the first pterodactyl-student anyone had ever seen?

Pattern is paradoxically central to the nature of unfolding chaos. Something about Chandra Xu's voice as she had said this—the extraordinary statement stayed with Shiels the rest of the day. What could it mean? How could chaos unfold in patterns?

Maybe . . . maybe it simply meant that one thing led to another, no matter what. But she could have had a dozen concerns on her mind—not just the band choice for Autumn Whirl, but ticket sales, promotions, volunteer recruitment, communications coordination, parking regulations, security, meetings to call, texts to send, stages to plan, plans to stage—and still she found herself that afternoon, when the school day was done, drifting outside with others toward the sports field. It was a spontaneous mass-consciousness thing—unannounced, in the atmosphere somehow, not even on Vhub. Everyone just knew.

They all wanted to see the pterodactyl flying around and around the track while Jocelyne Legault ran her crisp and steady laps.

The day had turned cold even, and misty rain blew from the north into their faces. Shiels had not worn a jacket.

Silly, really, to stand out like this exposed to the elements, getting wet. Shivering in her short dress.

She let her phone vibrate.

What was it about that dark form spearing through the air? When the crows flew—they massed in croaking billows high above, ecstatic—the act of staying aloft seemed simple, natural, as unremarkable as walking. But when Pyke flew, it was an athletic event. Those were muscles in his chest. As scrawny as he could seem close up, on high he looked substantial, heavy almost, like a man who had trained himself to move such powerful wings.

He looked like he'd flown across the ages, like he'd personally climbed out of a melting glacier and, seeing the world both old and new, had just taken it for what it was.

Was that where he had come from? Was he a cryogenic miracle? An ancient mutation? Some scientist's idea of a cosmic joke? She took out her phone and thumbed him a personal message: *Really, Pyke, where r u from? Y r u here?*

He wouldn't answer right away. Of course not. He was flying around and around the track at the moment. Probably he didn't even have a phone. He would have to reply from a computer in the library or something. If he bothered to answer at all.

God, he was beautiful.

Living in the suburbs, safe in an urban enclave, Shiels did not see large, nearly wild beasts very often. Once, years ago, a moose had wandered in from the bush and had trampled someone's vegetable garden, and crossed against the lights at a busy intersection close to the entrance to the freeway. Shiels had seen the photos in the newspaper, and that night had dreamed that the moose was banging at their back door, demanding to get in.

Until now, that had been her closest encounter with something truly wild and powerful.

She stood in the rain with so many others, on the slight bank near the tennis courts, looking through the fence at the runners, the football players, the majestic prehistoric flying beast so obviously smitten.

Around and around and around, his wings tireless, the crows screaming their adulation.

Shiels's phone was practically dancing out of the slim pocket of her clingy little dress, but it wasn't Pyke. Obviously not. She felt no great urge to answer.

"When you have a moment, dear," Shiels's mother said, later that evening. Shiels was in her room, on her bed, a chemistry text on-screen before her unfocused eyes. Why had the world invented chemistry, anyway? *Pattern and chaos.* Maybe they were both the same. But where Ms. Caitlin-Phillips saw pattern in everything—*Potassium permanganate and sulfuric acid. Add them together, what happens? Anybody? This is all about reactions, people!*—Shiels saw only chaos. Those chemicals created whatever Ms. Caitlin-Phillips said they created.

They created the need for brute memorization.

How could a pterodactyl just fly into her school and start going out with Jocelyne Legault?

"Shiels?" her mother said.

"What?" Shiels did not move from her position, buttressed by pillows, the computer digging into her belly. Her mother, as sharp as ever, traversed the room, sat, crossed her arms and legs.

Dark hair, severe bangs, newly dyed. Those calm, unwavering eyes. Why hadn't Shiels gotten her cheekbones? She'd gotten a slightly lower grade of cheekbone. She had nowhere near her mother's flawless skin.

"How's Sheldon?" her mother asked.

It was a safe, pawn-to-queen-four kind of opening. But danger lurked in the next few moves. Shiels could sense it.

"Busy, I guess," Shiels said. She knew enough not to seem withholding. "We're all busy. I think I told you we're doing a lot of the editorial work together for the *Leghorn Review*. I'm sure universities are going to—"

"You are spending an awful lot of time with him these days," her mother said.

"I guess."

"Is he coming over later?"

"I don't know." Shiels's phone vibrated that instant. She

didn't look. "He's a really great homework partner. I mean, he understands chemistry." Wrong thing to say!

Shiels's mother blinked, as if a patient had just admitted something incriminating—she hadn't been taking her blood pressure medication; she didn't walk ten thousand steps a day. "Chemistry is about the basic building blocks of matter, of life and health," her mother said. "I know it's difficult in the beginning, but it all becomes clear. Believe me. If you work hard enough, there comes a time when it all—" She leaned in, apparently to see what Shiels was reading, what problem in particular was stumping her.

"I know. I know," Shiels said in her defusing voice. She pretended to refocus on the screen. She would apply to all her parents' choices for a university, sign up for all the science and premed courses they expected. But if she got into Chesford . . .

If she got a chance to study with Lorraine Miens, as an undergrad—!

"It's just that your father and I have noticed that Sheldon is around a lot these days, evenings especially. And you're both working so hard, so late."

Shiels blinked noncommittally.

"You're obviously very good together. You know we love Sheldon. He's a gentle boy, he cares for you, he has a good future."

"We're not going to get married, Mom!"

The shadow of doubt floated across her mother's face, and then she smiled. Relief?

A suspiciously humorless smile.

"No, of course not. Not right away. You're both so young. And that's exactly what I'm trying to say. You're both so young. You have many, many years of serious effort yet, of real growing up, before you'll be in any position to . . ."

Undergrad, she meant. Then med school. Residency. Choosing a specialty, maybe more years after that. What did Shiels want to be—a surgeon? Psychotherapist? Ophthalmologist? A whole universe of unrelenting effort was out there waiting.

(She hadn't told them yet about studying with Lorraine Miens. Of course not. Why worry them until the possibility was real?)

"Are you saying I should break up with Sheldon?" Shiels could blink every bit as passive-aggressively as her mother.

"Of course not! Honey! He's great. In many ways you're like an old married couple. I mean, you do everything together. Do you know how long I've waited just to get you alone to have this chance to talk? He's always with you. It's like you're welded at the hip."

Shiels's phone vibrated again. Sheldon. She turned it off. Pyke was not going to reply to her, not tonight, if ever. Where was home even, some huge nest in a big tree?

"See other people. Have some fun. This is your graduating

year. After June everyone will take off to the four corners of the world. These days—literally. Keep your focus for what's really important. You know you are not a natural for some things. But you're really smart and you outwork everyone else. You always have. That's your strength."

Shiels could see that her mother was feeling better the further she got into their chat.

"I didn't meet your father until Saint Luke's," she said. "I had boyfriends. Of course I did. You don't have to be a nun. But stay on track." Her hand was warm. She squeezed Shiels's shoulder and then they were hugging, and Shiels felt herself brimming, brimming . . . then flooding right into her mother's sweater. *Stop it! Stop it!* she screamed at herself, but she couldn't. Her mother's warm hand at her back.

If things didn't work out with Lorraine Miens, if she didn't get into Chesford after all, then yes, of course, she could always be a doctor.

VIII

A pelting rain the next morning, wearying in the cold, and then, unaccountably, Sheldon was not waiting for her at Roseview and Vine. Shiels stood uncomfortably under her wind-tossed umbrella, looking down the street, waiting for him to come tearing around the corner, his worn treads slapping the puddles and his arms flapping, not quite like a girl—like a girl who couldn't run—but maybe like a chicken surprised and alarmed.

He had stopped texting her after midnight. That in itself was not unusual. Often when she became cataclysmically busy, she didn't respond, sometimes for hours at a time, and he had always understood it meant nothing. Roseview and Vine was a given. They always met here in the morning.

Now she fought with the wind and texted him and waited in growing unease as the gray sky, rain-lashed trees, the quietly shuddering shrubs and lawns gave her nothing. *We have been here forever*, they seemed to sigh. *You are an insect gone tomorrow.*

Where the hell was Sheldon?

She imagined, for a moment, him exploding out of bed in his way—he had described it to her—when he has over-slept and his limbs move all at once and in contradictory directions. Maybe . . . maybe he caught his foot flailing down the stairs and knocked his head senseless. Maybe he was right now speeding to the hospital in the back of an ambulance, his body strapped to a board, a paramedic checking his pulse.

She even heard a siren in the distance. She pictured herself wheeling him around, wiping the remnants of lunch from the crusty edges of his lips. "I'm sorry," she said, under her breath, as if rehearsing the line. "I'm going to have to go to Chesford. We'll stay in touch, of course we will. You know I care about you deeply."

A gust of wind blew her red umbrella inside out, and Shiels had to struggle to bring it back into shape. One of the struts was bent and dipped down ridiculously.

Five minutes late!

Shiels would not waste another moment. Sheldon was going to get an earful when she saw him at school.

As she approached the tired brick building—assemblage of buildings—Shiels began to sense something wrong. It was nothing she could see. All around her the usual assortment of teenagers spilled out of buses, traveling in packs or clumps of two or three with backpacks, earbuds, slouchy clothes. Everyone had an umbrella, which only made sense—it was raining.

But *everyone* with an umbrella? Normally half the school at least would just show up wet on a rainy day, with soaked hoodies, hands in pockets, shivering as if nothing could be done about inclement weather. In winter too, on the coldest day, most of the school would still be in sneakers, without gloves or hats, practically frostbitten. It was part of the unwritten code of the place: no care given to the weather. Now—umbrellas all around?

And black umbrellas at that. A shroud of them, bobbing as people walked. Was it a funeral? What could have possibly happened overnight that Shiels had not heard about? She checked Vhub quickly—the traffic was overwhelming. She really couldn't keep up with all the threads. . . .

She had a sickening thought again that it was Sheldon—Sheldon who had died. It would have to be something bizarre. Something falling from outer space. A dead satellite. If Sheldon were to go, it would be something like that.

Shiels felt as if she had lost a week somehow—just blacked out, perhaps—and so could not account for whatever terrible thing had happened.

She pulled open the front double doors and . . . everything was normal. Except that everyone practically, except for her, was carrying a soaked black umbrella. She spied Sheldon near the trophy cases horsing around with Rachel Wyngate, from the volleyball team, if that were at all believable, and some of the football players: Ellis Maythorn, Ron Fornelli. Sheldon was one of those boys who moved well in all sorts of company. They were sparring with their umbrellas, whacking one another and laughing.

Completely innocent. Shiels marched toward him. "Why didn't you wait for me?" was on the tip of her tongue.

And then when she was just paces away, Sheldon snapped open his black umbrella—*whump!*—and just as quickly shut it down again. It was an enormous one, golfing size, and Shiels found herself stepping back. Maythorn did the umbrella trick then too, right at her, and Fornelli, in a different direction, and Rachel Wyngate laughed in her athletic way—Shiels suddenly noticed her baldly interested manner of looking at Sheldon—and Shiels could see then all down the south corridor people snapping open and shutting down their black umbrellas . . . as if they were all Pykes, every single one of them.

"What the hell are you doing?" she said to Sheldon, who looked at her as if . . .

What?

As if she were the last kid in high school to grow wings.

• • •

Manniberg was not even in. Shiels found herself standing in the office in front of Ms. Klein, whose thick lids were raised at her, momentarily distracted from her screen. Shiels was ready to fire, to launch a new umbrella protocol. (That wasn't what she would call it; enough with the protocols!) "We can't have people opening umbrellas suddenly indoors!" she was ready to say. "It's not about some silly superstition. It's eyes being poked out! It's . . ."

But Manniberg was not in.

"Do you mean he—he's late?" Shiels sputtered. "Or he's not coming in?" Who would she have to deal with in his absence—Jimble? Or Ketterling? These vice principals were all—

"I'm not sure," Ms. Klein said.

"What do you mean?" Every drop of diplomacy had left Shiels; she could taste blood in her voice.

She tasted blood, but then she willed herself back from the brink.

(*What is the point of browbeating the school secretary, Ms. Krane?* she asked herself in the imagined voice of Lorraine Miens.)

(And—why had Sheldon been horsing around with a black umbrella? He was not a masses kind of person. Usually she could count on him. If everyone in the school were headed one direction, he was off in the opposite, out of principle.)

"I'm sorry," Shiels said. "People are exploding their umbrellas open in the halls."

Ms. Klein's heavy eyes shifted back to the screen, then again to Shiels. What was she looking at?

(Shiels wouldn't have thought Rachel Wyngate was an umbrella-masses kind of person either. But somehow the two of them together . . .)

"Students have brought exploding umbrellas?" the secretary asked dully.

"They're popping them open suddenly, right in people's faces!" Shiels sensed a great tide shifting against her.

"I can make a note of it," Ms. Klein said uselessly. She brought out a memo pad and waited for Shiels to say it again, to sum up the problem.

"Is Mr. Manniberg coming in today or not?" Shiels pressed her palms against the countertop separating her and the functionary.

(Functionary. What a lovely word. Why wasn't Sheldon here?)

Ms. Klein wrote on the pad—*STUDENT UMBRELLAS*—as if that explained the situation.

What else was spinning out of control?

Shiels left without another word.

Slashing rain. Cold gray sheets sprayed against the windows as if launched from some gigantic faucet far above

the Earth. The whole school felt submarine-like, underwater.

Shiels met up with Sheldon—or rather Sheldon caught
up with her—in the library just before lunch. "What? Why
are you looking at me?" he said, meaning *like that.*

Like he could be washed away in a slick of mud and she
probably wouldn't even go to his funeral.

"How are you?" she asked.

"Good! Waiting for some kind of response!" He was
thrusting his jaw out, which he did sometimes when he was
miffed about something she had done. It normally lasted
about ten seconds before he unthrust his jaw and agreed
with her over whatever it was he had been confused about.

"What are we talking about?"

They weren't standing in a particularly quiet corner of
the library. Computers were humming, students were cutting across to get to the cafeteria—which Mr. Wend had
forbidden, but they still did it—and Mr. Wend himself was
fiddling with a collapsible bookstand well within earshot.

"Pyke's band! Morris came through. That's what I was
bleeping you about all last night. You never answered. They
were heat source. Total freaking rummage!"

Sheldon flicked his hands, a sort of chicken-wing gesture that erupted when he was excited.

"Are you face-raking me?" she said calmly. "Pyke has a
band? He just arrived!"

"They were on last night at Dead Papyrus. Didn't you look at anything I sent? I missed the first set because I was waiting for you to get back to me. But the second was cellular. I'm not exaggerating. And Morris talked him into doing Autumn Whirl."

Sheldon had his phone out, despite the in-library ban—Mr. Wend was right there, still—and he thrust the screen at Shiels. At first she could make out nothing—someone's writhing back, people jostling, ugly sounds from a bass guitar offscreen—and then a bouncing glimpse of Pyke, onstage, wings folded, his body in a crouch almost, as if about to spring into the air.

"Does he sing, or—what?"

Mr. Wend was looking at them. Not only were they using Sheldon's phone, but it was making weird noises.

"Wait for it. Wait—"

More bouncing. Sweaty bodies. Sheldon must've been changing positions, trying to get a better view.

"Could you not have edited this?" Shiels said.

And then the shriek. Pyke rose to his full outstretched grandeur, and his jaws were wide open. That beak . . . and the eyes. Even with this crappy phone-quality video, she could see the intensity of spirit there. And the sound—

"What in God's name is that?" Mr. Wend said.

The video stopped.

"That's all I got," Sheldon said. "My batteries died. But

the show went on and on. Everybody was wailing—we just stood there and spilled our noodles."

"Did you dance?" Shiels asked.

"It's beyond dancing. You just—emote pure sound. It's like—better than drugs. You don't even want to dance. Your body does whatever."

He was hopping in place as he talked, almost like Jonathan with his rehearsed board moves.

"Since when do you do drugs?" Shiels said. The boy would not even take mayonnaise on his cheese sandwich. But he glanced away for a second, as if he might not be all that she thought she knew. "Anyway, Autumn Whirl is a dance! Why would we hire a band that made you *not* want to—"

The way he was looking at her, as if—

"I'm not face-raking you!" she said. "I honestly believe—"

"It's so much more than dance music!" Sheldon practically oscillated in front of her. She could feel her own feet tingling. Was it from Sheldon, his heat for this shriekiness, or was it from the small taste she had had on video of the shriekiness itself?

"Would you please take your caterwauling outside?" Mr. Wend said, and then the bookcase he was fiddling with eased itself to the ground, like a wounded horse kneeling, about to topple over.

IX

The Autumn Whirl standing committee met for lunch in the theater arts room in the basement. Rebecca Sterzl chaired but looked to Shiels for approval on everything—and sometimes, such as today, Sheldon sat in just because he was Sheldon. They were talking about Pyke's band and how this new brand of music—could it even be called music?—would change the nature of the event. Without Shiels's direction they would all just roll over in the face of this new thing, this pterodactyl craze that was taking over the school, and what was going to be a lacerating opening event to the social calendar would instead be . . .

Shiels sat listening to Rebecca go on and on about the electric nature of the shrieking experience, how everyone who'd been there last night vibrated freakishly and how other shrieks ruptured out of people like glorious teen vomit. "Only better," Rebecca said. "We're going to have to take a hard line on limiting access. No one from outside Vista View. It's going to be insane." Her face betrayed that same loopy glow that Sheldon's had had when spewing about the weird music.

He was standing beside Rebecca in front of the circled committee. Showing his few seconds of video over and over.

"We could double the price and still overfill the gym," Melanie Mull said. "What about another venue? The Steadhouse?" She was a quiet, conscientious sophomore, the kind of girl who often showed up on school committees. Her head seemed full of this new possibility, Autumn Whirl with Pyke's band.

"The Steadhouse is jammed with seats," Rebecca said. "Nobody's going to be sitting. And anyway—"

Shiels shifted her chair. She was chewing a quinoa bun and made a soft sucking sound with her teeth. Everyone's head turned toward her.

They all seemed highly aware that she hadn't spoken yet.

"Autumn Whirl hits in a week," she said in her dead calm, assassin's voice. "We don't have time to change venues. And I hear what you're saying about this band, Rebecca, but yesterday you seemed to think you'd hit a totally other righteous band. Maybe tomorrow—"

"But Morris really liked them!" Sheldon said.

Shiels turned her smiling, cutting eyes on her boyfriend and waited to see if he was going to continue to advertise this divided front before the entire committee. His words shriveled. But he wasn't sitting down.

"Morris isn't here," Shiels said finally. Reasonably. "Maybe a lot of kids will be into shrieking their heads off. But is that what Autumn Whirl is all about? If we return to the mandate"—Shiels flipped back in her open binder—"we'll see it's all about school spirit and community-oriented socialization. I don't see anything here about descending into the primordial ooze."

She knew Sheldon would appreciate that last phrase. But he was looking . . . as if he somehow still disagreed with her.

"I think we need to keep looking for a band," she said curtly, finally. She glanced at her watch, took another small bite of her bitter muffin. "How are the ticket sales going, anyway?"

"We've barely hit a quarter of our target!" Rebecca blurted. "I know if we hired Pyke's band, we'd—"

Shiels signaled, with a glance, that the meeting was over. Rebecca's lips flapped noiselessly. Nobody else said anything.

Shiels closed her binder. "We'll have to redouble our efforts. This is our first big event of the year. Let's nail this down. Walloping Wallin is next, and that's going to be a struggle. We all know that. What's it been, seventeen years? There won't be a lot of joy. So we have to get this one right. Shall we meet again tomorrow?"

Sheldon would not let it go. He should have taken the east corridor to Family and Society, but he just had to get in one last word.

"You knew you were wrong back there. You just won't admit it. If *you* had thought of it—if *you* were the one who'd been trying to bleep *me* all night, then the outcome would have been completely different. Admit it, Shiels!"

He grabbed her arm and stopped her midstride. She stared at his fingers until he unhanded her.

("Unhand me, sir!" she imagined herself saying.)

"You get this way," Sheldon said. "I've seen it over and over. You get hyper, your brain is like a gerbil on a running wheel, you're just going to keep scrambling till you crash and I have to pick you up. And when you're like this— Shiels, listen to me!"

What was that fire in his cheeks? From her mousy Sheldon.

"When I'm like this, what?"

"You make crappy decisions. You're not really in control of yourself!"

She almost laughed at him, he was so serious all of a sudden. Over a shrieking dinosaur bird boy. Over Autumn

Whirl, for God's sake! He never cared about politics. But now his hands were cramping with it. It made him . . .

"A gerbil!" she said. "You think I'm a gerbil on a running wheel?"

"No," he said, backtracking. Because he was Sheldon. Now he didn't seem to know where to look.

"Do I make you nervous?"

"No. I—"

But he was nervous. He was standing in front of the janitorial closet, and she knew it would be unlocked because that was the way the universe lined up sometimes. She pushed him in then closed the door behind him, and he nearly sat in the bucket, he was moving back so fast. She turned on the light and tugged at his shirt.

"So you think I'm hyper. Just going on fumes."

"No, I—Well, yes. What are you doing?"

"You are so cute when you get agitated."

"Am I?"

Off with the shirt. Buttons flew in odd directions. The closet smelled of chemicals, of eons of accumulated high school dirt never quite rinsed out of the ancient gray mop. Sheldon pulled at her shirt, but she fended him off.

"No. No. This is just you," she said.

"Is it?"

She snapped off the light and unzipped him. His hips were so skinny, she barely had to yank to lower his trousers.

He was ankle-bound now, back against the cinder-block wall, trapped on one side by the stinking buckets, on the other by a set of shelves.

Why had she turned off the light? She wanted to feel his ribs, his bony nose, the hardness of him. She didn't want to see him . . . and the thought surprised her. Guys want to see—she had read that somewhere—but she wanted to *feel* him, to breathe him in. (Beyond the stench of the closet? On top of it. It all went together.)

He was hard in all the right places. This boy had angles. She kissed him, bit his lip until he squealed and she shushed him down. *"Not a sound,"* she breathed.

Tendons. Muscles. Boy sweat. Naked in the dark. In the old dark. This could be the ooze, she thought. This could be primordial.

"Shiels," he said. His voice was strange, like he was mumbling underwater.

"Shhh."

"But I don't . . . I'm going to . . ."

She held his tongue with her teeth until the noises stopped.

She was breathing hard. It was as if they were both running somewhere. In the wild. Out of the woods, across some grassy plain.

Running hard and getting nowhere.

Staying right where they were.

"Shiels. I think I—"

He was right. They were *all* right. It just hit her in the dark and sweat of that little black wild box they had wandered into.

Pyke had to do Autumn Whirl. It was the only solution that made any sense at all.

And then, once the decision was made, everything fell into place. Shiels was hardly prepared for it. (Yet she should have been, she thought later. Surely this was close to the same phenomenon as when she'd taken Manniberg's simple suggestion to let the student body know they should keep Pyke as their own secret. There it was, both times—the power of so many suddenly pulling in the same direction.)

Rather than simply an announcement over the PA along with schedule changes and activity notes, she waited an extra day, until the Blaze of Fall Scholars' Awards assembly. By then, of course, everyone knew already. A few well-placed leaks by Sheldon and others, and the news spread like a grass fire on the savanna. *Pyke's band is playing Autumn Whirl!* It didn't even matter that the band had no proper name. They weren't the Acid Toads or Sacred Disaster or, as Sheldon had laughingly suggested, the PteroTunes. They were just Pyke's band, a bunch of boys from different garages with a smattering of equipment and, oh yeah, a flying ancient screeching monster everyone was in love with.

By the time of the official announcement, some tickets were being reverbed on Vhub for double, triple, quintuple the face value. How to stop the practice? Even when they limited initial sales, the tickets disappeared like a whisper.

Sheldon, and others, were right. Shiels could see it. She didn't necessarily have the best ideas. The gym was not going to be big enough for the whole school, but if the weather cooperated, they could set up a video link to the athletic field scoreboard, and the overflow crowd could gather there. Pyke could perform a flypast at the end of the evening—he'd have to go home anyway—and everyone would be delirious.

By the time of the official announcement, at the assembly, all the plans and more were already in place. The student body could barely stay in their seats. They had waited for an hour as the likes of Chandra Xu and Natalie Micau and, yes, of course, Sheldon, had trouped across to pick up various plaques and certificates for their brain-bending work during the early part of the academic year. Blaze of Fall had actually been Shiels's idea from her first term on council, to get the school honoring academic stars throughout the year rather than waiting until June, when everyone was desperate to be free of the place and not likely to be inspired to sweat their homework. Pyke sat near the back with shades on, of all things, like a jazz musician, with Jocelyne Legault tucked under his wing. From Shiels's place on the stage, where she was sitting beside the department chairs and helping to organize the certificates and plaques, she could just see the two of them. Pyke turned his beak toward Jocelyne and murmured something, and then she laughed—when did Jocelyne Legault ever laugh?—and Shiels felt that something, that worm in her gut, chew a tender spot.

When Shiels took the microphone near the end of the assembly, she could feel too the coil in the room, like they were twelve hundred starlings suddenly braced for flight.

(Or were they all turning into Pyke's crows?)

"I just have one quick announcement," Shiels said. Why did she pause? Did it have anything to do with the way Jocelyne Legault ran her hand over Pyke's naked purple chest? "But first," she said, "one final round of applause for the brilliant brains of Vista View!" The tepid, ironic applause of the last hour—all right, the student body had not fully embraced the idea of honoring academic achievement—gave way to something entirely different. Now the students erupted, cheering, Shiels realized, because they knew already what Shiels was going to say next.

They were boiling over to hear the actual words.

"Some of you might have heard that the first VV social of the year will be held this Saturday—"

And then it was like the roof blew off. All at once the whole student body was on its feet, howling, stamping, hopping about, and exploding black umbrellas over and over. Shiels glanced, nervously, back at Manniberg, who looked startled.

"*And the band . . .* ," she screamed. She could not hear herself. She waited and waited, but they would not stop, so she shrieked as loudly as she could, "*The band is Pyke's!*" Then the auditorium itself seemed to be bouncing in an earthquake. She held on to the mic, as if she might think of something else to say that could at all be relevant. And she glanced at Pyke—at where Pyke and Jocelyne had been sitting—but they were gone.

Sheldon stood at floor level by the stage, close to Shiels's shoes, laughing and exclaiming and pointing at her, as if much of this glory somehow was hers. And maybe . . . maybe it was hers. It hadn't been her idea, but she was the one who'd made the decision—the right decision—and now the shock wave was unleashed and there was nothing to do but hang on and ride the crest of it all the way to shore.

Wherever that might be.

The strange, silly, euphoric wave of Shiels's announcement jaggered through the halls. It was hard to think. Everyone wanted to talk to her, congratulate her, ask her how she had come up with such a brilliant idea.

But there wasn't much time to celebrate. Rebecca Sterzl dragged Shiels to the cafeteria, where the roar of the students sounded almost as loud as in the auditorium. Shiels pushed through the heavy double doors. The dull gray tables were the same as always, but the place was packed, everyone was on their feet. Where was Pyke? There—in the middle, on a table, grinning. Football players around him chanted, "Food fight! Food fight!" Jeremy Jeffreys, the VV quarterback, had a sandwich in his hand. Pyke was waiting. . . .

"They're throwing food at him!" Rebecca said.

Shiels's gut clenched. Was this, finally, the hazing of Pyke she'd cut short when he'd first arrived?

But no food was in the air yet. It was all potential, like a buildup of static waiting for the touch of a metal doorknob. The wrong word now, and the entire cafeteria would erupt in flying pizza slices and worse. Shiels didn't want to be the one to call out. She didn't want to be the heavy.

Jeremy Jeffreys might not listen, she thought.

I will look like a fool.

Jeffreys fired his sandwich. Not at Pyke at all but high above the pterodactyl's head. Pyke stretched up, up, his neck, his beak—he spread his wings and snagged that sandwich in a flashing, stabbing motion that released a roar from the students half again as big as anything in the auditorium earlier.

Or that was what it sounded like in the crush of the cafeteria.

Then Jeremy Jeffreys had another sandwich in his hand. How long before the whole room would be smeared in projectile lunch bits?

Shiels knew she should say something. She should—

She turned, and there was Manniberg, standing beside her, his eyes squidged together as he tried to understand this new unfolding affront to order.

"Wait!" Shiels screamed, her voice suddenly bigger than the room.

(She knew it. She felt it.)

Jeremy Jeffreys turned. He looked like he would be just as happy to fire apple jelly and chocolate spread right into the middle of her chest.

He hadn't seen Manniberg yet.

"There'll be one more shot!" Shiels yelled. "And then it's over!"

She picked up someone's applesauce fruit cup and thrust it at Manniberg.

With her eyes she said to him, *If you say no to these people now, the whole place is going to be flying food.*

She held the fruit cup out to him.

"Mann-i-berg! Mann-i-berg!" the football team began to chant.

You can still salvage this moment, Shiels's eyes said.

"MANN-I-BERG! MANN-I-BERG!"

The principal took the applesauce cup. The cafeteria

froze into delighted silence. Pyke turned to Manniberg as if the pterodactyl might lance the cup from Manniberg's hand if the principal didn't throw it in the next few seconds.

"One throw," Manniberg said in his strongest voice. "Then—lunch!"

Even as she stayed serious on the outside, Shiels could feel herself laughing. The wrong signal could still ruin it. But—

Manniberg brought his arm back awkwardly.

Leadership is about managing moments, she thought. *The big and the small.*

Manniberg threw it surprisingly hard and fast and straight at the pterodactyl's face. There wasn't time to duck or—

Zzsht!

Pyke snatched the cup in midair, then lifted his beak and shrieked in triumph. Shiels, like everyone else, watched the applesauce disappear down the elongated gullet, plastic container and all.

An explosion of cheers, applause, thunderous banging of tables. Even Manniberg was smiling.

"All right! Only twenty minutes left for lunch!" he announced. And the football players sat down, so everyone else did too. Thunderous chatter still, but the crisis was over.

Manniberg's squidgy eyes sent Shiels a quiet *Thank you.* His first of the year.

Sheldon liked being pushed into the janitorial closet.
He pretended he didn't. He looked around nervously, to
see if anyone noticed. He claimed he wanted the light on.
He tried to pull at her clothes, to bite her lip, to be stronger
than her.

But he wasn't. Shiels was the one who said yes and no,
whose glance fried his nerve ends, who directed where his
hands might or might not stray and decided whether today
was cold or hot or broiling or frigid.

She said whether there was time or not.

She knew what wind might blow where and how and if
and whether.

She did not say why.

She was not sleeping much—she never did close to an
event—but the dreams she had were vivid. In all of them

her clothes seemed to fall away and her body yearned for wilderness—for the cover of trees, or tall grasses, the slap of broken ground on resilient soles (sometimes her feet were yellow, or she was wearing yellow shoes), or for fresh air gulped into deliriously freed lungs. In one, she was crawling out of a hole in the ground, her usual spot, close and warm and smelling of earthworms and black soil. She knew where the surface was, but it took a while to stretch herself, snake-like, far enough, and to pull up her hind body (slither, slide, sneak along). Her skin was . . . skintight, sexy. She liked the luster of it, its tautness, how silkily she moved.

Up finally into the air, out of the gap between two gnarled roots of a rain-soaked giant tree that stretched sky-ward beyond imagining. That little snatch of blue between the branches impossibly high . . . that was some other world she would never truly see. Unless she climbed it, slithered up its moss-soaked slippery sides.

Ooze-covered sides, dark with warm slime she did not mind touching. The bark was tough and soft at the same time, as warm as pungent sweat that seeped out of the tropi-cal air. Higher and higher, but what was the rush?

The bark soothed her skin, and the higher she got, the slower she . . .

What did it matter where the sky was?

It was as if, in climbing the giant swaying tree, crowded in amongst its towering branches, she was also burrowing deep, deep again into the earth. Both at once, just as she was thinking of her dream yet also standing with Sheldon in their dark closet, all at the same time.

"Shiels," Sheldon said, when a heavy roll of brown paper toweling fell off the shelf in the dark and clunked him in the shoulder.

"What?" she breathed.

"Do you think . . ."

She was like that snake in her dream, oozing deliciously with every slight movement.

"Do you think we should . . . find a room somewhere? Maybe . . . with a bed?"

She clamped her teeth on him, and he yelped in his adorable way and a second roll clunked down, on his head perhaps, although she couldn't really tell in the darkness.

"Don't be silly," she murmured, and slithered her tongue along him.

How to explain what was happening, especially explain it to Lorraine Miens. (If Shiels ever got to the personal interview stage. But she felt she would—surely, now, with all that she was achieving?) It wasn't just that Shiels had instinctively followed Manniberg's suggestion about keeping news of Pyke on Vhub, or had sensed a moment of crisis in the cafeteria and acted upon it, perfectly defusing a potential disaster. The more she thought about it, the more she realized that the larger feat had been simply when she had changed her mind. It was how, by being wrong, but firm, and leader-like in the beginning—immovable, really, and completely in control—she could then overcome her own constructed mental garrison (to use a Lorraine Miens term, first coined, Shiels believed, in *Motherlode*, although she would have to look it up). She'd constructed barricades against the best idea, she could see that now. But that was only natural. All humans do it. We are creatures of habit; the world is too complex and too much in constant metamorphosis for any of us to ever be able to keep up. Better to think with your gut *and* your brain. (With both your brains; science had found the gut brain. Shiels knew that too from her explorations in the further reaches of the Internet.) Think fast, know, act, be firm—that's what any good leader will do. Followers need to know that they are being led with energy. (She had followers, and she was just beginning to realize the implications of this. When she had stood before the multitudes about to announce what was already known—and so highly anticipated—she'd felt the quivering of the followers in the room. And then in that moment in the cafeteria, too—the vibration, the tremors . . . were for *her*, not just for Pyke.)

She'd changed her mind, and later in the cafeteria had even channeled power to Manniberg. A leader's prerogative.

To be firm and absolute and set on a course, and then to reverse . . . It's the leader who can do that, straight-faced, without an eye-bat of embarrassment or apology (she imagined herself saying this to Lorraine Miens, who had written in *Abandonment* about how confused and apologetic and embarrassed almost on the cellular level most women were raised to be) . . . it's those armor-plated leaders who whirled the tank around because of better data, a stronger hunch (both together) . . . those leaders whom people adore and follow anywhere. Off the cliff.

Into the next valley.

They adore the commander who changes course.

(Because she didn't have to. She could have staged Autumn Whirl to a half-filled gym of socially damp types who hadn't gotten the message that Pyke's band wasn't playing after all.)

"I felt the will of the student body," she imagined herself saying to Lorraine Miens. "It's hard to describe. It was like a gravitational pull. As a leader I have become intensely interested in tuning into the social, psychological, emotional, and intellectual pull of the mass of people around me."

Would that be too insane a thing to say? Maybe not to Lorraine Miens.

Should Shiels write it in her application essay?

Better if Miens could see her as she said it—her shoulders

set, her lips pulled down in a thoughtful frown (like Miens in most of her portraits), her eyes frank and humble.

She wasn't congratulating herself. She had almost steered her student-body chair year into the ditch on the very first social of the season.

By fate or by luck, this was the year of the pterodactyl. She'd better use it, she realized, or else she'd be buried.

XI

Late Saturday afternoon, Shiels and Sheldon were downtown, running for a bus, leaking supplies—Sheldon was dropping plastic cups, and Shiels was trailing crêpe paper bought from the dollar store, last-minute acquisitions for Autumn Whirl. They had to get back to the auditorium for the sound check; they were the ones with the authority to pay the techies who were setting up the stage and installing the video feed to the sports field scoreboard. It had rained earlier, and the footing was still slippery. Shiels had a slippery sense inside her too—a sort of meeting between the fog of fatigue (there hadn't been many hours of rest lately, given the avalanche of organizational responsibilities) and the bright sun of her own formidable will. Nothing was going to get in the way of Shiels making this an unforgettable social extravaganza.

Then Shiels saw it in a storefront window—a yellow running shoe just like the ones that had been popping up periodically in her dreams, on Sheldon sometimes, but more and more often now on her, whether she was climbing up through the undergrowth of pulsing rain forest or was alone on the savanna running, running.

She glimpsed the flash of yellow, turned . . . stopped. She was highly conscious of the tightness of her current stiff shoes, not meant for running, for anything wild. Sheldon ran on for another half block before he even realized she wasn't with him anymore.

"What are you doing?" he yelled. He was carrying his black umbrella, along with the supplies, even though it wasn't raining now. He went everywhere with his black umbrella.

"You just go on! I'll catch up!"

She wasn't looking at him but could feel him hesitate from a distance. He didn't believe her. What was she up to now?

Keeping him guessing.

"I'll be there on the next bus!" she yelled, and then she stepped into the shop.

It was not a place she would normally even notice. Darkish, in the gloomier part of town, with old wooden floors and distressed brick walls—from age, not design— lined with running shoes.

When was the last time Shiels had bought running shoes?

She saw white ones, blue ones, red, black . . . high tops, leather, synthetic, thick-soled, thin, for different sports, obviously; sections of the store were labeled for basketball, tennis, cross-training, gym, running, walking. . . .

She didn't see the yellow shoes. Just the one in the window.

A thin old man shuffled out of the gloom in the back of the store. He was wearing some kind of sport shirt, but it was untucked in front. White wisps of hair would not stay in place on his mostly pink head.

"Something I can help you with?" he asked.

She mentioned the yellow shoe in the window, and he seemed surprised it was even there. "Don't know if I have any of those left," he said. "What size?"

Shiels allowed for an eight. Her feet were quite large, out of proportion to the rest of her. They seemed like duck flappers most of the time to her—her least elegant body part, she felt. But these shoes . . .

"Doubt I have any left," the man repeated on his way back into the gloom.

Shiels was holding the window shoe now. It seemed to float in her hands, barely a slipper, a stretch of fabric that would mold to the foot, a wafer of rubber on the soul to keep the skin from bleeding. This particular shoe looked too narrow for her, but she cleared room on an old bench littered with shoes boxes and sat down anyway to try it. The fabric did stretch; the toes were cramped, but—

"No luck," the man said, suddenly upon her again. "What kind of training are you looking to do, anyway?"

"This one fits," she said. "Where's its mate?"

He smiled in a frowny sort of way. "I had a pretty good look. What exactly are you—"

"I'm looking for this shoe's mate, exactly," Shiels said. "You have one. You must have the other. Unless you sell single shoes?"

His gaze seemed to take in everything: the shelves and shelves of shoes; the piles of shoe boxes; the benches with their worn fabric, purple once perhaps, now turned to gray; a rack of cobwebby shoelaces; a broom leaning incongruously against a pile of newspapers.

"Are you looking to run races or something?" he said.

She did not feel at all inclined to submit to interrogation about her motives for buying a simple pair of yellow runners. One was already on her left foot. Where was the other? This should not have been difficult.

"I've always wanted to take up running," she said. "Do you mind if I help you search?"

"If you're not a runner already, these aren't the right shoes. They're for people who've been running barefoot for a long time. Africans, mostly. If you're not a barefoot runner already, you want more cushion, more arch support. I have a good selection. . . ."

Shiels was already pawing through the front window

display again to see if the other shoe had fallen down some-where, perhaps was lodged under the dismal turf-colored fabric blanketing the booth. "Where do you keep the mates of all these other display shoes?" she asked.

"Running creates a lot of impact," the man said. "It's hard on the knees, the ankles, the hips. . . ."

The old man looked pretty creaky. How long since he had run anywhere himself? "You must have a system," Shiels said. "I can't believe you regularly lose companion shoes like this. Where do you put them?"

He showed her to the back storeroom, lit by a single dull bulb, where leaning towers of boxes tilted high into the shadows. "Depends when I did it," he said vaguely.

Many of the boxes were apparently unlabeled. But it was not a huge room. It would not take forever to look in every box. And maybe Shiels would get lucky. Certainly Sheldon could handle the last preps for the dance, or what-ever Autumn Whirl was becoming. The Event. "I'm just going to have a quick look," she said.

Her phone then. A text from Sheldon: *Pyke awol sound chk need u now!*

The old guy was moving shoe boxes from one tempo-rary pile to another. She needed to warn him. "I have to leave in, like, two minutes," she said. "But I am going to find this missing shoe. I'm asking for your pre-forgiveness."

He scratched his neck, as if he did not understand.

"Just nod, and know that I will pay for the shoes and I will clean up. Thank you," she said. "If this shoe's box had a name on the label, what would it be called?"

"Meteor," he said.

She scanned through the boxes with labels, the ones she could see, letting her brain reside in her eyes—was it fair to think of it that way? Meteor, Meteor, Meteor. It was a faster way of thinking. She trusted her eyes to find the printed word before her brain could process all the images, the towers of identical or nearly identical boxes. When she was through with one tower, she moved on to the next. When the labels were scanned—no Meteor shoes anywhere—she turned to the unlabeled boxes, this time not methodically at all. No time for that anymore. She just went where her muscles thought to go. Her brain was in her hands, her fingers. Eyes still scanning but now for yellow, for the lone shoe.

She wasn't trying to make a mess. Empty boxes flew behind her, tissue, laces, random shoes this way and that.

She had asked for pre-forgiveness.

The yellow shoe was somewhere in the room, somewhere near.

And then . . . there it was. On its own, in a box, not tucked in a corner or anything. In her hand. She'd barely torn through half the storeroom.

"I will be here tomorrow morning to clean up this

room," she declared. "I always keep my word. What time do you open?"

The man looked stunned, as if a bear had shambled into his shop and he was alone, without weapons.

Shiels whipped out her parents' credit card. She had already used it anyway, to pay for the last-minute supplies. "I think I will wear them now," she said.

It felt like nothing was on her feet, or that her feet were nothing—weightless, just like in her dreams, her body lifting subtly off the ground as she was easing her way forward. The first few steps were just like that, full of a burst of pleasure from somewhere lost inside her, a lovely breath.

The first few steps.

Out the door and down the block, and she thought, *I don't need to take the bus. I can run there.*

She pumped her arms. Like she'd been running long distances all her life. She'd be a bit flushed when she arrived. . . .

Like Pyke after heaving himself into the air with his beautiful wings. Those glowing chest muscles.

She would glisten.

Like Jocelyne Legault rounding the corner of the track. Those first few steps—a half block to the corner—Shiels was at least as fast, as efficient, as effortless as Jocelyne Legault.

But she didn't get the light, and a truck rumbled through,

so she stopped and noticed that her heart clanked, and her breath was ragged, and if she thought about it (how could she not?), her feet actually were starting to weigh something.

Her beautiful yellow feet were turning into . . . blocks of wood.

The light changed, she sped off . . . lurched off, and was most annoyed when the curb at the other end of the crossing seemed unusually high, so that she had to physically lift herself. She was not flying. The pavement grabbed at her, slowed her knees, her thighs. Her breasts jiggled. *And they aren't even big,* she thought. But she wasn't boobless.

She wasn't Jocelyne Legault.

She pushed to the next light, praying for a red, for a break, but it turned green just as she got to it, so she had to keep running.

People were watching. People in cars going by her thinking, *Who is that clumsy girl with the flapping, thumping feet and bouncing chest carrying all those crêpe streamers and wearing those championship yellow sneakers pretending she's a runner?*

She wasn't a runner.

She was breathing like she had a bird's nest in her lungs.

She was dizzy after two and half blocks.

One and a half blocks!

She looked back and could not tell how many blocks she had run.

Her soles felt like they'd been beaten with a hammer.

She was not a runner.

Was not.

Could barely breathe.

Cramp, cramping in her gut.

She started again. It was an elemental human thing— running. We all started out . . . on the savanna . . . running after our food.

That's how we started.

Slowly.

Huff . . . huffing . . .

And if we didn't . . . If we . . . couldn't . . .

If dinner got away . . . If we looked like dinner ourselves . . .

Why was this so fucking difficult?

Jocelyne Legault made it look like . . .

Shiels glanced behind her. Tried to focus. No bus. No bus was coming to save her.

She was going to have to make it back on foot whether she wanted to or not.

Was it ten blocks to the school . . . or two hundred? Shiels willed herself forward, prodded and slapped her feet against the hard concrete . . . up every evil curb. How could she feel so feeble, so clumsy, so joltingly out of step in her beautiful new yellow shoes? The breath gurgled out of her. She felt her head rolling. She had a vague sense she ought to pump her arms.

She dropped the bag of crêpe paper and did not stop to pick it up.

She dropped her old shoes, her leather, sensible ones.

The world became a tiny moving spot of focus on the pavement a few steps ahead of her feet.

It started to rain again. When? Hours later? When she was still running . . . heaving herself forward.

Her lungs knotted.

She breathed with her mouth.

The tiny spot ahead of her shrank.

Her fists were tired. Was she even running anymore? She was shuddering forward.

She lost track of where she was going.

The rust in her knees seemed to be grinding against other rust. But how could it be there? She used to run places. Didn't she? She remembered playing soccer with her father and all his side of the family at that reunion. When was that? She was almost in high school then.

She could run after a ball then.

She remembered.

She ran a bit back then.

And then . . . at Vista View . . . well who ran, anyway? Jocelyne Legault. She was practically the only one. She ran for the whole school because she was good enough, and whoever could keep up with her anyway?

Shiels realized she was no longer moving forward. The world was moving forward, but she was teetering over someone's flower bed.

So she was not downtown anymore. She must've been close to home. Where was she going?

Nowhere. The flower bed . . . the dirt of it. Cleared of flowers. Ready for . . .

. . . the student-body chair of Vista View High School to lean over, gasping, waiting to see if the contents of her stomach were going to return to the world.

Silliness, to arrive in the auditorium so long after the sound check should have been completed. To show up soaked from rain and sweat, crying practically from the pain, the stupid pain of running such a modest distance. Throat burning from breathing so hard. The whole world listing, spinning, broken.

"You're green," Sheldon said to her. "Where's the hand stamp?"

Shiels had to lean against the stage before words would form. Why had she ever thought she could run more than a block to save her life?

Because she'd run after Pyke, when Pyke had been a monster, and it had been effortless. Her feet hadn't even touched the ground. She'd run after him when everyone else had stayed back.

The volunteer team was setting up the tables. Where was the dance floor supposed to be?

Where was Pyke now? Where was the band?

"What hand stamp?" Shiels said.

Instead of enveloping her in his arms, Sheldon stood back at least two paces. He seemed to be accusing her of something.

"It was in the bag with the extra crêpe paper," Sheldon said. "We have to stamp hands when people show their tickets. What took you so long anyway? I texted you, like, half an hour ago."

Half an hour? So, she'd been running for, what, twenty minutes?

Ten?

"Did Pyke show up for the sound check?" she asked finally.

Sheldon's look said no. The stage was littered with instruments, but no musicians were apparent.

"Nobody's seen him since yesterday," Sheldon said.

Stay away part of an afternoon, Shiels thought, *and what happens? Chaos.*

For a moment she felt herself leaving her body, she was so wrung-out from her little run. There she was, a few feet above herself, vibrating vaguely while Sheldon, in a shimmering fog, keeping his distance, explained about the band. What was he saying?

They never did sound checks anyway, it turned out. Sound checks were redundant.

How could Jocelyne Legault run so fast for so long and never look tired?

Shiels retreated to a corner of the gym where tumbling mats had not yet been put away in the equipment closet. She rested her head for just a moment. Autumn Whirl was going to require every ounce of her attention soon enough, if she was going to save it from unraveling. No Pyke!

She was going to have to rouse herself.

A horde of ticket holders was soon going to descend upon her. Momentarily, after she raised her head and opened her eyes, she would check her phone and so know the hour. How late it was.

Everyone counting on her.

Blaming her.

She was the student-body chair.

She had a sense of them, already, gathering. A boy from another school—how had he gotten in?—began pulling the banners and posters from the wall. "Pyke is shit! Pyke is shit!" he was screaming, leading others—they were all screaming, even the members of the organizing committee.

"Shiels is shit! Shiels is shit! Shiels Krane can't explain!" The boy, the leader, was tearing her name off an iron sign she hadn't noticed hanging near the stage. Using a crowbar. The nails creaking loudly, because there was no music.

There was no music.

Autumn Whirl, organized by Shiels Krane, student-body chair, had no music.

"He's coming. He's coming!" Shiels said, looking around for Sheldon—who filled in the gaps, whenever she did something stupid, like run to the school and exhaust herself instead of taking the bus. He could be counted on.

Sheldon had her back.

But even Sheldon now was gone.

"There she is!" the boy yelled. He had a ferret face, and a strangely ridged back, as if he had just stepped out from the bush and into decent clothes last week. "In the yellow shoes. There she is!"

Shiels started awake—what a brutal dream that had been!— and saw two lights, red and white, chasing each other all over the gym. It was hard to see anything else because of all the bodies bouncing, writhing, spinning in the darkness. And because of the noise.

The screaming.

They were all out of their minds.

Shiels pushed herself into the mass of them. How had

she slept through all of this? The exhaustion of the preparations and of the run must have come to a head. She squiggled between sweaty girls, jiggling boys. "Sorry. Sorry!" she said, hopelessly. No one heard anyway, and no one cared. They were all one big pressing, gesturing, screeching beast.

Shiels plunged her fingers into her ears. Everyone had gone insane. Howling like . . . like they were giant birds of prey blaring the pain and victory of the world.

Closer, closer. "Sorry! I'm sorry!" she yelled, and then she stopped apologizing. She didn't recognize anyone. Were they all strangers? In the dark, who could tell? Everyone was dressed in black, and they all had umbrellas dangling from their bodies. Purple lines painted down the ridges of their noses.

Closer, closer to the seething middle of the mass. What was pulling her? Something as strong as the primeval tug of those yellow shoes she was still wearing.

She hadn't changed for the event. She was in her soaked organizing clothes. But it didn't matter. No one saw her. No one recognized her.

They were all different.

A lone dancer flashed onstage, a sharp-shouldered tiny girl in raven black, head to toe, and not only the ridge of her nose had been purpled but the entire appendage, which looked substantial now, a whirling, slashing beak, almost, as she hopped and dipped, angled high again, stabbed out with her elbows, her knees, the sharp proboscis. A dancing, screeching, swirling blur.

Shiels couldn't help but follow the movements. Everybody followed them. They were all whirling, hopping, stabbing in time . . .

To Jocelyne Legault.

What had happened to her?

And there was Pyke at last, tiny and giant at the same time. Shiels was so close, she could feel the heat of him. When he lanced his beak forward, it looked like he could draw blood. When he hopped and stabbed, he did it as one who'd been living off the move since before the last Ice Age. When he screeched . . .

When he screeched, Shiels felt the worm in her gut coil itself, squeeze as if time had sped to the jolt of the universe and molten rock would spurt in an intake of breath.

She howled out the pain of it, the shatter kick, the boom. *Do you like the world as it is?* a voice scratched deep inside her. *Do you like the world as it is?*

Do you like the world?

Already, already, already . . .

Already that world has gone.

Omigod, omigod, omigod, omigod!

She was not a girl who said such a thing, who thought in such . . . teenage terms.

But—oh my God.

Nothing was the same. In the space of one afternoon—and one long, unexplainable night—the axis of everything began to do its own dance. Its own dance with everyone.

Pyke raised his beak at a certain angle, he sang out something so old and bloodboiling yet soft and beguiling . . . He was beguiling. How did he do that? He never left the stage. He stayed where he was, hopped this way and that—anyone else who hopped like an oversize crow would just be laughed at, but when Pyke hopped . . . sentences unraveled. Thoughts spilled out like someone had reached in and pulled your intestines and you watched them, feeling . . . a certain pleasure?

Feeling something.

Feeling everything.

Everything came out on the dance floor.

Nobody was sitting. Nobody was standing around. They were wriggling earthworms together, earthworms on steroids. Was this what drugs were like?

Sheldon had as much as said he had tried drugs. He had said this was better than drugs.

He was wriggling in front of her, and she had to hold his face still, to climb him and wrap her legs around his torso . . . oh, his bony thin torso, her aching tired legs . . . didn't matter. Nothing mattered.

They kissed to the bottom of the endless ocean.

Everyone was kissing. As far as Shiels could see. Pyke screamed, the band played, Jocelyne Legault melted onstage and regrouped, melted and regrouped. Was that dancing?

Was anyone dancing?

The whole world was melting molten red hot wet and flowing . . . How long did Sheldon carry her?

Who knew he was this strong?

"Why don't we . . ."

Carried her around like he owned her. Her legs locked. Pressed in the seething mass.

Practically public.

"Why don't we . . ."

She couldn't stop kissing him down to the bottom of everything.

How deep did it go?

How deep did it . . .

How?

XII

Blue walls. Everything still. Light.

The slant of the attic, just like Sheldon's room.

Blue.

Sleeping on her stomach with her jaw twisted into the pillow. Like she was trying to eat it. For breakfast.

Shiels was ravenously hungry.

Where was this dream?

A typewriter, ancient clacker, nailed to the wall just like in . . .

And Don Quixote—Picasso's squiggles—on the other wall, the non-slanty one.

All familiar.

She blinked. Doesn't happen very often in a dream, that she was aware of. Blinking.

"Oh shit," she said. Her throat gritted with sandpaper.

Sheldon raised his unshaven face from the mound of blankets. His nose was still ridged purple. "Good morning to you, too!"

"Oh shit. Oh shit!" she said, and she grabbed the sheet instinctively and drew it to her. Wrapped herself like a big wad of refuse.

"Are you cold?"

He was in his vintage Astrolab T-shirt and what looked like train engine boxer shorts, his boy hairs poking out of everything.

"How did I get here?" It felt like she had fur growing on her teeth.

Pterodactyl fur?

Even as he said, "You're kidding, right?" she remembered the dream of it—hauling him here as the night broke up, the comical pull-grab dance up the darkened stairs. Of his house.

Did that all happen?

"Are your parents here?" She looked out the window. It was a two-story drop to the back garden. How would she ever get out?

"I believe that's them downstairs cooking breakfast." He knew she was torqued, could see it in her face—he must have—yet he still leaned as if she might be inclined to kiss him.

Or more.

Bacon and end-of-the-world eggs. Shiels could smell them now.

"You are going to create a diversion." She could barely breathe, her brain was working so fast. "So I can get out. They don't know I'm here, do they?"

Sheldon was balanced midlean between his rejected advance and this other emotion he seemed to be having. What? He wanted her to saunter down the stairs and have Sunday breakfast with his freaking parents?

"They'll be cool with it," he said. He was holding his teeth stiff.

Like he both did and didn't expect this from her.

Had they. . . Was she . . .

Sweet flying murder of crows. One crisis at a time, please!

Why couldn't she remember anything?

"Diversion, Sheldon," she said. As if she had to keep things elementary. She reached for her clothes—her bra tied to the bedpost, her pants inside out. Her shirt and sweater twisted like a rope hanging from the corner of his grade school desk. With each movement she kept the sheet wrapped around her.

"It's not as if I haven't seen you." Sheldon's hair was a sat-upon loaf of bread.

"I need to get out of here." Her voice a feeble scratch. Had she really spent most of the night screaming her head off?

Had she really just gone to bed with Sheldon?

She felt stretched and raw . . . down there. Was it . . .

No. Sheldon would never drug her. She couldn't believe it. It was something else. Pyke. The head-banging churn of Autumn Whirl.

The mother of all crashes.

"Should I go out the back . . . or the front?"

She was dressed now. Sort of. Nothing fit anymore. It felt like she'd walked into the Salvation Army and randomly pulled things off the shelves.

"You should comb your hair and wash your face and walk proudly with me into the kitchen and say good morning to Eugene and Nancy. They already love you, you know that. They have been asking me, in their way, if we have slept together yet. They aren't against it."

Shiels looked at him dubiously.

"They aren't!" he said, so loud that she shushed him.

Dear, stupid, deluded, dense-brained boy. He looked like he was going to be hurt.

"This isn't the way I want to do it," she said. The kitchen was in the rear of the house. The stairs led straight down to the front door. That would be best. One of the advantages of living in a shoe box.

"How do you want to do it?" He was trying so hard to keep the hurt out of his voice. To just be Sheldon—never angry. Never surprised. Rolling with everything.

She kissed him, to get him to shut up, to not be so . . .

To get her one step closer to out the door.

"You might want to wash up," she said to him, and she touched his purple-ridged nose. That look! My God. "I'm not face-raking you," she said.

So furry in the mouth. They both were.

"You keep saying that to me." Dangerous voice. He was looking at her with weird eyes. "You're embarrassed," he said. "To be with me. To be . . . *with me.*"

"No. No. Sheldon . . ."

"It never has been about me, has it?"

"Sheldon—"

"It's about you. And now it's about you and Pyke."

Where was all this coming from? How did she ever end up here, in this freaking moment?

From the kitchen—the house was so small, they could just yell—Sheldon's mother called out, "Breakfast is ready, dear!"

A strangulated, broken silence.

"Just trust me, please," Shiels said. "I'm not face-raking you."

Outside now. For once a plan had unfolded properly. She had just walked out the front door, hopefully unseen and unheard. Wearing the yellow shoes, it was almost as if she *had* to run, or at least try. What time was it? She was too tired to check her phone. But her parents never slept in. They would be in their cozy twin flannel dressing gowns staring dreamily into their locally crafted pottery mugs of fair trade organic coffee with the *Times* burning brightly on their respective screens: New York for her mother, London for her father. The sun would be flooding in from the east window.

Had they checked her room? Probably not.

Her legs creaked like they were made of wood.

(Had she really just ruined things with Sheldon? Because she couldn't face his parents at breakfast?)

Maybe if she slipped through the front door at home . . .

Jolt, jolt, jolt went her feet.

(It would be all right. Of course it would be. After all this had blown over.)

She didn't have her key. Probably the door was still locked.

(So why was she shaking? Why did her insides feel coated with ice?)

She walked. Too much to think about. Last night . . . last night was one of her weird dreams of late, but come to life. She remembered the shrieking, remembered wrapping herself around Sheldon, being carried around.

She remembered it as one endless kiss.

They must've done it. At Sheldon's house. In his bed. They'd been too molten not to have done it. Sheldon was a prince but he was not superhuman. He would have done it.

She would've throttled him if he hadn't.

So he had done it. *They* had done it.

Finally.

And it had been late, and they had been drunk—drunk on something. She couldn't even remember it.

She'd done it blacked out.

She'd missed her own party.

God, God, God, God.

What did God have to do with it?

And God said: Thou shalt use a condom, because if not, you'll become rotund with child and become a teenage mother, bottom wiper, and human milk dispenser.

And the Lord God said: Teenagers who do it while unconscious do not deserve to be student-body chair, much less be considered for a personal interview with Lorraine Miens who said, "A woman who treats her body like a highway deserves to be paved." And who also said, "A man who treats a woman's body like a highway deserves every crash coming to him."

Jolt, jolt, jolt. She was walking as fast as she could. But she felt like roadkill, or not quite—like she'd been winged by a passing truck so was lurching along, almost a hop-hop-hop.

Had it been that bizarre last night? Everyone in black, hopping and lurching? Everyone shrieking?

It hadn't been bizarre from the inside. From inside it had been . . .

Molten.

Her ears were still aching.

And she felt . . . raspy down there. She'd done it with Sheldon, obviously she had. She must've felt *something*.

Maybe she was pregnant. Maybe that was why the morning sky was purple and the grass gray and all her joints felt gritted with sand, including her jaw.

Her jaw?

What did her jaw have to complain about?

She imagined herself waddling in front of Lorraine Miens. The famous black-rimmed glasses would get pulled down for closer inspection.

"You're pregnant, Ms. Krane."

"Actually, it's a thyroid condition. I'll go on a grapefruit diet during the semester."

Those dark-pooled eyes that had seen everything forty times already.

"I want to work on . . . the cultural implications of inter-species hyper-communications."

"The what?"

"I'm the student-body chair of Vista View. You might not believe this, but our high school—"

"I think as little about high school as I possibly can. And I certainly couldn't contemplate taking on a student who is going to give birth. Our program is highly—"

"We have a pterodactyl-student. I'm the chair through

the whole thing. And what we've found . . . as I'm studying the various reactions to his—"

"Ms. Krane—you're pregnant!"

"I don't know if you'd call it charisma. I think that's too lame a word. He . . . gets inside us in amazing ways. So I'm calling it 'interspecies hyper-communications.'"

"Did he get you pregnant?"

"I'm not pregnant. I just—"

"Did the pterodactyl get you pregnant? Is this what you mean by 'hyper-communications'?"

Shiels was outside her own house, shaking, when her phone rang. The earth was solid and unchanging before her—there were the elm trees, shedding their leaves; there was the water tower in the distance, as green and bulging as ever; and inside her, glaciers were melting and canyon cliffs falling into surging rivers.

It was her father.

Her father was calling her ten seconds before she would have been able to slip through the front door and possibly fool them.

Three rings. Four. One more, and Shiels's confident answering service voice would pick up. But she hit the button.

"Hello? Hi, Dad. Hi." She was trying to find the right tone.

"Good morning, Shiels. It's your father speaking." His phony formal voice. Shiels scanned the front windows to see if he was standing there, on the phone, watching her arrive. After being out all night. After spending the night with Sheldon, and doing it, and probably getting pregnant.

Maybe.

"Hi, Daddy," she said. A flex of her little girl muscles.

He wasn't standing at any of the front windows.

"Your mother is worried that perhaps you didn't get your entire eight hours of restful sleep last night." He was trying to keep a light tone. Shiels could hear her mother breathing over his shoulder.

"It was a long night," Shiels said. "Amazing, though. Huge turnout. We were doing the cleanup, of course." Breathe, breathe. Dark purple sky. Gray grass.

Yellow shoes.

"So you're just getting out now?"

Yellow shoes. The store. She remembered now. She'd said she'd clean up there. An excuse! A good reason to not go home right away.

"I'm okay. I'll sleep this afternoon. It was really a great, great event." She could hear her mother wringing her hands. "Love you, Daddy," Shiels said.

"What has happened to you?" the old man said, at the door of the running-shoe shop.

"Nothing. I'm quite fine," Shiels asserted. "I'm here to fulfill my pledge." When the old man failed to respond, but just kept standing there, blocking the door, she said, "Cleaning up the storeroom. I said I would do it this morning."

"Why is your nose all purple?" he said.

"It isn't," she said, but her hand went up to her nose anyway. It felt perfectly normal. She thought of Sheldon looking at her in bed, that weirdness in his eyes.

"Looks purple to me," the man said.

Shiels pushed her way through. There was an employee washroom at the back, an odd, old-fashioned cement chamber with a showerhead, a sink, a toilet, a mirror, a garbage can, and a drain in the middle of the floor.

She examined herself in the mirror. Her nose looked like it had been coated in purple shoe polish. *Sheldon!* She bent to wet her face. Where was the soap? She spotted a hulking yellow bar resting on a piece of wood on the floor behind the toilet. It smelled like it might dissolve metal. Was that the soap?

Cautiously she wet the bar and rubbed, rubbed. The purple wasn't oily at all. It wasn't thick. It felt . . . like her skin.

Like the skin of her nose had simply turned purple.

The pigment wasn't coming off. She closed her eyes, breathed through her mouth, waited for this stupid nightmare to pass.

Blink. Blink.

Purple.

"*Sheldon!*" She screamed his name into the phone, but he wasn't picking up. He was probably still having breakfast with his sunny-morning parents. He was probably punishing her.

She longed to face-rake him that instant. She wanted to . . .

"Is everything all right, miss?" the man called from outside the door.

"No!" she yelled. "My nose has turned purple!"

He didn't seem to have an answer to that. He waited forever, and then he said, "Just take your time."

She stared at her face. She looked fierce, somehow, her purple nose beak-like. Dipped in ink. The pores on her nose were larger than those on her pale cheeks. She scrubbed and scrubbed, with her hands, with a rough cloth she found by the moldy garbage pail, then with a brush that she demanded the old man bring to her. The harder she worked, the more tender the skin became, until fresh-rubbed blood oozed like cherry sauce on sick chocolate.

"Is it coming off?" the old man asked through the door.

She had to hold herself against the crusty sink to keep from falling over.

"How did it get all purple anyway?" the old man asked.

"Go away. I'm sorry. Just . . . go away." She could still hear him breathing outside the door. "It's all right. I'm not going to kill myself." *There must be a solution*, she thought. *Don't people get tattoos removed?*

Maybe she could get her nose removed.

And replaced, of course. A nose replacement . . . Her parents would know the right specialist. They knew all the right—

"It's just . . . this is the only bathroom," the old man said finally.

In a crisis Shiels had learned, through her years in leadership, to turn to the closest thing at hand. Do that task. Focus, focus. Give your brain time to unglue.

She tackled the mess in the storeroom. Quietly, efficiently, with all the concentration she could summon. Did it make sense to sort the boxes by style and make or by size? Size made sense. Style and make might change regularly, but size is eternal, maybe. Size is orderly and predictable. Small at the bottom. Largest on top. But broken into manageable clumps so that the shelves were used to full advantage. And midsizes, presumably the ones most often in demand, would be at chest to eye level. Easy. Predictable. A touch of organization.

She was an organized person. An energetic and intelligent and disciplined person who dismantled the entire storeroom's structure—if near chaos could be called a structure—and rebuilt it along reasonable and practical and even scientific lines.

She swept and dusted, threw out more than twenty empty

boxes that had been taking up space, pretending to hold shoes. She found three single shoes without mates. There were no more yellow ones—she was wearing the last pair.

She kept the door shut and did not look out. The old man came in twice, looking for a particular size and brand, and both times Shiels was able to retrieve the box within seconds and send him on his way.

She could organize a storeroom. If she didn't get an interview with Lorraine Miens, she thought, if her nose stayed purple and she lost all hope and couldn't even get into medical school, she could always organize storerooms.

Who knew how long she stayed in there? Her phone was off. She began to feel vaguely hungry, but that could be ignored until every last box was checked and stacked in its appropriate place in the universe.

In the end, when she could delay no longer, she had to open the door. The old man stood with his hands in his pockets and his eyes large. Others were there too—customers who looked like they might be runners, and who (perhaps) had come to gaze at the miracle of organization.

"It's beautiful," the old man said, evidently for everyone.

Shiels buried her nose in her arm so it could not be seen.

XIII

Step and step, all the way home, no one answering her calls, not Sheldon, not . . . Sheldon. She was the student-body chair of Vista View High. That changes a person. The office had seeped into her posture, into how she thought of herself. Yet . . . she was hungry now, and cold, and terribly tired, and the whole of her world was a different place since yesterday, beginning with her foolish run, leading to other things. To the dance. To spending the night with her boyfriend, who now had fallen off the face of the earth.

It had led her to an unexplainable but apparently permanent purple nose.

Step and step. She would not bow her head. She would not walk around anymore with her hand in front of her face. She was student-body chair. She would not look away as the eyes of the others on the sidewalk, across the street, in the windows of the shops and restaurants she passed, registered their surprise.

A permanently purple nose.

(If she were pregnant, by her apparently disappeared boyfriend, would Babyface emerge with a purple nose too? Had the pigment seeped into her skin? Was the change encoded in her DNA?)

Step and step. Heading home to double-physician parents who would press her to recount every detail of the last twenty-four hours.

Maybe, she thought, she could just keep going. Grab a bus to somewhere large and anonymous where a purple-nosed girl would blend in with all the others who congregated there, waiting for their surgeries.

As if there were such surgeries.

She slipped into the house quietly, as she had learned to do. All still. Sunday afternoon. Her father would be in one of the dens, watching the game, whatever game it was. His hour of relaxation in the frantic week. Her mother would be reviewing her case files for tomorrow, because she never relaxed.

She could relax after she was dead.

"Shiels, is that you?" her mother called. Shiels had been soundless. But her mother could still feel Sheils's footfalls in her womb.

"Yes, I'm home." If she pushed herself upstairs, she could barricade herself in her room, postpone the inevitable for an hour or two. But she was starving and would have to face inspection sometime.

Sure steps of doom headed toward her. Shiels waited. Her mother emerged from the western dining room carrying her tablet. Her reading glasses were still on. "I can't imagine you've made a dent in your assignments this weekend," she said. "Don't you have that biology lab to do? And what about your—"

She was going to say "college applications," Shiels knew it, but she stopped in the hall while her tidy chin kept working for another beat or two. It was rare to see her mother lost for words. "Have you taken a look at yourself lately, dear?" she asked finally.

Shiels's phone then. Sheldon. She turned it off.

The boy had slept with her when she hadn't been in her right mind.

He had let her leave the house without telling her that her nose had turned into night.

Probably he was the one who had inked it purple.

"Yes, Mother, I have seen."

A standoff in the doorway.

"Is this some . . . fad or other? I think it's in terrible taste. Why don't you clean it off?"

"I will," Shiels heard herself say. And then she was

hurrying up the stairs—her feet seemed to have made the decision for her—and very quickly she was in her room. Door locked. She took out her phone and called her brother.

"What?" Jonathan said. He was just in the next bedroom.

"I want you to go downstairs and fix me a plate of mixed green salad with slices of tomato lightly sprinkled with olive oil and feta cheese, and I'd like some of those biscuits in the cupboard, the special ones in the russet package."

"Why are you calling *me*?" he said.

"I'm starving, but I can't go down to the kitchen right now."

"What, you're home?"

"Don't waste time. I'm famished."

"You're at home and you're calling me to go get you food?"

"Just do it, all right? I'm not going to explain. Did I not just organize the best high school social event in the history of the universe?"

The boy was silent. As much agreement as she was ever going to get from him.

"You know it was beyond scalding. Please, Jonathan. I will owe you. If there are any olives—"

"I hate olives. I can't even touch them. They smell like rotting puke."

"Forget the olives. Please. Anything. A plate of food. *I will owe you.*"

She closed her eyes and willed her impossible brother to connect with some remnant of humanity left in his pubescent body. Leaders got things done. She was a leader . . . still.

When at last the boy had given his burping, grudging acquiescence, she called Sheldon. "You didn't tell me!" she said as soon as he answered.

"I'm sorry—"

"You let me leave your house without telling me. Not a word. You let me . . ."

"I'm sorry. I just—"

"You let me sail into town looking like, like . . . a purple-beaked white bird. You didn't say one word. You didn't . . ."

"I'm sorry."

"You are. You are very sorry. You were going to march me down to have breakfast with your parents looking like this. Now, what is this shit on my nose, and how do I get it off?"

"I don't know." He didn't sound like himself. Sheldon wasn't an "I don't know" kind of person. He always had an opinion, a bright idea. He always . . . "Did you try soap and water?"

"Of course I tried soap and water! I almost peeled my skin off! Now tell me!"

"Well, I didn't put it on you," Sheldon said. "It was after

you went up and wrangle danced with Pyke. You came back, and your nose was done. I didn't see—"

"I never wrangle danced with Pyke. What are you talking about?"

"Everyone saw you. You and Pyke. You have to remember *that*."

"I don't remember two molecules about what happened for a lot of last night, Sheldon. You'll have to tell me. I'm sorry. I wrangle danced with Pyke?"

Someone rattled her doorknob then—Jonathan. "Just leave it outside the door. Thank you!" she called. "Back away and don't look."

There was half a microbe's chance that Jonathan would look away. She pulled on a hoodie and cloaked her face, then opened the door and grabbed the plate he'd left. She didn't even glance to see where he was.

Slam! Safe again.

He'd made her a peanut butter sandwich with a tired purple grape on top. Did he know already? She bit into the sandwich, chewed dryly, threw the grape into the wastebasket.

"Are you there?" she said again into the phone.

"The most important bit about the whole thing," Sheldon said—he sounded an odd mix of himself and some gravely serious person—"is what happened at the end of it. You do remember that?"

"Yes," she said dubiously. "I think. I'm sorry, I'm just going to say this," she said, because he was Sheldon, after all. It felt like the world had righted itself somehow, slightly at least, to simply be talking to him. "I'm just going to say it. I know we woke up together. Did we . . . Did we . . ."

"Say that we loved each other? Yes, we did."

It didn't sound like he was joking.

"But did you . . . Did we . . ."

"Fall asleep in each other's arms? Yes. Wake up together . . . yes. Have breakfast with my parents . . . no. You would have been fine. Even with your nose. Mine was still lined, and I would have kept it that way."

"Sheldon!" She bit more of the wretched sandwich. The peanut butter tasted like it had been buried by ancient Egyptians. "You know what I am asking."

"You mean did we swim the English Channel together? Did we walk on the moon?"

"Any of those things."

Silence, as if he were reveling in this occasion to be indignant. Of course he wanted her to remember. Ordinarily she would. This was not an ordinary situation.

"After you wrangle danced with Pyke," he said slowly, "you practically dragged me into my own bed. I've got scratches still from where you ripped my clothes. What do you think we did?"

Was he breathing anymore? She couldn't tell. He stopped talking, and the silence stretched between them like an eight-lane highway.

She couldn't think of what to say. She didn't want to hang up. She wanted him to be right there. She wanted to be alone with him, in his bed again, skin to skin, as they must have been, after the storm had passed. They must have been lying together, cobbled, breathing. He must have wrapped his arms around her. She must have felt his strong hands, the thrum of his heart, the heat of him. She must have said it first. *I love you.*

She could almost, almost remember.

"Sheldon?" she said. But the boy was gone, gone, gone.

Shiels gazed hard into the bedroom mirror at her tender, purpled, rubbed-raw nose. The color wasn't going to come off. The skin would not heal quickly.

She had wrangle danced with Pyke? How could she not remember? Yet, somehow the mention of it brought back a niggle of a memory. She remembered Pyke, gesturing with his beak, looking at her. When she'd been dancing with Sheldon. When they hadn't been entirely grappled together. Had she gone onstage then? Had she moved her own feet, or had the crowd propelled her? Was that what everyone had been shrieking about?

Shiels and Pyke, onstage, coiling and uncoiling.

She had a terrible thought—that it was all on Vhub. At this very moment. That people had videoed it—of course they had. What important moment went unvideoed these days?

Sleeping with Sheldon. Doing it finally with him. Apparently. Maybe getting pregnant. That all had gone unvideoed.

Why had she no memory of these seminal events?

(An unfortunate choice of words. What would Lorraine Miens think?)

"I will not interview any young woman with an unintentionally purple nose," Lorraine Miens said then in some basement corner of Shiels's mind.

Unintentionally purple.

God, it looked enormous like this, like it was growing into a beak in front of her eyes. (Literally. "That's where a beak would grow, Ms. Krane.")

She had a thin tube of concealer. For little spots, sun-caused things. She almost never used it. She spread some now with her tiny, soft brush. Had some unbelievably cute furry animal died so she could try to brush over the scaling of her face? (What if her face turned to purple scales?)

"Makeup is the hardening over of the human face," Lorraine Miens had said. "It's the iron grip of patriarchy flexing within your own fingers."

Beigy dust, like fine desert sand blowing in, caking in the humps and hollows.

Shiels would have to buy this stuff by the crate load to do this every day.

A mottled beak. She looked like some space creature now, an invading species attempting to look human.

Her hand stayed steady, despite the free fall inside. She changed brushes and powder. Flesh tone. Cakey in spots, but she could smooth it out.

Some of it.

Better.

How to erase the borderline, to smooth it all out? Just keep going. A multitude of sins can be plastered over.

Not plastered. Powdered. She tried to keep a light, light touch.

She started breathing again.

Turned on her computer.

"Shiels—Shiels dear, are you hungry?" her mother called. Shiels glanced at the digital time in the corner of her screen. How could it be dinner already?

"In a minute, Mom!" she called.

She was still starving, actually. But first things first . . .

"We're eating a little early because your father and I are going to the thing," her mother said.

Shiels logged into Vhub. Crackers!

"You go ahead then, Mom! I'll be down in a bit."

Blurry shots and video of Pyke at the microphone, Pyke blaring out at the crowd, Pyke and Jocelyne Legault entangled, doing their own wrangle dance.

"I want us all to eat together tonight!" her mother called. "It's family dinner night!"

A cluster of videos. One still shot of Shiels climbing up onto the stage, Pyke's beak angled right at her . . . right between her legs.

Her nose distinctly non-purple.

"Now, please, Shiels. I insist!" Her mother was standing just outside her door.

But she wasn't coming in.

Shiels put on her headphones and watched as the blurry figure in the yellow shoes—with the white nose—stumbled onto the edge of the stage then righted herself. She lowered her shoulders and shimmy-hopped—how had she learned how to do that?—and cradled in close to the pterodactyl. The noise was unbearable, but she didn't turn down the volume. The camera jumped and jostled, making it look like the two of them—the girl and the beast—were folding together. He raised his beak and screamed something out, and she had both hands on his glistening chest, and his wings fanned out and he shimmy-hopped against her. She was holding him, holding him up.

She was burning in her seat, watching herself. The

whole boiling crowd seemed to be out of its mind.

She was whirling him, whirling him around the stage. What was she holding? His little legs. When he folded his wings, he was a handbag with handles. When he opened them, she was pulled off her feet as if attached to a kite in a high wind.

Her body twisted. He circled and thrashed, and she was limp and laughing, and when he caught her, in his beak, it looked . . . it looked like she was impaled. Like she was riding him.

Oh God.

It looked like sex.

It looked like she was having pterodactyl sex onstage in front of the entire student body. And now on video for the whole leering . . .

He set her down. He leaned against Jocelyne. Shiels was staggering off. . . . She looked drugged. She looked . . . gloriously, stupidly happy.

She staggered into somebody. The camera was on Pyke and Jocelyne. Shiels was almost out of the frame. But she remembered something. . . . She remembered . . .

. . . staggering into Sheldon.

Last shot—yes—staggering into Sheldon's arms. All of her molten. Hardly able to breathe for laughing, for feeling it.

She paused the video. Was that a shadow . . . or an unusually dark nose?

• • •

It took about three seconds, after Shiels had sat down at the table, for Jonathan to shoot off his mouth. "What's happened to your nose?" he squealed, and then—"She was wrangle dancing with Pyke last night!"

"Shut up!" Shiels said, as if the words could be withdrawn. As if the horror on her mother's face could be peeled away.

"I didn't say to cover it with makeup . . . badly," her mother said. "Just wash it off! Won't it come off?"

Her father was staying neutral, as he often did, looking on but remaining cool. Knowing, probably, that anything he said now would be superfluous, and maybe harmful.

"I'm having trouble getting it off," Shiels said in a small voice. Dinner was linguine with cream sauce and lightly fried tofu squares, with a five-lettuce walnut salad bought from a specialty store her mother worshipped.

Her father raised his glass of white wine. "To family harmony," he said. Her mother shot him a look, but eventually raised her glass as well. Shiels drank her water. The toast was sacred.

"Why did you ever agree to having your nose colored?" her mother said. "I just don't understand it."

Shiels kept her voice modulated. Dinner was good. She needed to eat. "I didn't agree. I don't remember how it happened."

"How can you not remember how it happened?"

"She was wrangle dancing with Pyke!" Jonathan blurted again. "That's how it happened!"

"I don't understand anything about that statement," her mother said.

"It's wrangle dancing. It's all over the Internet. Shiels was up there, alone with the pterodactyl, in front of everybody for, like, ten minutes. Maybe more!"

Jonathan didn't seem to understand the enormity of his statement—the spilling of the secret!—until he noticed Shiels's eyes drilling into his skull.

Her mother twisted linguine on her fork but did not glance away from Shiels. "You were dancing . . . with *what*? A pterodactyl?"

"He's a pterodactyl-student," Shiels said. "The school board approved it. It's no big deal."

"A *pterodactyl*?" her father said.

"He's cool," Jonathan said hastily. "He speaks English . . . sort of."

"Our principal brought him in," Shiels said. "We're a pilot project. It's all right—there were adult chaperones last night. It was completely organized."

The PD exchanged glances—how much of this could be real?

"He's actually quite shy and . . . very talented musically," Shiels said, trying to keep her voice normal.

Her father said, "And he thinks he's a pterodactyl?"

Shiels exchanged glances with Jonathan, then seized the moment. "We're trying to create an open and accepting environment for all kinds of students," she said.

Her mother looked at her watch. The PD were going out. This dicey questioning was not going to last forever. Shiels stood up and began to collect the dirty plates. Her mother took a quick sip of wine. "So you were dancing with this . . . pterodactyl-boy," she said to Shiels. "And somehow you blacked out. What were you drinking?"

"Nothing! I had nothing to drink. Maybe I became dehydrated!" Shiels's tone sent her mother leaning back in her seat.

"No one gets dehydrated after dancing for only ten minutes." Her mother glanced over at her father, and he cleared his throat, ready to take over the interrogation.

"Somehow something happened to your nose because you danced with this fellow?" he said.

Her mother sprang up then. Shiels had no time to react, and knew better than to try to defend herself. In an instant her mother had dipped the cloth napkin into Shiels's water glass and was dabbing, wiping the makeup off her face.

"*That's* what happened!" her mother said. "Look!"

Shiels sat as still as a burning mannequin, being stared at.

"It does look awfully dark," her father said. He approached too, and took out his glasses. "It doesn't look like ink," he said. "There are raw patches. . . ."

"I scrubbed myself pretty hard," Shiels said. Her father touched her nose gently with the tips of his fingers. "Fascinating. So you think it happened . . . how?"

"Every girl who wrangle dances with Pyke gets marked," Jonathan said. "Everyone knows that. It happened to Jocelyne Legault, and now it's happened to Shiels."

"I have no idea what you just said," her father said then, but patiently, echoing his partner in parental unity. "How did this . . . Pyke . . . mark your sister?"

"He just did. It just happens. Nobody knows how. It's part of the wrangle dance!"

"The what?"

Shiels would not wait around for complete humiliation. "Whatever it is, it's my problem. I'll deal with it," she said.

"Do you . . . Do you have feelings for this . . . this boy?" her mother said.

"She's totally in love with him!" Jonathan called out.

"*I am not!*" Shiels slammed her hand onto the table and spilled the water glasses.

Everyone gaped at her, shocked out of words.

"I'm in love with Sheldon Myers. I slept with him last night. That's where I was. All night. And now I'm probably pregnant. Are you satisfied?"

And then a personal wind was blowing her, blowing, out of the room and up the stairs and safely behind her slammed, locked bedroom door.

XIV

She loved Sheldon Myers.

Shiels Krane, student-body chair . . .

No: Shiels Krane, girl, woman. She loved Sheldon Myers.

She loved the tiny black hairs on his skinny forearms. She loved the points of his elbows when he leaned over, on the desk, and left behind whatever it was he was immersed in—an explanation of how black holes affect the literary theory behind graphic novels—and held his face inches from hers. Cell-widths. And how the molecules he breathed seeped into her lungs and she could see the heartbeat pulsing in his baking red ears.

She loved that he had baking red ears.

She loved the smell of him. He was pears and apricot and . . . shoe leather. Not new, slightly old. He fit her nose. He was clean—he showered most days—but he wasn't antiseptic. His mother did his laundry, but she didn't iron and neither did Sheldon, and Shiels loved the rumpled charm of him. If his socks matched, it was serendipity. Maybe a mistake.

But no, no. It wasn't just all the superficial things. She loved the boy. She loved him for his skin and for what he was underneath. He stood by her. He was steadfast. He was . . . quietly Sheldon, anchored while she flew off with her usual this and that. She needed him. Obviously. Tethered to the ground meant just that, not flying, not going anywhere fast.

They needed each other.

She could see that now. She was not just . . . Shiels Krane, person. She was one half of Shiels and Sheldon, the untethered half. The half that would simply let herself blow onstage and wrangle dance with the first pterodactyl boy she came across. No wonder Sheldon was angry.

He was jealous.

Jealous and upset and . . . put out by her untetheredness. She had stayed on the string—she'd come back to him—but she had gone too far. With Pyke, and then with Sheldon himself. She'd gone too far and hadn't honored it—how could she have? She hadn't even known. She hadn't been conscious.

She had sleepwalked through the most important moment of her life so far.

She needed to apologize. To make it up to him. She still was on his string. Of course she was! And he was on hers.

You don't just bury a kite because of one wrangle dance in the clouds.

"Shiels honey," her mother said, knocking gently. "Can I come in?"

Solicitous mother. Gentle mother. A careful inquiry. Shiels could've said no. She crossed the room and unlocked the door because certain things were now clear to her.

She was not going to let her mother—or anybody—put her off Sheldon Myers.

"Oh, that nose!" her mother said, but quietly. Without rebuke. Shiels returned to her bed, surrounded herself with pillows. Her mother sat on the edge, squeezed Shiels's shoulder just the way she used to when Shiels was young and it was bedtime.

Oh, that nose. What was Shiels going to do about it? Sheldon would never love her—could never—while she was marked this way by a . . . a pterodactyl.

Who would've thought this could ever be a problem?

"So . . . ," her mother said, and smiled sadly.

"Yes, *so*," Shiels said.

"You and Sheldon have in fact . . . become closer."

Closer. Shiels supposed that was one way to look at it. Closer, yet it also felt like they had become oceans apart.

"You know I was trying to anticipate this," her mother said gently. "It's hard, as a parent. You want to respect your child's autonomy, her privacy." Her mother had tears in her eyes! Shiels was not going to be able to keep it together. "And yet, some things need to be said—"

"Mom, I know about birth control!"

"Yes, and I'm a GP. I have this chat every day with young women like you who know all about birth control, and yet, when it comes down to it, they have not used it. And they're smart, they have every advantage, they know the statistics." She set her jaw, wiped her eyes. "Shiels, I'm sorry, I'm not good at hiding my disappointment. In myself as well as in you. I have failed to prepare you—"

"Oh, Mom!"

"No, no, hear me out. I tried to tell you, but I didn't actually say the words. I want you to think seriously. If you're going to be sexually active, there are so many better options than just closing your eyes and hoping. And there are STDs to think about—"

"Mom, I know this. I know!"

"I'm sorry. I've been thinking of you still as my little girl. I should've headed this off months ago."

"It's not your fault, Mom. And I'm not sure how getting fixed up now is going to help me if I'm already pregnant!"

Her mother shook her head, apparently still stuck on figuring out how any of this had come to pass. Well, it had.

Sometimes a pterodactyl just lands in your neighborhood and everything goes wrangy for a time.

"I'm pretty sure you're not pregnant, dear," her mother said. "You slept with him once, last night, yes? Probably that means it's going to happen again. So I would like to make an appointment for you—not with me, I can't be your doctor for this—but with one of my colleagues."

"If I am pregnant, then I'm going to have this baby!" Shiels blurted. "I love Sheldon, I love him! I can get a job, I can put off school, Sheldon and I can do almost anything together—"

Shiels's mother let her run out of steam; it didn't take long.

"I know, I know, you're a passionate young woman, you have a formidable will. I have no doubt you would make an amazing young mother, and we do love and respect Sheldon. I have said that before too. Certainly your father and I would support you in every way that we can. You know that, yes?" Shiels's mother was holding both her hands now. "But having a child now, at your age, is not a great strategy, is it? Ideally, so many other things ought to be in place before you can even think of starting your own family. Anyway, it's highly unlikely that you actually are pregnant, dear. Just because there's a big wind, it doesn't mean a tree is going to fall on your house."

"How can you possibly know? We did it, we did it! Are

you just hoping that because it's your daughter, everything's going to be all right?"

Her mother was staying extremely still, even smiling slightly. "We have talked about your cycles, yes?" she said softly.

"My cycles!"

"If I'm not greatly mistaken, I believe your period is due in the next day or two. So if you slept with him last night, and that was the only time so far, then you weren't really fertile. Your eggs are ready, as you know, in the middle of your cycle—"

Shiels stood abruptly. "How could you possibly know when my period is due?"

Her mother pressed her lips together, sort of frowning but not really. "I buy the supplies, dear. Our cycles have been pretty well synchronized for the last couple of years. It's not uncommon. It's a well-studied phenomenon, though not proven definitely. But once you move away to college, if you're living in a girls' dorm, you'll probably find everyone gets in more or less the same rhythm."

Shiels put her hands to her face. Was she really hearing this?

"When you're really trained," her mother said, "when you start to approach life in a more scientific way, you just might find there's all kinds of heartache and confusion you can avoid by keeping a simple grip on the facts."

• • •

A simple grip on the facts.

She wasn't pregnant. Probably. She had lost her virginity—probably—but had no clear recognition of any of it. And her nose was . . . definitely . . . still purple.

Why could she not remember any of the details? She did remember, in Sheldon's house, the clumsy, gasping, half-laughing passage up the stairs. Having seen herself wrangle dancing on the video, she felt she could now remember part of what had happened in his bedroom. Or was she fooling herself, creating false memories?

How could she have been so absent when clearly she had been right there? After scrambling up those stairs, she must've thrown him into bed. He must've been beside him-self trying to shush her so his parents wouldn't hear.

Why had he not texted her, or called her, in all these long hours that she'd now spent lying on her bed, staring at her phone, willing him to notice her?

He must have forgiven her.

Forgiven her?

Forgiven her wrangle dance with Pyke.

When he had woken up, he hadn't been angry with her. He'd been loving. Drowsy. Stubbled. He'd wanted her to have breakfast with his parents.

He'd thought . . . God knows what he'd thought.

It wasn't like him to not call.

She stared at her phone and stared. She felt cold all over,

shivery and light, as if her bones had been hollowed out.

Maybe her mother was right, maybe she wasn't pregnant. But she was still going to have to show up at school
tomorrow with a purple nose and no Sheldon, and everyone knowing . . . or thinking that they knew . . . that in the
course of just a couple of days she'd fallen from the heights,
in plain view, with her entrails hanging out for all to see.

XV

Monday morning. Snow falling. The first of the season, like little lost flakes blurry against the steel-gray sky. The ground cold and hard underfoot. Bitter wind. Students without hats and gloves, in sweaters only or light Windbreakers, undone, open to the elements, trudged into the brown-brick buildings of Vista View High clutching backpacks and cell phones and black umbrellas.

Shiels was intensely conscious, as she approached the school, that no one was staring at her purple nose. Sheldon was not with her. That was expected. She had not even taken the route past Roseview and Vine. She had staged, as it were, a preemptive strike against the loneliness of that moment when he would not be there.

He had already skipped out once before when they'd been still officially together.

Had they split up? She felt in her bones that they had.

She could feel the blood throbbing in her nose. She looked like Cyrano de Bergerac. *'Tis a rock—a crag—a cape— A cape? say rather, a peninsula!*

She would not look at the ground. She would not melt under anyone's pitying or gawking gaze. . . .

But no one was looking. Yet. With the snow and the biting winds, they were all just trying to get indoors to start their Monday in the prison of high school.

She pulled open the heavy doors, stepped inside. It smelled like elementary school, like wet wool and sweating mittens.

¯(Where were all the woolen mittens of elementary school? There were none here.)

Now her eyes fell. She did not want to wipe out on the slippery floor in front of everyone. She just wanted to blend in, be any anonymous senior student, hurrying to class and—

"Ms. Krane."

Manniberg. In the middle of the hall, hands on his hips—"Akimbo," Sheldon would have whispered, had he been there—looking at her. Her body turned toward the stairway, as if she might pretend . . .

"Ms. Krane, what the hell happened this weekend?"

Now, there was a question. She could not possibly begin to explain anything that had happened over what was probably the most extraordinary weekend of her admittedly so far fairly short life.

"Uh—"

She was stopped now in front of him in the crowded hallway. They were a spectacle for others to eye-grope.

He was staring at her nose. "Promise me that is not a tattoo."

"Not . . . as far as I know, Mr. Manniberg." He liked to hear his name spoken with some reverence.

"Well, what in hickory happened to the gym? I thought you had the cleanup plan in place? In fact, I distinctly remember signing and approving the cleanup plan you and your committee presented to me."

Oh. Oh. The floor felt uncertain beneath her feet. "Did Rebecca not stay and—" she mumbled.

"Whoever it was, they definitely did not. You are in charge, Ms. Krane. I hold you personally responsible. Athletics classes are going to have to be held outside in the snow this morning because the gym is not available. I'm going to have to make that announcement. Your name is going to be all over it. And before you set foot in any classroom, you are going to assemble your team and do the work you should have done Sunday morning. As planned. Understood?"

Rebecca Sterzl had been on cleanup. She'd had a whole crew of volunteers. All right, Shiels had said she would look in later on Sunday to do a final inspection. There had been slippage. She hadn't done it. She had been managing her own crises. But still—

"Yes, Mr. Manniberg."

Shiels whipped out her phone and began texting. For one day . . . *one day* . . . she had ignored the beeping and vibrating of others. That was all. One sniveling—

"Get moving, Ms. Krane!" Manniberg roared.

For a moment Shiels yearned to be back in the storeroom of the running-shoe shop. That was tiny, at least—chaos contained in a manageable space. This was an entire gymnasium, a vast chaotic scatter of plastic cups, puddles of stinking pop, overturned tables, fallen posters, even cobwebs of crêpe paper—hadn't she dropped the crêpe paper while running back from the shoe shop? But here were cobwebs of green, blue, black, red, purple crêpe paper hanging from the walls anyway, sodden with drink, already looking like some ancient wreck.

And clothing. Twisted leggings, a shirt. Someone's panties. Black jeans leaning back on an overturned chair as if—

—as if they'd been ripped off in some jet-thrust of a hurry.

Where to start? She picked up the first thing at hand—the panties—then threw them down again and righted the table instead. She nudged her toe into a puddle of sticky soda. She checked her phone. No response. Not from Rebecca, not from any of Rebecca's team, not from Sheldon.

Not from Sheldon.

The mop was in the janitorial closet. That much she knew. And the paper towels. And the garbage bags.

Twist their noses, she thought.

They are going to ignore me.

They sign up for student government. They want the glory, they want the responsibility, they want to be on the inside of a major event like Autumn Whirl. . . .

She marched to the janitorial closet. Unlocked. She freed the ancient mop and tub set, ran fresh water, added liquid cleaner—righteously harsh. She would not wear gloves.

She would not check her phone again.

The bell had already rung for class. Now Mr. Manniberg was on the intercom. Shiels willed herself not to listen.

They had no loyalty, Rebecca and her gang.

He was not worthy—craven Sheldon.

Craven? Was that related to crows somehow? They were all as bad as craven crows.

"When the glacier groans, that's when you know who is a mountain and who is a rockslide," Lorraine Miens had written. As the mop squelched to the puddles, as the garbage—the panties; the leggings; the soggy, disappointing cobwebs of crêpe paper—cragged into bag upon bag, she pictured herself in Lorraine Miens's office, leaning across her desk, eyes locked, matching her quip for quote. "You want students who are going to grow into mountains," she said, out loud, alone, in the gymnasium. "I am student-body chair of Vista View High. Do you have any idea what I've had to do to make it the best year ever in the history of the institution?"

By herself, she started in a corner and worked toward the middle. A gymnasium, too, is finite. She would work all day if she had to. It was her watch. She could not afford weakness.

And if Sheldon showed up, she probably would not be able to unclench her jaw. It was a good thing he didn't.

She heard the squeak of the heavy door opening. She would not look. What time was it?

The reverse-groan upon closing. Probably some snivelly kid looking in on the disaster.

More mopping. More crêpe and cups and stupid stinking paper wads. What had they been for?

She was nearly out of bags, would have to return to the closet. It was the end of some period—which one, she didn't care to think about. She heard students crushing, cruising in the halls. She'd wait, wait before showing herself.

Another squeak of the door. Who this time? Across the gloom Pyke stood with his wings out—enormous, magnificent—clutching a carton of black garbage bags.

"No zelp here?" he said in his funny accent, like he didn't know humans, didn't understand at all what they might get up to.

Something about him was different. What? He looked gigantic. It was his crest. . . . His crest had turned scarlet. He was standing there . . . waggling his knifelike scarlet crest at her. When had it changed? At Autumn Whirl it had been purple. Her nose had been white. Now she was standing before him purple-nosed, and he was red-crested, waggling . . .

"You've got to be kidding!" she said.

When he folded his wings, he was smaller again, just a bedraggled kid really, short and dark. He picked up something with his beak, a sharp quick movement—someone's jacket that wouldn't be wanted back, not now.

He hopped a few steps toward her.

"It's all right. I'll do it," she snapped.

Hop, hop, a few more steps. She happened to be holding a bag open, and he stuffed the jacket in with silvery quickness. She had a sense of him perched by a riverbank waiting, hunting, staying still and then exploding into movement.

Was this all some mating display? On her account?

He speared something else, and when he jabbed it into the bag, his lance of a beak rubbed against the outside of her thigh. It felt strong and gentle at the same time, precise somehow, as if he knew exactly how much pressure to use to graze her, rub her, without knocking her over. This close, a fierce heat radiated from him.

"Too long, juzt we," he said. His voice was strange. It was a miracle he could talk at all, she thought. She remembered how stunned she'd been when he'd spoken on that fateful afternoon when he'd crash-landed on Jocelyne Legault.

Jocelyne—that was what he meant, Shiels thought. "Juzt we" had to include the other girl with a purple nose.

Pyke's two girls.

Hop, step, hop, stab, and each time his beak rubbed some part of her—her arm as he pulled out of the bag abruptly, her hip when she turned away, the inside of her knee when she spread the bag wide.

Two girls.

How had that happened? How did she become . . .

She tied shut the top of one full bag and bent to open another, and when she straightened up again, he had vanished. She hadn't heard or felt the rush of his wings, hadn't noticed the door open or close. Then she spied a window high in the far corner, the sliver of outside glistening on the tilted glass.

An opening big enough for a pterodactyl.

They came in waves, bursts of black spitting through that one open space and then scattering around the cavernous gym. Thousands of crows, Pyke's gang, streaming through endlessly, it seemed. Shiels stood for a while trying to hold open bags here and there, but then she gave it up and retreated to a safe wall, out of the diving, veering, wheeling path. They squawked and squabbled, heckled, pecked, jabbered, screamed, but it was not all madness. They seemed to know what they were about, pecking at the clumps of mess, picking up the wads of crêpe, flying off with them. A mass of crows—a murder—seemed to start a war over some piece of clothing underneath the basketball hoop, but as soon as it started, it was over, with the winner zooming off with the pink, gauzy thing—a tank top? a bra?—in its beak. They pecked their way into the bags that Shiels had already tied shut, but soon she realized it would be all right. Pyke had grasped the essential nature of the problem and had implemented a solution.

They flew off with everything, and it did not take long. Pyke did not reappear, but it was all his doing. He had set his fellows to work . . . just as Shiels had completely failed to mobilize her own.

She found herself leaning against the wall, her back cold on the painted cinder block, watching the window where crows flew in and out like bats. She kept wishing it was just Pyke and her again, the two of them. She pressed herself where Pyke had pressed—placed her hand where his beak had been.

Like probing a tooth that is not sore but is not well either, that's heading toward a greater awareness of pain.

It took hours to clean the gym, even with the help with the crows, but eventually order was restored. When she was done, Shiels retreated to the washroom and scrubbed her hands. At least they could come clean, even if her nose stayed unsightly. Pyke's odor lingered despite all the cleansing—he smelled of the bush and the ocean at the same time, it seemed, pine gum and salt air and fishiness, of black earth and depth and darkness. When she closed her eyes, his scent seemed to take her over. She was standing by a window left open despite the cold, and wondered if somehow he was hovering just out of sight on the other side of the fogged glass, letting the breeze blow his essence into her lungs.

Was he there really?

Her face in the mirror: still, relaxed, older somehow. Shiels but not Shiels. The purple nose was a bit of a mask. It was letting something else come forward in her character. What was it?

She had just a niggling thought, on the periphery of her imagination. When she tried to think straight at it, it disappeared.

And then . . . she felt something release. She'd been holding, holding it but now was not. Her period, of all things! She had supplies. It wasn't unusual. After her mother's words she'd been pretty well expecting it. What she hadn't been expecting was this feeling that somehow Pyke had brought it on, the pull, the gravity of him. That he was affecting her in ways far beyond her knowing.

Manniberg texted her shortly afterward—a meeting in his office, now! Had he even looked in the gym? He couldn't still be angry about the delayed cleanup. It must have been something else. She checked her other messages . . . but there were none. Sheldon was maintaining his radio silence, and all her other contacts had gone dead. No one would give her a heads-up. What could Manniberg possibly—

"I've been hearing from parents all day!" the principal said when she walked in. "They've been told stories about Autumn Whirl. Kids have been showing them videos of what all went on." He was agitated, his face twitchy and red. "Shiels—what all went on?"

Manniberg had not been at the dance. That was not surprising. Certainly some of the vice principals had been there. Why wasn't he interrogating them?

Everyone had been dancing, writhing, shrieking. When it got down to it, after a while everyone who'd been there had just been . . . in a molten state. There'd been no adults, and no kids for that matter, left in the room. Just human beings, being human. And one pterodactyl. As far as she could remember.

Of course, she didn't remember a whole hell of a lot.

"It was a blisteringly good party, sir," Shiels said. "I think everyone was safe. The gymnasium's completely cleaned up now, if you want to have a look."

"I have parents telling me it was an orgy, a complete bacchanalian I-don't-know-what! I have parents who said it took them all day yesterday to figure out where their kids ended up spending the night. And with whom!"

Shiels blinked, blinked. She was not going to give in to his hysteria.

"And I have parents thinking we've got some kind of monster lurking in the halls here. I'm calling an open meeting for the whole school community tonight. I'm going to have to stand up there and tell them that Pyke is just as normal a student as any other and that there's no danger or—"

He was sputtering. His hands were moving up and down with nothing to do.

"He *is* just a normal student," Shiels said evenly. "There is no danger. He's an extraordinary asset to the educational experience of every boy, girl, and even teacher in the school. I would be happy to stand up in front of a thousand parents and say just that."

"In front of your own parents?" Manniberg said. "Because your mother was one of the first to call me. She's furious! She thought Pyke was a student pretending to be a pterodactyl. She thought maybe you gave her that impression. But then she ran into some other parent this morning who told her otherwise."

Shiels felt a slight smile coming over her face. It was much better, this sense of control. She wasn't pregnant! The rest of life could be put into perspective. "I'm sorry you caught my mother's anger," she said. "She chose to believe what she chose to believe. Hold the meeting. You say your piece, I'll say mine. Then we'll bring Pyke out, let him say a few words too. Pack the auditorium with students. We're *all* on his side. Our parents will see that above everything else."

"Have you seen yourself in the mirror lately?" Manniberg said. "I'm not going to let you speak to parents with a flaming purple nose. One look at you, and I'd have a full revolt on my hands!"

Had he really not thought this through? Why had he ever brought the pterodactyl to Vista View anyway? Surely he realized the parents would have to be informed someday.

"He was a cross-boundary transfer," Shiels said. "Where was he before this? How did they deal with him? Why is he here now?"

Manniberg pulled a handkerchief from his pocket and blew his nose. He ran a hand through his thinning hair. "The school board said they were going to get me those answers. But I have a feeling they're dealing with smoke

and mirrors. Wouldn't be the first time they've lost someone's paperwork. As far as I can tell, he's here because he's
here. But he seems to be fitting in all right, wouldn't you
say? Until now?"

"Everyone's in love with him," Shiels said.

Vhub was boiling with talk of the scheduled meeting, but
Shiels felt oddly above it all. She had been through her own
mess. Manniberg was responsible for handling the parents.
He was smart enough to figure things out thus far. And . . .

. . . she was not pregnant. And . . .

. . . Pyke had flown to her, come to her rescue when
everyone else had abandoned her. Maybe there was a reason why her nose had turned dark, something she could not
yet figure out.

On the way home, alone at the end of the day—an
entire day at school in which she had not run into Sheldon,
and had not heard from him, smelled him—Shiels dodged
snowflakes and thought about how the world could be.
How just when her heart had sought clear to the wide plain
of knowing that she loved someone—Sheldon—then the
planet shifted, and Sheldon slid out of reach.

But now it seemed the pterodactyl was attracted to her.
He had branded her, chosen her, come to her aid. Hadn't
she always known, from that first glimpse, that worm biting
her gut? Just like that, she could feel the world leaning away

from the boy who only the day before she'd realized was the love of her life . . . so far.

That was the thing. Her life so far had not yet been long. If Sheldon had shown up at the gym holding a box of garbage bags, she might have married him on the spot (maybe just to see the look on her mother's face).

She would've melted into his arms. If he could have forgiven her purple nose, and put away his pride, and understood how she would've felt about tripping into his parents' kitchen on Sunday morning with sleep in her eyes (and her head not too clear) and her nose so purple (he hadn't even told her!).

If he could have just been himself, steadfast, understanding Sheldon for one more day, the way he'd been for practically the whole of the last three years in which they had been inseparable . . .

If he had stood up for her, grown his own red crest, or whatever.

But he had stayed away. Like the others. Whose noses weren't fully purple. They had drawn those ridgelines. They could wash them off.

They had not wrangle danced with Pyke.

The building was boiling over, practically, with talk about what the parents would do when they found out for real that a pterodactyl had been going to school with their children. But surely once Pyke stood up and said a few things into the microphone, once everyone could see how harmless and fragile and magnificent he was, the whole thing would blow over.

On the way home, on one of the backstreets, Shiels heard a gasp of wind behind her, above her. A series of gasps . . . She turned to see the wings. The black bright eyes she was hoping to see.

Oh, that red crest burning for her!

Pyke circled, circled, his shadow skimming the road beside, ahead, around her. She ducked as he came in for a halting, awkward, semi-controlled crab of a landing.

"I thought you'd be better than that!" she said to him. It felt like her whole body was smiling.

He hop-hipped, hop-hipped toward her, his beak gesturing to something, the road in front of her.

"Where you?" he said.

"Right here," she said. "What do you mean?"

"Where you? Where you?" he repeated.

She was freakishly warm, just being near him. And she wanted to run her hand again along his chest. She remembered that fragment of it, the wrangle dance.

She loved the look, the slope, of his scarlet crest.

"Where you?" he said again, glancing at her feet.

She looked down. She was in a pair of her mother's flats. Black with wide toes.

"You mean what am I wearing?" she asked.

"Wear you . . . yellow zhoe!" he said.

He reached down with his beak and untied one of her shoelaces, as if she might have the yellow runners with her right then.

"Wear you . . . yellow zhoe!" he said again. "Run-run! Zomorrow. Run!"

She laughed. "You like my yellow shoes?"

"Run-run!" he said.

"I hope Manniberg has talked to you," she said. "There's going to be a meeting tonight in the auditorium. You need to be there. You should stand up and say a few things to our parents. Maybe—do you have parents? Where are they? Would you bring them to the meeting?"

He waggled his crest. He seemed to be flaming at her.

"You must come! You'll be fantastic! It's going to have everything to do with your future in the school."

Hop-hip, hop-hip. A sudden stretch of wings. As he took off, flying away from her, he looked back, like a pilot in a biplane, glancing her way.

She watched him fly—watched him work his leathery wings into the distant fabric of the sky—until he was hardly a speck in the gray reaches.

XVI

Manniberg was going to handle it, but he wasn't at dinner with Shiels and her family, when her mother was in full Inquisition mode:

"What do you mean a pterodactyl *is* attending your high school? They're extinct! How does he even exist?"

"Well, he does. He showed up one day out of the blue—"

"And he speaks? He sits at a desk? He takes tests and exams?"

"He's in Jonathan's grade. I think so far his marks have been okay. Nobody's mentioned—"

Jonathan spoke up. "He might've come to us through a disturbance of the time-space continuum."

Their mother glared at him until he returned to his dinner.

"Science can't explain everything." Shiels tried not to

sound patronizing. "But the fact is he's here, he's delightful, he's unique."

Her mother's gaze did not indicate a softening of any sort. "This has been going on for how long? And the administration is just now getting around to—"

"I think it's fair to say there's been a settling-in period—"

The two women in the family kept at it while Jonathan and their dad, though still listening intently, were tucking into the seven-cheese lasagna with Creole garlic and portobello mushrooms.

"This is the creature you danced with? Who turned your nose purple? When you said he was pretending to be a pterodactyl?"

"I never said 'pretended,'" Shiels said. "Dad said Pyke thought he was a pterodactyl."

"But you didn't correct him. You let us both continue to blithely assume—"

"I'm sorry there was confusion," Shiels said. "But you're against him simply because of his species orientation," Shiels said.

"His *what*?"

"He's different from us. He's not from our tribe. So you're against him. You have been from the beginning."

"This isn't the beginning. The beginning, I gather, was some time ago, and yet—"

"If he were a student of color, you would be all in favor of integrating him," Shiels said. "If he came from a different country, or had an unusual sexual orientation—"

"Do not call me a racist, or a sexist, or—"

"It's speciesism," Shiels said simply. "You can't believe someone from a different species, from a whole different era of evolution, could benefit from a normal high school education. Or could teach us anything—"

"This is ridiculous!"

"Is it? I spent half of today cleaning up the gym after Saturday's dance. And you know who helped me? About a thousand crows. And they were so much more organized, efficient, and pleasant to deal with than any of my own team of so-called volunteers."

"Now you are just raving!"

"Parents never understand!" Shiels said. She clapped her cutlery down. This was so. . . satisfying. To get to say those words.

"I can hardly wait for this meeting," Shiels's father said, and he helped himself to another glass of wine.

"Thank you, folks. Thank you all for coming tonight on short notice," Manniberg said. The microphone screeched. He had to step back from the podium—and someone in the back, Jeremy Jeffreys, yelled, "Pyke! Pyke!" which got everyone laughing.

Well, the students laughing. The parents didn't seem to know what to make of it.

Pyke was sitting alone onstage beside Manniberg in one of the skinny, wooden orchestra chairs. His wings were folded, his beak was tucked, as if perhaps Manniberg had advised him to stay as small, as unthreatening as possible.

Shiels was not sitting with her own parents. She preferred to roam an event like this—not that there had ever been an event like this at Vista View. But since she wasn't speaking, she needed to be free to see, to work the room.

Sheldon was on the other side of the auditorium, sitting with that same group of cronies he'd exploded umbrellas with some days before—Ron Fornelli and others. Rachel Wyngate. (Why did Rachel Wyngate look like she always belonged wherever she happened to be?)

Sheldon was texting someone.

"Yes," Manniberg said, finding the right distance from the microphone, "this meeting is about a new student we all know as Pyke. If you remember in the fall newsletter, I did make reference to the Vista View Cultural Outreach Program, about how we are embracing many forms of diversity just as a lot of you have asked us to do—"

A father with a black stubble beard, sitting near the front, yelled, "What does this have to do with a freaking pterodactyl?"

Pyke raised his beak slightly. He seemed to inflate with the implied threat.

It was hard for Shiels to take her eyes off him. *If I need to,* she thought, *I will rush the stage and get him out of here.*

(But, no, this would not be the time for any reckless rescue attempts. This meeting was for talking it all through.)

Pyke looked a little lost, up there without Jocelyne Legault. It was painful for Shiels to realize. Probably Manniberg had warned Jocelyne away too, because of her own purple nose.

Shiels imagined herself sitting up there beside Pyke. They were on the right side of history, she knew. This might be one of those moments.

"Pyke, who is a pterodactyl," Manniberg said, "is right here beside me. He's a student, he has a name, he has as much right to respect and privacy as anybody else's children in the school. Let me just say"—his voice was picking up confidence; he could be a strong speaker when moved— "that in a short while I have come to know this young student very well. I am so impressed! He does come from a remarkable background. He brings his own wealth of cultural knowledge and experience—"

"Where the hell *does* he come from?" another father yelled. "How sharp are his teeth?"

Others called out as well. Manniberg smiled gamely. "I *will* take questions. This is meant to be your session.

Let me just explain, though, that there are strict privacy regulations, the same ones that protect your child, ensuring that I do not divulge personal information in a public forum like this. So I can't discuss background except to say Pyke came to us with the proper credentials. The board is behind this initiative, which, frankly, I think is an excellent opportunity to expose all of us to new ideas and ways of—"

"Would you stop marble-mouthing and just answer the question?" a woman barked. "You sound like a bloody politician!"

Laughter. Nervous energy snapping in the room.

"Someone asked about his teeth. Pyke has none." Manniberg turned to the pterodactyl. "Please, son, if you could just stand up, open your beak . . ."

Pyke did so. He was being careful not to stretch his wings, not to look frightful.

"You see, not a biter," Manniberg said. "He eats in the cafeteria with the other students, with his friends. Just ask any of your kids. I think you'll find he has integrated quite—"

"He looks like a freaking monster!" the first dad yelled, the angriest one.

"I assure you, sir—" Manniberg was starting to lose control of the room. If he'd ever had it. Shiels moved quickly, quietly back to Jeremy Jeffreys.

"What exactly does he eat?" someone else yelled. "What was all this shrieking business over the weekend?"

"Jeremy," Shiels hissed, and pulled the huge boy aside from where he was standing by the back wall.

"Maybe we need to hear from Pyke himself at this point," Manniberg said.

"What?" Jeffreys asked.

"Get a football. Now!"

"What? Why?"

"Just do it!"

Jeffreys was practically twice her size, but he could not stare her down. He was gone in a moment, out to his locker.

Pyke hop-hipped to the podium. It was hard to see him. At the bottom of the podium was a small box that could be pulled out. Shiels tended to use it to stand on whenever she was speaking in the auditorium. But no one had told Pyke.

Shiels texted Sheldon: *Rescue him now!*

Pyke clicked his beak and shuffled awkwardly in front of everyone. "Hllo hum," he said. "Zorry, zorry trubbled maker. Hah?"

When I say, Shiels texted. *It's about W Wallin.*

Sheldon turned around, trying to see where she was.

"What bloody planet are you from, you freak!" the angriest father yelled. "Do I need to get my shotgun?"

It wasn't funny, but some people laughed. Pyke glanced

at the man like . . . maybe he might skewer the guy for dinner.

Jeremy Jeffreys, at last! Hands wrapped around a football.

Make it about fb, Shiels texted. At the same time she said to the quarterback, "Do you think you can throw it onstage from here?"

Manniberg rose to join Pyke at the podium.

"Of course!" Jeffrey said.

"Show me!"

Manniberg said, "There's no need for threats or even jokes about—"

Jeffreys reached back and sent a perfect spiral arcing over the heads of the audience. Even Shiels could appreciate the strength and accuracy of the throw. It snaked left a bit near the end. Pyke had to leap and stretch . . . but he nabbed it out of midair as fast as an eyeblink.

"Hey! Don't give away our secret weapon for Walloping Wallin!" someone yelled—Sheldon! And Ron Fornelli leapt to his feet too. "Hoo, hoo!" he yelled. "Vista View!"

"Are you kidding me?" the angry father yelled. "This guy plays football?"

Manniberg retrieved the ball from Pyke's jaws and tossed it—not badly at all—to the man with the stubble beard. "Try to get one past him!" Manniberg said.

The guy had a rifle arm. He sent a bullet straight at Pyke's head. Shiels winced—but Pyke nabbed the ball like a natural, and even flipped it back to Manniberg like the principal was his caddie or something.

Did they have caddies in football?

A half dozen fathers, and one mother, in the audience took turns throwing the ball to Pyke, who only dropped one pass, a wobbler that slipped from the hand of the passer. "Sorry, son—sorry!" the embarrassed dad called. "It's been a while since I tried this sort of thing."

Manniberg picked up the ball and tucked it under his arm. The student body gave Pyke a standing ovation. Shiels was worried that Pyke might ruin it all by opening his beak and shrieking . . . but he knew enough to just bathe in the applause.

"All right, okay," Manniberg said, giddy with the moment. "We don't want news of our secret weapon to get out, do we? Vista View hasn't beaten Wallin in, what is it, eight years now?"

"Seventeen!" Jeremy Jeffreys called out.

"Seventeen years. So we'll just keep this under our hats until game time, all right? When is it, next week? Thank you all so much for coming tonight. Thank you for your understanding, your sense of community, your generosity of spirit. The society we're building here at Vista View is inclusive, it's supportive, it's striving for acceptance of diversity every day. Thank you again. Thank you!" He smiled, he waved, he laughed and shook the football at

Coach, who was standing with his arms crossed, scowling.

Well, the man was always scowling.

Jeremy Jeffreys slapped hands with teammates and well-wishers. And Sheldon—

Where was he?

Gone already.

Jeremy Jeffreys's arcing pass stayed in Shiels's mind: the elegant spin of the ball, the snake to the left, the coil in Pyke's movement as he spied the incoming shadow then leapt and stretched, wings gigantic, to gather the ball into his wide-open beak.

It was an exquisite gesture for that moment, the whole thing a complex act of grace—how Shiels had pictured it happening, and found exactly the right words and movements—the order to the quarterback, the texts to Sheldon, all while keeping an eye on the unfolding disaster at the podium. Shiels had been invisible at the center, calling and executing the play, almost like a quarterback herself, or a coach, an unseen mover.

Perfect.

Too perfect.

As the assembly broke up, there was Jeremy Jeffreys surrounded by acolytes, reenacting the pass like he'd just won the Super Bowl with seconds draining on the clock. And there were Rebecca Sterzl and Melanie Mull and others from the council laughing with one another. "And now he's a football star!" Rebecca exclaimed, without a glance in Shiels's direction.

Of course Jeremy Jeffreys was not going to say, "Shiels Krane told me to do it!" And Sheldon Myers, who did not hang around, was not there to say, "Shiels texted me just before I yelled." (He would have before. He had deflected all light to Shiels, almost to a fault.)

Pyke of course was gone seconds after Manniberg turned off the mic.

In the lobby after the event, in the press of people talking, laughing, reenacting the whole unbelievable spectacle, Shiels felt herself standing alone, still the girl with the purple nose.

Walloping Wallin was not going to happen all by itself— her council would have to lay on the buses, organize the rally, negotiate a block of tickets for as many people from the school who wanted to go (which now would be everybody, practically). It was the forty-seventh year of the rivalry; Wallin and Vista View had been the first two high schools in town, and although now there were fifteen schools, this was the game that counted. Or at least it used to count, before Wallin had became a football power.

Seventeen years since the last Vista View victory! In truth, Shiels had not been expecting to have to do much organizing for Walloping Wallin. Last year, when Vista

View had hosted the game, fewer than a hundred people had come from the home side. But now, thanks to her invisible manipulations, her almost instinctive grasp of how to influence a nearly chaotic situation, another amazing event was set to unfold.

Why did she feel so miserable?

Alone in her bedroom that night: Was it just her purple nose, the wrangle dance? Was that why she'd been so abandoned? She was not the only one who had lost her head. That disaster zone of a gym after Autumn Whirl!

But it was as if something unthinkable — unspeakable — had happened. Shiels actually called Rebecca Sterzl and began to leave a pleading message — the weakness in her voice! — but stopped herself.

She had more pride than that.

She lay on her bed in the evening with her phone in her hand, smelling the sudden shift of the winds. It was like some elementary school romance. She remembered her grade six crush, Robbie Lewis, who had had a way of looking at her and not saying a word, as if he'd known exactly what she was thinking. In choir he would stand at the back and let his angel voice soar over everyone's head. Shiels was not musical, not really, so she didn't know how else to describe it. Robbie Lewis's voice had lifted them all like a set of wings.

She remembered standing with him for some reason

outside the library in their old school. She wasn't used to being so close to him. His skin seemed to quietly hum something to her, something warm. He looked at her, and she almost leaned right into him. It got hotter and hotter until finally she said, "Where did you ever learn to sing, anyway?"

She was standing just below his chin by then. She remembered straining her neck to look up at him. He said, "I just do it because they make me. Only morons like singing." He snickered, and tapped the top of her shoe for some reason with the dusty toe of his runner. That single touch — those two ugly sentences — broke the spell. She couldn't look him in the eye anymore.

He didn't even sound so good to her in choir either. It was like the milk had curdled. When they passed in the hallway, she drifted toward the wall to be as far away as she could get.

That was what this moment felt like too, as the air went out of the evening and Shiels returned to the reality of her life. What had her political team seen, when she'd been gyrating, purple-nosed, so close to the beast? What had she shown them? How had she betrayed herself?

"I didn't even know I was doing it," she said aloud, to no one, to the four walls of her too-quiet bedroom.

Robbie Lewis played for the football team now. He had grown enormous, his voice had dropped, and his eyes now looked like old flat unremarkable discs. Who knew what he was thinking anymore? Who cared?

Not Shiels.

And somehow . . . somehow she wondered even if she cared about political success the way she had before. This manipulation of the public meeting had been almost accidental stagecraft, as much luck as anything else, she thought now. Even her parents had been won over, sort of, by the sleight of hand, the bold-faced changing of subjects. And the triumph at Autumn Whirl had not really been hers. She could admit that to herself now, alone, in the silence of her room. Sheldon and others had grasped the importance of Pyke long before she had. They had even done most of the setup and organizing. As leader, she had simply not stood in the way.

As leader she cared about things like crowd control, beverage revenues, the implementation of the cleanup plan. But as Shiels . . . as Shiels she found herself thinking for long stretches about the shocking changes in her nose, about Pyke's magnificent crest, about being chosen, and choosing, and standing in the chaos of the gym feeling her body moving closer, closer . . .

And now what? Walloping Wallin might become even more of a triumph than Autumn Whirl. But maybe no one would ever treat Shiels like student-body chair again—ever give her any credit, or respect; ever volunteer for another of her committees; ever look her in the eye in the hallway or elsewhere.

And why?

Why?

Because they had seen the real her, stripped of her title, her costumes, her armor, her aura—they had seen her in the wrangle dance, another of Pyke's girls. Chosen by him, marked by him, slave to him.

Slave?

She was nobody's slave. Yet she did find herself glancing across the bedroom at her beautiful yellow shoes. She had worn them at the dance. That was why Pyke had picked her out. He had confused her for a runner, another Jocelyne Legault.

She was no Jocelyne Legault.

But she got out of bed and slipped on the shoes and imagined herself clip-clip-clipping along, tirelessly, like Jocelyne, her body an elegant, light transportation machine, the wind blowing, fresh against her face, deepening her lungs. They were heartbreakers, those shoes. Robbie Lewises. The first touch against the feet made you feel like you could cruise through a marathon, uphill, and hardly break a sweat.

Who was she fooling?

In the darkness, in the cold wind, Shiels stood outside the door of Sheldon's house with her hands shoved into her pockets, listening to the sad fury of her heart.

She had not warned him.

He had followed orders; he had responded on cue perfectly in the auditorium, reading the situation as if he and she did indeed share the same brain. But that had been to save Pyke. She was not confident that Sheldon would have responded to another sort of text from her.

But if she showed up in person, if she sat by him in his room, where they had slept together not all that long ago . . . then this could be fixed. Couldn't it?

She rang the bell. Sheldon's mother answered.

"Mrs. Myers, hello." Shiels was throbbingly aware of the other woman's eyes on her purple nose. She felt like she was wearing a face tattoo, some kind of punk aggressive message to the world.

"Shiels . . . hello," Mrs. Myers said.

Normally there would've been a hug. Sheldon's mother wouldn't be blocking the doorway.

"I was hoping . . . Is Sheldon in?"

A stilted moment. Then the woman stepped aside. "You know where it is," she said.

By "it" she meant Sheldon's bedroom.

The sadness on Mrs. Myers's face. What had Sheldon told her?

Mr. Myers was sleeping in a stuffed chair in the living room. Shiels walked as quietly as she could up the stairs.

When Mrs. Myers called out, "Sheldon! It's Shiels!" Mr. Myers didn't stir at all.

Sheldon did not race out of his room to greet her. Shiels stole down the hall and pushed open his partially closed door. He was sprawled on his bed, in his Aching Angels band T-shirt, on his phone . . . to somebody. Not her.

He said, to the phone, "Call you soon!" then clicked off. He didn't get up.

She sat in his desk chair—after moving his socks—and he stayed propped against his pillows. How often had she angled herself against those pillows too, and rested her head in the hollow of his shoulder while they wormed their way through some assignment or other?

(Wormed? Why did that word occur to her?)

"I thought—" she began, and all that she had actually thought fled from her mind.

"That was amazing tonight," he said. "Really. Now I've seen everything from you. It wasn't planned, was it?"

"It was Manniberg's meeting," she said simply.

He was staring at her nose; she touched it self-consciously. "It really isn't coming off," he said, meaning the purple. He scratched his own nose, which was clean, clean.

"Apparently not."

The silence twisted between them.

"Sheldon," she said, and her thought was this: *If I cry now, he will hold me, and then we can get through anything.*

She said, "I'm sorry that I hurt you. You know I never mean to. You know I just get wrapped up—"

She dipped her head. She could not bear to look at the dark edges of his eyes. She was almost crying. But she fought it.

She didn't want to get him back that way.

"—I get wrapped up in myself and what I'm doing. You know I don't mean to—"

His phone rang. He glanced at the screen, and for a moment she thought he might actually take the call. But he didn't.

He didn't move toward her either, or grasp her hand. He didn't envelop her in his arms or—

"Oh dear," Shiels said. "What can I do? To make this right?"

He tapped the edge of his phone against his black-jeaned thigh.

"Here's the thing," he said. "I think we need to take a break."

She heard the words and then felt their kick, unexpected, straight to the gut.

"Do we?" She almost launched herself at him. But he might resist her.

It would be terrible to be resisted.

"*I* need to take a break," he said. "I don't think straight when I'm with you. When you look at me—Shiels, be honest—half the time you're looking past to something I don't even see."

Pyke, he meant. She was looking at Pyke, red-crested, immense, the whole improbable fact of him, monopolizing her mind's eye.

She could be honest. She could sit in Sheldon Myers's little office chair and not touch his foot which was so close to hers, and not pay any heed to how baking hot her face felt now that he had called her out like this. She could be.

Honest.

She loved him enough.

(She wouldn't cry. She wouldn't.)

"All right," she said. "I'm just going to say this. After the dance, I dragged you back here, I remember that. We ended up in bed, I remember that, remember . . . the morning. But did we . . . I mean, in the night did we—"

"You asked me this before. Do you think I would lie to you?" Sheldon said.

"About this. I mean in the heat of it—I mean . . . maybe, yes you would lie. I think, maybe, I dragged you up the stairs and ripped off your clothes and then . . ."

"And then you fell asleep. In my arms. And we slept together. As in, dreaming. As in—you snoring into my armpit. I would never do it to any girl who was unconscious. You know that about me, don't you?"

She did. She did know that.

Sometimes, when all the world was theirs, they would both look up at the same time from whatever they were doing—their plotting, scheming, working, joking, laughing—and his eye would catch hers and lock and they would stay that way, not speaking, for about half a millennium, leaking into each other's souls practically.

"You were desperate to make love to somebody that night, but, Shiels, it wasn't me."

Those times, she didn't look past him, she thought now. Those times, she was all his.

They looked now. She didn't want to break it. She felt if she didn't . . . didn't move, then maybe they wouldn't be over. Not really. There wouldn't be this . . . taking a break.

If she didn't . . .

But he didn't either.

His gaze was stronger. Calmer. Truer.

So she had to break it.

(She had broken it anyway!)

She had to be the one to walk away.

A hard dream that night. Shiels saw herself at a train station, an old one, with the steam from the locomotive fogging the air. It was night, and she was carrying two of her parents' old suitcases—the kind without wheels. They felt like they had rocks in them. The train came slowly into the station, but it didn't seem to be stopping. She understood that she was going to have to board while it was moving. She started jogging down the platform, the suitcases unwieldy. The train really wasn't going very fast, but it would take some coordination to leap onto the stairs by one of the doors. She didn't have a hand free to grab the rail. She would have to time it perfectly and swing one suitcase into the opening—the left one—and then follow with herself and the right suitcase. She was jogging more slowly than the train so that the car would pass and then the doorway would appear.

Gradually she became aware that Sheldon was standing in the crowd. His body was angled off. He was reading something—his phone—not paying attention to her. He could've helped her, could've taken a bag, or even both bags. He was strong in the hands. He could've made sure she grasped the rail and swung herself at the right moment.

But he was pretending he didn't see her.

The train jolted, slowed . . . then picked up speed just as she was getting ready to swing. So she had to hurry up. And now the end of the platform was nearing. . . .

Nearing but not swallowing her. "Sheldon!" she said, but the boy didn't look.

The cases were heavy; she couldn't set them down. She was tiring yet still ran, on and on. The door would not line up, but she kept trying. . . .

What else was she going to do?

She had to get on that train.

And then she was on an elevator, just herself, a tiny gray metal box she could stand in, barely, going down. She was supposed to meet the others in the mine, at least that was her understanding. The buttons were subtle, she had to feel along the wall, like feeling along the side of an old gray file cabinet, the kind her mother had in her office. For the old files, before everything went digital.

She was going down, down. The world turned hotter. The box seemed to get smaller, the air ached, it was difficult to breathe. Why did she want to go there anyway? To work in a mine? Just because the others wanted it?

She searched for the buttons, searched . . . woke up on her back with her extra pillow partially over her nose and mouth.

Awake.

And . . . and . . . *anyway*, she thought, why the hell shouldn't she have wrangle danced with Pyke? Any girl in that sweaty gym would've done it. They were all shrieking out of their minds. The video showed it, and Shiels remembered it. She had wrapped herself around Sheldon. They'd almost mated right there under the basketball hoop. Like the writhing mass of other couples. Practically an orgy. So now just because her nose had turned purple . . . stayed purple . . . she was tainted somehow? She was . . . *curdled*. . . . Even Sheldon caromed off the wall and spun away from her like some anti-magnetized satellite. (Shiels wasn't sure how to think of it—she'd heard Sheldon go on about this sci-fi series and that, but she hadn't really been listening.)

She repelled him now. The boy she used to tug so effortlessly into the janitorial closet, she now sent reeling off.

XVII

Quiet steps, soft, her feet felt light. Early morning. Yellow shoes. Yesterday's snow had not stayed. Immediately the world warmed again, slightly, and it was still autumn. The low light slanted with a cool edge on everything: on the too-vibrant green of people's lawns emerging after the first frost; on the sloped black roofs of the neighborhood houses; on the shrubs and the fences and the glistening wet metal skins of the parked cars.

Yellow shoes. Light steps. The sun was barely peeking between the trees, and it was quiet except for the wing rustles of the black crowd of crows slowly filling the sky in the east. She could feel their wings inside her chest, somehow, even though she was so small and far away, on the ground. (She saw herself, oddly, in an instant from up above the tree line, looking down—a tiny girl with loose clothes and vibrant yellow shoes. As if she were still dreaming. As if she could spin the world like that.)

The crows saw her, and she saw them. *They know me,* she thought.

Yellow shoes, soft steps, light, all the way to the school and then behind, to the track. She eased herself past the chains of the gate. And then she was alone on the running surface. No one else there, not Jocelyne Legault, not the football players, just Shiels Krane, whoever she was now . . . and some thousands of crows alighted along the top of the chain-link fence that surrounded the compound. Black shadows, all quiet. (Weirdly—when had she ever seen so many crows not shrieking over something?) All watching her.

Pyke's spies, she thought. *His eyes in the world.*

At least they are not repelled by me, she thought. *They want to know who I really am.*

Who am I?

Yellow shoes, soft steps, a bit of a run. Not too fast this time. That was the trouble before, she thought. Before the dance, when she'd first bought the shoes, she'd tried too hard. Soft steps now, arms moving, lungs engaged, feel the ground. Through the sole. The track slightly springy, nicer to run on than the road. Those beautiful white lane markers. When does life ever supply clear white lane markers?

Now. On the track. All alone, with no one watching . . .

just the crows. Her new crowd. Her new . . . constituency.

No, no, not that. Just . . . (She took the bend in her yellow shoes, soft steps, breathing easily, moving . . . slowly. But not killing herself.) Just what?

The crows were fellow creatures. That was all.

And she was just running . . . jogging . . . woggling. Not fast. But steady.

The sun reached through the battleship gray of the low-sailing clouds and lit the lane before her feet like some special effect in a movie. She made it around the track once, and a man showed up with his dog, scaring the crows. They flew off in a massive scramble and lit on a stand of trees behind the tennis courts, complaining loudly even long after the man and dog had left.

Another lap, and another. Her body was doing it. Slowly. She was not Jocelyne Legault, but she was not a wreck either.

Sheldon, Sheldon, Sheldon, Sheldon . . . , she thought. *I have loved you, loved you, loved you.*

Slower, slower, slower. Keep breathing. *Loved you, loved you.* Breathing, breathing, breathing. *Don't outrun your shoes,* she thought, as if that might be wise advice for someone like herself.

And then, a lightening. It was a new day after all. *Robbie Lewis, Robbie Lewis,* she sang to herself, a silly little song, when she was walking down the hall, and there he was.

My grade six crush.

You beefcake slabhead selfish lush.

All right, it was not going to win a Grammy. But it gave her the courage to angle at him in the hall. He was walking toward her in his relaxed, football slouch, his chin tucked into his neck.

Not looking.

Like all the others, not looking at her.

So she lowered her shoulder, braced herself, caught him on the flank even as he was twisting slightly to get out of her way.

"Hey!" he said, like he wasn't used to getting hit. Like she'd hurt him or something.

"Robbie Lewis!" she said, and batted her eyes. "How are things fixed for Walloping Wallin?"

He didn't want to be standing in the middle of the hallway talking to her. But she was blocking his way, making herself big, willing it.

Pure personality.

"You know, big game," he said carelessly. "We're getting our focus. Gonna be something else with Pyke playing."

"Don't I know it's a big game." She could talk sports with the sweatiest of them. "Wallin has beat everybody so far by two touchdowns. And you guys—"

He turned to get by her, the way he might pivot

around an oncoming linebacker—was that what they were called?—not through force but the opposite, by releasing one side, becoming a revolving door. She spun along with him, matched his strides down the hall.

"—you guys have lost most of your games by two or three field goals at least. What's the plan? How you going to make use of the pterodactyl?"

She had not talked to Robbie Lewis, said anything directly to his disappointing face, since that deflating encounter at the school library in grade six.

You beefcake slabhead selfish lush.

She could do this. It wasn't real, this shunning, just like her victory in Autumn Whirl had not been real either.

"What's Coach going to get you doing differently?"

She sounded like a sports writer, a groupie.

"Who knows?" Robbie Lewis said. "We haven't practiced with Pyke yet."

He was headed for Spanish class. He would be beyond her grasp in a matter of seconds.

"What position is he going to play?" she pressed. "Ball catcher? What's it called?"

Robbie Lewis laughed. "All that stuff—that's all for Coach to decide."

Coach. Who never in a million years would've thought of adding a pterodactyl to the lineup. And here was Robbie Lewis, who had no idea how that had ever happened, Pyke catching a football in the middle of an angry meeting. Miracles never cease.

"Well, you guys just make us proud," Shiels said. "If you're having troubles, I don't know, communicating, maybe I can help."

"You?"

"You know what I'm saying." She didn't have to point to the purple on her own nose. She didn't have to remind him, or anyone else for that matter, about the wrangle dance. "We have a bit of a link," Shiels said.

"Ha!" Robbie Lewis said. "That's one way to put it! I just hope he shows up at game time."

"He's a star," Shiels said. "That's what he lives for!"

It was hard not to imagine it: Jeremy Jeffreys with the ball, the Wallin boys charging at him, and he launches a pass high in the air, way over everybody's heads, and then from nowhere comes a dark shadow, a red-crested superplayer who swoops down on the what, what was it called? Not goatskin. Pig. Pigskin. The ball! Who caught it every time and flew into the end zone for touchdown after touchdown, humiliating Wallin once and for all. There were no rules in football against flying, of course not!

Not yet.

Everyone pulsed with the anticipation of it. The halls surged, Vhub reverbed, even the teachers were giddy with the thought of future glory. Football. Really, who cared?

Everybody, if they thought they were going to win.

And yet . . . and yet, at lunchtime, at the regularly sched-
uled student council meeting in the theater arts room, it was
Shiels, the sophomore Melanie Mull . . . and no one else.
From an elected body of twelve, only two showed? Really?
Shiels worked her phone, she scatter-texted, she received only
a smattering of responses. *Sory, big civics thing. Nxt time 4 sur.*

"I guess there is the transportation issue," Melanie said.
She was as small as Shiels, a spark plug with striking, arching eyebrows; she had her notebook open. "Do we have to
order buses, is that how we do it? Is there a budget?"

"Manniberg will be on board for whatever we require,"
Shiels said. Melanie made a note. Shiels said, "Maybe you
could be the point person for that." She didn't say, "Are you
looking to take on more responsibility?" because clearly the
girl was. She didn't say, "Are you thinking about running for
student-body chair next year?"

It was all rather apparent.

"Probably we'll hold the rally here beforehand, in the
parking lot?" Melanie said. Her voice didn't sound tentative
at all. She'd been thinking through the details, obviously.

"You know what?" Shiels said. "I think you're going to
be really good at this."

Melanie blushed. She had no control yet over her
reactions.

Shiels thought: *It's all right to be grooming a successor.*

And: *Vista View is not forever.*

And: *I want to see him. Pyke. I want him to know who's really spinning the world in his favor.*

She wanted to see him, and there he was in the east wing, near the biology lab. Or at least that was where the crowd was, a frenzy of students chattering like they'd all been turned into crows. Yet she wanted Pyke now. Alone. For herself.

He was the one who had purpled her nose, changed her life.

She wanted him to know what she was doing for him.

Every day he seemed bigger, different, older. That spectacular crest! Maybe pterodactyls grew faster at this age. She wanted to tell him that she was running now, that she wore the yellow shoes, that he could see her in the mornings at the track if he came early enough. His crows would tell him, but she wanted to tell him too.

She wanted him to hear it from her.

And she wanted . . . she wanted to be close to him, to feel that warm surge again, the heat pulsing from him.

He pulsed with heat.

She walked toward the commotion.

Everywhere he went, commotion!

She was changing, because of him, she wanted him to

know. She wanted to run her hand along the length of his beak, his spear, just to feel it.

There were flashes. People were taking photos, like he was a rock star or royalty.

What was he doing in the center of that scrum?

She wanted to walk slowly toward him and to have the crowd part for her because she was marked, had been marked by him, they had wrangle danced and everyone at the school knew. She was not a fan, she did not have a camera, she—

She just wanted a little respect for her position!

"Hey. Hey! No cameras!" she said to a girl with red hair down to her waist that looked like it had been brushed out a thousand times for a shampoo commercial. She was tall and stretched up on her tiptoes with her phone to record something in the center of the mass.

"No cameras, I said! This isn't a circus!" Shiels might as well have been invisible. Instead of opening up, the wall of people tightened against her.

Crows, freaking paparazzi crows who . . .

She didn't recognize the students. It was odd. Shiels didn't know everyone in the school, but she knew a lot of people. . . . "Hey! Where are you from?" she said to the tall redhead.

"Mind your own business!" the girl snapped.

"You aren't from here. Where the hell are you from?"

"Clamp it!" the girl said.

But her backpack tag said Claymore, and Shiels recognized another girl from Wagleigh—they had sat together on Interscholastic Youth Council last year.

"Clear it!" Shiels yelled, in her largest student-body chair voice. "Anybody not from Vista View, clear these hallways right now!"

Normally her voice could rattle the roots of anyone's hair. But these people, they turned with their cameras. Shiels could see them all staring at her nose.

"You're the girl!" somebody said, and flashes blinded her, but she did catch a glimpse of dark purple somewhere in the mass. With a scarlet slash.

Probably Pyke didn't know what was going on.

Probably, if he'd known it was her, he would have hop-hipped out and slipped his wing protectively around her.

Probably he would've done what he could.

But as it was, Shiels was driven back down the hall by what felt like a wall of photographic flashes all aimed her way, bleaching her insides, scrubbing clean any notion she had of who she might have been or who she might be now.

And Sheldon was not there either. How often had she relied on him to pick her up after a particularly public defeat? She relied on him, she took him for granted, she knew it. . . . She knew it especially in moments like this, when she was steaming toward Manniberg's office, ready to strip the paint off the school lockers to get the changes she was demanding.

Sheldon was usually there to temper her anger.

To smooth out her prickles.

Just to hold her.

I'm being stupid, she thought. *I'm being stupid. I should go to him again, just say whatever is needed to make it right with Sheldon.*

She stormed into Manniberg's office alone. Manniberg was standing in plain view, looking at papers as always, vulnerable to her, almost defenseless.

Sheldon was not there to rein her in.

So she raged about the paparazzi, about the students from other schools, and disorder in the halls, and the security lapses, and the potential danger to Vista View students, and breaches of privacy, and what was going to happen now if the whole world knew? She fumed long after poor Manniberg had gotten the point. She backed him into the seating position of his desk and dictated the APFSP, the Anti-Paparazzi Foreign Student Protocol—another protocol! That was what came out of her mouth, and Sheldon was not there to edit out the invective. And Manniberg—he just wrote it all down. When she was subtle, he caught her passes. They worked together uncommonly well. Something in the back of her mind realized this. But when she was in full hurricane mode, he had no resistance against her. He got rattled, he didn't really know what he was doing.

Everyone she truly cared about—Sheldon—could stand his ground when the winds were so foul.

And yet . . . and yet . . . She had driven him away.

Everyone she loved—Sheldon—could put strong hands on her shoulders and slowly get her to stop foaming and then could hold her and bring out his phone and write up something sensible from her anger.

It wasn't that her anger was misplaced, or wrongheaded. It was just too . . . Shiels.

It was too Shiels.

She knew it in the middle of blasting but could not feel a way to be both Shiels and Sheldon at the same time.

And Manniberg had no resistance to her.

So the APFSP was dictated, typed, announced, and distributed by the end of the day.

And everyone knew who was behind it—the girl with the purple nose who had wrangle danced with Pyke, and turned his crest scarlet, but was not known for running.

Anti-Paparazzi Foreign Student Protocol (APFSP)

Vista View High School values and protects the privacy and safety of all its students, regardless of species orientation, and safeguards the basic human rights of each to not be mobbed by fawning, shiftless, overly aggressive, camera-wielding, screaming crowhead sewer vermin from other educational institutions. As extraordinary as the achievements and talents of Vista View students are, the school and all its members vow to protect each and every member, wronged or not, from these lizard brains.

Consequently, *there will be no unauthorized use of cameras or any other photographic or otherwise recording instruments in the school at any time especially by students and other individuals who do not belong to the Vista View High School community;*

Specifically, *no student or other individuals from outside the school will be allowed entry without express consent of Principal Manniberg;*

Furthermore, *any student or other individual found to be in contravention of this protocol will be subject to the full prosecution of the laws of trespass;*

And in summation, *the Vista View High School community vows to protect and value the privacy and safety of all its members, across species, to the highest extent and especially to keep irresponsible and bottom-feeding students foreign to our community away and clear from school property and uninterfering in the lives of its especially most talented and extraordinary members.*

XVIII

An avalanche of electronic invective smashed down on Shiels's head. She could not look at very much of it.

What gives u the right to dictate to us, slime-nose slut?

Her phone jerked out of her handbag almost, in the backlash.

Where'd u have to shove yur gob to purple it up like that?

Her laptop fumed with the fallout.

Wrangle dance with him all u want. Yur just acting like slutshit!

Shiels sat on her bed with her knees drawn up, holding herself. Trying not to shake.

One brief text from Sheldon: *Sewer vermin? Lizard brains?????*

When she texted him back, he did not respond. When

she called him, she didn't even get his service. It just rang and rang for nothing.

Her mother knocked softly on the door, and when Shiels did not answer, she let herself in carrying a hot mug of cocoa and an oatmeal cookie.

"You're working so hard these days." Her mother put the tray beside Shiels and sat on the edge of the bed. "Taking a break for a moment?"

Shiels's face felt as gray as a wrinkled sky.

"I wanted to follow up on our conversation from a few days ago, before all the . . . pterodactyl business," her mother said. "I have made an appointment for you to see Dr. Russell—"

"There's no need," Shiels said, keeping her eyes down.

"There's no need . . . you have made your own arrangements, or there's no need—"

"There's no need," Shiels said slowly.

"I see. Well, as you know—" What was it in Shiels's eye that made her mother stop talking, swallow slowly, shift gears? "Well, then. I also wanted to remind you about the Stockard application. I don't want to nag or anything, but it's due in a matter of weeks. I have heard that they look more favorably on the early applicants. Joan Lumley, who is on their board of directors, said this to me recently. You have met Dr. Lumley before?"

Shiels's mother was chewing her lower lip, just the

corner. Holding back. Shiels had a vague sense of Dr. Lumley standing eagle-eyed on three-inch heels at one of her parents' parties.

"I know you will do a fabulous job on the application. Stockard is small and elite, but with your record I think you're a lock, although you will have to apply yourself once you're there. They have a phenomenal record of placing people at Johns Hopkins. I know you might prefer Harvard, but if you look at the research possibilities now at Johns Hopkins—"

If Shiels did not say anything, her mother would just keep talking.

So Shiels said, "Stockard sounds good."

"I'd be happy to look over your draft. Your father as well. The essay is key. A lot of people don't have your . . . experience and interesting take on life. Maybe . . . maybe Sheldon could help you with the writing? I mean just to get your thoughts together? He is good with words."

The dam held, somehow, a last membrane behind Shiels's welling eyes. "Sure," she said.

It was a war, practically, to keep important things from her mother. Shiels had to change the subject. So she said, "Walloping Wallin," and forced a smile. "It's going to be great, don't you think?"

"I saw the pterodactyl," her mother said. "We all did. That's lovely that he plays a sport." She squeezed her daughter's shoulder. "But you, you must focus on what's important. That's the challenge now. There will be time for all kinds of fun and games after your applications are done!"

The next morning Shiels was back on the track in her yellow shoes. Earlier than before because sleep had not visited, not at two a.m., not at four, not at five thirty.

Not a disaster. She needed to stay conscious. To think it all out in tighter and tighter circles, like Pyke flying around the track while Jocelyne Legault churned out her countless laps.

Her mother had said to focus on what's important. Not football. But maybe not applications, either. Shiels's spinning thoughts kept coming back to this essential truth: Jocelyne was Pyke's real girlfriend. He'd been smitten with her from the beginning. Everyone knew that. He might have wrangle danced with Shiels, but his wings flapped for just one girl. And who knew, really, why his crest had turned? Maybe it was just his age—pterodactyl puberty or something. He had wrangle danced with both Shiels and Jocelyne. Maybe both of them had set him off.

Yet Shiels donned her yellow shoes before sunrise and settled into her steady, reliable low gear around and around the track. Cool air, blue-gray skies. Almost foggy. The crows were out again to watch her. Should they not be escaping south for the winter? Did crows escape south? Why not?

Ugly weather was coming. Bitter winds, frozen ground, snow upon ice upon more snow. Months and months of it.

The dictator of the Anti-Paparazzi Foreign Student Protocol settled into a chugging, quiet rhythm. Small steps, arms pumping, breaths regular. This was the stride her shoes wanted her to take. Slowly, slowly . . . just keep running.

Why had Pyke not yet come to watch her? She was in full view of his spies, wearing her yellow shoes (he had practically commanded her to wear them). Running.

Learning how to run.

She needed him to seek her out.

She had engineered him a role in Walloping Wallin.

She was doing everything right, as far as she could see. And yet . . . And yet . . .

Sheldon was gone.

There was no loyalty left amongst her team.

The students hated her.

Stride, stride, breathe, stride . . .

Maybe . . . they were right.

Maybe . . . she had no legitimacy left. Maybe she'd never had any. Who was she fooling? She was not going to get into Chesford to study with Lorraine Miens. Not as an undergrad. Maybe not as a grad, either. She couldn't even write an Anti-Paparazzi Foreign Student Protocol without landing a ton of crowshit on her head.

Where was Sheldon when she needed him?

She rounded the bend at the north end of the track, and Sheldon was not there—she had no right to expect him to be—but suddenly Pyke was. He landed so abruptly, with so little grace, she felt the fear jolt through her the way a field mouse must experience the instant before the grasp of a hawk.

"Crowshit!" she said, because that word was on her mind.

He was standing just a few paces away, his wings opening and closing, looking huge, as if he might take off again any moment.

He stared at her now, visually pulled her to him. Lowered his beak as if he might use it.

For what?

"You came to see me," she said.

Again, a certain heat surrounded him. It wasn't just the running. She felt so close to him. How far had he flown just to be with her? She put her hand on his heaving, purple hide. It just felt like the thing to do. She remembered now the moment of first touching him in the wrangle dance— not just a video memory, but a real one. This pulsing through her body. Boiling her oil.

"Run you," he said—a whisper, really. He wasn't learning much English, despite the classes he sat through day after day.

Maybe he didn't need it. He seemed to have a whole other way to communicate.

Where . . . where to kiss along the beak? *Is that what pterodactyls do?*

The crows started to clamor then. Shiels was going to ignore them—who ever paid attention to crows?

Pyke snapped around. It was a miracle Shiels was not disemboweled by the slashing beak.

Shiels strained to see . . . Jocelyne Legault arriving at the track in her warm-up gear, an athletic bag on her shoulder. Her nose so dark, like Shiels's. She carried her shoes.

Her yellow shoes.

Jocelyne stopped when she saw Pyke, the two of them. *What are they doing?* she must've been thinking. Pyke and the new girl.

The new girl with the purple nose wearing yellow shoes too.

On Jocelyne Legault's track.

"I better . . . I have to get going," Shiels said to the ptero-dactyl. And she started running—clip-clip, clip-clip—in her slow way. It was just down the home stretch. It had to be toward Jocelyne Legault.

That was where the only exit was.

But by the time she got there, Jocelyne had already pulled on her own shoes and taken off around the bend. Uncatchable.

Unstoppable.

Shiels had no idea what she might want to say to Jocelyne Legault anyway.

"I love Sheldon but I covet your boyfriend too."

"I can't describe what he does to me."

"I'm like this river that cannot stay within its own sensible banks."

Already waiting at the school when Shiels arrived to begin her academic day was the real paparazzi—news vans, photographers, journalists with video cameras, staking out the front doors of the school. Shiels wanted to charge into them (that instinct reared its head whenever Pyke was concerned), but she held back. Had her own foolishly worded protocol summoned the press, unwittingly leaked the news of Vista View's most extraordinary student?

Unlikely. Those non–Vista Viewers yesterday had already found out about Pyke. The wonder was that the school had been able to keep a lid on so far. And this scrum . . . was not her responsibility. Manniberg was already holding court, looking grim and leader-like in his overcoat and not letting anybody in. Shiels kept her distance but could hear clearly.

"I have a duty to protect the privacy and person of every student under my care," he said. "There can be no photographs, no interviews, no video shot without permission, and the student in question has not granted that—"

"Is he playing in the football game, Principal Manniberg?" a woman yelled, leaning in with her microphone.

"Those decisions are Coach's responsibility," Manniberg said. "What we are most concerned with here at Vista View is providing safe, challenging, appropriate education for every student who—"

"Is it true that he's a pterodactyl?" another reporter asked. "Where does he come from? Have paleontologists been alerted?"

"Vista View is a school, not a circus," Manniberg said smoothly. "Now if you'll excuse me—"

"We've heard reports that some of the girls of the school have been sexually marked by the pterodactyl—"

Shiels turned and headed for the side entrance, her face down. They needed to bar the doors, call the police!

But it wasn't her responsibility. She'd already authored the APFSP. Manniberg had gotten the drift and knew his lines. Maybe they should call in the National Guard!

Or maybe it wouldn't be such a big thing. It hadn't taken long for most of the Vista View students to get used to having Pyke around. Maybe the whole world was going to fall in love with him too.

Maybe Shiels didn't have a lot of time.

But, with the world slowly turning its eyes, with the press at the door, hungry, how to think about anything else? Pyke had not shown up for practice yet. The football team was in disarray. Was he going to play or not? How would they do it? Where was he now? He seemed to drop into classes only occasionally, a period of urban geography, a session in Spanish (which he seemed to speak better than English, although that was not saying very much).

Pyke is a game-day performer, Shiels posted on Vhub, to try to calm people down. *He didn't even show up for the sound check at Autumn Whirl. But everybody knows . . . he sure came to play!*

U 2! some troll wrote back. *U played wrangle dance till ur nose turned blak!*

She didn't look at any other comments.

Another issue of the *Leghorn Review* was due soon, and Shiels was dreading it. Normally she and Sheldon would've been watermashing the topics all week—texting, emailing, calling, gabbing. They would have already hashed out something on People Who Text Too Much, and Why Watching Music Videos without Sound Should Become an Olympic Sport, and on Seven Unusual Facts about Sober Dating. They would have talked it out. And then in the stuffy control room off the library, they would have sat together and pounded out the articles, concocted the graphics, mixed the music.

Until now it had always been a Shiels-Sheldon coproduction.

And the new issue was supposed to go live in a matter of hours.

Hours!

Life seemed to be conspiring. Shiels's stomach felt wobbly. Her palms itched. Her scalp seemed to channel a rogue electric current, not strong enough to burn, not weak enough to ignore.

Her breath felt like it was going in her nose and then directly out of her mouth, missing her lungs; her chest was too tight to let in fresh air.

There was Sheldon now, walking away from Gendered Society. Talking with Rachel Wyngate. Again! So tall and leggy. Her forearms permanently red from volleyball. Shiels picked them out with her gaze across the whole length of the eastern corridor. A moment later Sheldon turned, as if he could feel in his cells that she was watching him.

A naked stare. She would not look away. Not this time. Even across that riotously populated hallway, that stupid distance, she saw the hurt still in his eyes. Then Rachel Wyngate turned to see what—who—Sheldon was looking at. And others, too, turned to look.

Though not at Shiels. The commotion was behind her. The fire doors opened. Shiels, too, turned. Pyke burst through, tottering as he walked, leaning upright with Jocelyne Legault beside him and the usual mob trailing them both. Pyke halted when he saw Shiels. He stretched his wings so that Jocelyne had to step away. He waggled his crest at Shiels, and made low squawking noises. He hop-hipped toward her.

"Stop it," Shiels said, but without conviction. "You're making a spectacle of yourself."

He waved his beak. His shriek sent a roar of approval from the crowd up and down the hall.

"That's too loud. That's not appropriate," Shiels said, too softly to be heard.

Pyke circled, he warbled. Where was Jocelyne? Standing back. Watching the display. Where was Sheldon? Sheldon should step between them. Knock the pterodactyl flat on his back and say—

What could he say? Nothing. He wasn't there anymore, and neither was Rachel Wyngate.

It was Jocelyne who said, "Pyke," in her quiet, cutting voice. Who yanked that bird back by his invisible leash. "Go to class."

The pterodactyl slunk away. Leaving the two purple noses to face each other. With about eighty onlookers still crowded in.

"This is no one's business but ours," Jocelyne said in a voice taut enough to hold an ocean liner stiff to a dockside. When Shiels added a glare, the other students melted off.

"He can't help himself," Jocelyne said finally. *But you can*, her eyes were saying.

"I have no interest in a freshman," Shiels said. What a relief to hear her own voice, more or less normal-sounding, to have a sense that her life was not over. (Her life as herself, Shiels Krane, the self she had built so consciously over the years and thought she knew so well.) "Don't misunderstand me. I'm not out to steal Pyke. We need him for Wallin. Why isn't he going to practice? Tell him he needs to go."

Those shallow blue eyes. Jocelyne Legault would never have thought of Pyke for the football team. She had no ambition for her boyfriend. *Forgive me for seeing the big picture,* Shiels thought.

Forgive me for not being like everybody else.

Jocelyne shook her head in tiny, jiggly movements, as if her neck were a spring. "They can't practice on the field. Everyone's watching. So they're doing it in secret in the gym. Behind closed doors."

"And Pyke is actually showing up?" Shiels said.

"He will," Jocelyne said. Her eyes narrowed. She was staring at Shiels's shoes, brighter even than her own. "Why are you . . . Why are you running?"

"I just want to get in shape," Shiels said. "Don't worry. I just like to jog around. And," she repeated, "I'm not after Pyke. My nose to the contrary, he doesn't affect me the way he seems to affect everyone else. You can have him as long as you like."

Shiels felt the corner of her mouth turn into a little

smile. A trace of fear passed Jocelyne Legault's eyes, like the brief shadow of a bird flying overhead. "Really," Shiels said then, and touched the other girl's arm lightly.

It wasn't a lie. Was it? It felt perfectly true in this moment. "We all have the will and means to reshape reality," Lorraine Miens had said. Shiels was just thinking of the good of the school. Wasn't she?

Then, later, there was Sheldon already sitting in the office off the library, in their little space, working away on the *Leghorn Review*. Shiels had the door key in her hand when she gazed through the glass and saw him in his dingy blue cable-knit sweater—his holey garment, he called it, because of the patches—his rounded shoulders leaning toward the monitor, his jaw thrust forward, fingers dancing across the keyboard. Composing. The words flying on-screen. If she opened the door, she would distract him. She wondered if she should walk away, let Sheldon have *Leghorn*.

Clearly he could do it himself. She was prepared to do it all by herself as well, and she knew his *Leghorn* would be miles ahead of hers. He was the writer. She was the . . . facilitator.

Those fingers were flashing. Facilitating just fine without her.

She pushed open the door anyway. He turned, startled out of his thought. She could see in his kind eyes—his dear, gray, lovely eyes—that he'd been far away for a moment, even in the middle of something funny, and that the something evaporated the moment he saw her.

No, no, not precisely. The moment he saw her, his eyes lit more, but then something seemed to leak out of him, obviously with the realization, the memory, of where they were now, who they had become.

"We don't have much time," Shiels said, just to say something, to get them past the awkwardness. She took her seat beside him. They could do this. "What are you writing on?"

His fingers were still poised above the keyboard. "I've been horsing around with flying dreams. Ever since Pyke got here, I've been having them. I have this sense of lifting off, floating above the ground with every step, like I'm walking but not walking. It turns into flying, only it feels completely normal. Like walking on the moon, maybe."

"It's running for me," Shiels said. "In my dreams. Same as you." She hesitated. Were they really talking like this, as if everything were normal? "It turns into flying. But often I'm naked, except for my yellow shoes."

"Really?" Sheldon glanced down at those shoes, his fingers tapping something out.

"Don't write that!" Shiels said.

"It's not about you. But you did buy the same shoes as Jocelyne's, didn't you?"

"Maybe the whole school is dreaming about flying," Shiels said. "We could put it out there. Ask for people's flying dream stories."

"We could call them 'Pyke dreams,'" Sheldon said, and he couldn't help it, he was a smiling little boy over his pun. Shiels thought: *Two minutes sitting with Sheldon, and already the ideas are brimming.*

"I don't . . . I don't think of him directly in my dreams," she said. "I mean, obviously it's him. I see him, but at the time of the dream, I think that it's you. You with muscles."

"I have muscles," Sheldon said. He was writing, writing away. The way that he did. She didn't watch the screen. He was a composer, obviously—the writer. She was the facilitator.

The muse? No, that would be Pyke.

She said, "I find myself running, like I'm in Africa or something. On the savanna. Or I'm pulling myself out of the jungle, looking for sky. That's what I want. And his muscles and his heat."

"You want his muscles and his heat?"

"It's not sexual," she said. This always happened when she was with Sheldon. The barriers broke down. It was like they were one person. She could just say what she had boiling in her brain. "It's just physical."

"Like the wrangle dance? Like the way his crest flares whenever he sees you?"

So—Sheldon had stuck around long enough . . .

"I don't know what that was," she said. He was writing and warm now too, in his sweater, a hand width away from her. She could reach over. Their whole life together had started in this very room, working on a different version of this project many issues ago.

So easily, she felt like she had dialed back the clock and none of the coldness of the separation had happened.

"You're going out with Rachel Wyngate," she said suddenly. When he didn't react, she said, "Does she have Pyke dreams too?"

"Everyone has Pyke dreams." Sheldon's fingers did not slow down. "We're going to be inundated with Pyke dreams as soon as we put this out."

Words slapping up on-screen. She didn't read them.

"You're in love with Pyke," he said, and she nodded, because it was a dream (sort of) that they still were in. This was a dream kind of truth. She had just told Jocelyne she did not love him, and that too was true. From a different dream.

"Everyone's in love with Pyke," Shiels said.

Everyone was in love with Pyke. Sheldon was right—as soon as *Leghorn* went live, the Pyke dreams flooded in.

It's water. I'm swimming but I'm flying, too. Breathing underwater. I'm a dolphin with wings, my skin is stretched all tight around my body, and I have a way of jumping that turns into something else. Diving in reverse. I'm doing all the steps. Watching myself and doing it at the same time. The water is warmer than the air.

For me it's all about the umbrella. I'm late for something, class I guess. And I just wish he would come and pick me up. Swoop down and cradle me. He's so gentle. The way he was holding Jocelyne. That's how he would hold me. And my umbrella. When I open it. It's kind of hard to explain. I open the umbrella and the umbrella starts to cradle me, and then we're flying together. I can't believe other people have had almost exactly the same dream!

My Pyke dream is about being on my motorcycle. I'm rounding a curve, it's a jump. I rev it and rocket, and then I'm off-ramp. I turn the way I would on a board, just slow and casual, looking down, staying calm, one big loop, and my engine cuts—it's quiet. I'm going so slow, I might as well have stopped in midair. I had this dream before Pyke came to the school, but now it's like the dream is in hyper-view because I can see the colors in the bike. I mean, I could always see the colors, but now the colors see me, too. Does that sound weird? I didn't even go to the dance. I felt like bonking my head against concrete when I found out how great it was and watched it all later online. Every

time I *have this dream, it gets clearer and slower, so now
it doesn't even feel like flying anymore. Is that still a Pyke
dream?*

*it's twisting maybe a propeller or a tail whipping round
like a crocodile in one of those nature shows that grabs the
calf and brings it under and then whips around and around
and i step into the blade but i know the blade will slide off
me if i'm loose enough and not just me but a better me the
gentle me i'd like to ride his back to tell you the truth i could
wrap my arms around his chest i could hold him with my legs
i could hug him not hard just right i don't really dream all
this the twisting yes but that's the way i feel*

XIX

Robbie Lewis tracked down Shiels near the portable outside when she was heading to Postlethwaite's forgettable English class. It was another gray, cool, wet day, and Robbie Lewis was not in Postlethwaite's class, so he had clearly gone out of his way to reach her.

"Is Pyke a go for Friday?" he asked. "Because Coach has to submit the lineup sheet now. So we have to know."

Robbie seemed smaller. He was shivering in his Vista View colors, the gray and gold.

"I thought you were practicing in secret," Shiels said. "Haven't you been working out plays and stuff?"

"He hasn't come yet. But you said he would. You practically guaranteed him!"

"Did I?" Shiels was enjoying her little moment of teasing. Finally she said, "Of course he'll be there. Put his name down."

He almost needed to bend double just to talk to her. "But what position does he play?"

The same question she had asked him when she'd nearly knocked him over in the hall. "Anything where he has to catch the ball."

"Tight end? Wide receiver? How about special teams? Punt returns?"

"Sure. You saw him in the cafeteria, in the auditorium. Just get the ball to him! It's not rocket science."

"Catching the football is a whole lot different from playing in an actual game. Does he even know the rules? Has he ever been hit? He wouldn't swallow the ball, would he?"

"He grew up in the Himalayas playing football with his brothers and sisters," she said.

"Really?" Was it getting bonked on the helmet that made Robbie Lewis so credulous all of a sudden? Shiels took a moment to enjoy him shivering in his flimsy shirt, trying to figure out if she was kidding or not.

"Every day on the mountaintop. Football, football, football," she said. "That was his whole life. Just you see. It'll be a game for the ages."

I have always wanted to be a doctor, Shiels wrote in her application essay for her mother's choice, Stockard College. *I suppose it was simply in my genes, in the soup of my childhood. Having two doctors as parents helps a great deal, no doubt. I took it for granted that every girl grew up surrounded by microscopes. At breakfast, conversation revolved around the latest in cancer research or what an elderly woman might do to prevent bone loss. It is simply a given in my family that we serve others, that our lives were meant to be dedicated to improving the health and well-being of the ill and suffering, patient by patient, neighbor by neighbor, friend by friend.*

She paused. The opening paragraph had just poured out, almost without thought.

But what I wasn't expecting, what took me by surprise, is my fascination with political society. The science of groups, I suppose it might be called. Beyond the microbes in our gut, beyond the workings of various viruses and other physical instabilities, what makes the body politic tick and twitch? What are humans? Who are we and who could we be? And why are we like we are? When our hearts thump in certain directions, when life seems to have laid down an honorable and worthwhile course, why do we turn away and follow another distraction? Why can't we love who we are meant to love, simply and without doubt? Why does the blood boil in such uncomfortable directions?

Who are we?

Who are we when we dream, when we close our eyes and the good sensible sweet smart guiding judgment of our magnificent brains turns off for the night and what emerges is the soup of our desires with its clashing tastes and its talent for mixing the uncommon with the unnatural? Who is that naked woman with the purple beak running in the tall grass after the winged boy with the dark skin and the probing eyes and other things . . . other things that should probably not be included in a college application essay?

The truth of the matter . . .

Dear Committee, the truth of the matter is that you will be taking a big risk if you admit me to your esteemed program. I might be fine, I might settle down, I might yet get my act together and use your excellent faculties to springboard my way to a life in epidemiology or clinical obstetrics or forensic parapsychology . . .

Or I might fall in love with a pterodactyl.

I might sit in class dreaming of his glowing pectorals, of those arching wings. I might fly off.

I might fill my lab notes with descriptions of his odor.

He smells like: leather boots that were stored wet last season and now are moist and grainy to the touch, an unexpected slap to the nose;

like running hard in the rain with winter coming on but your heart and your body, everything is oiled, and suddenly you are awake to what the ground and the air and the moist trees and the dying leaves and the very world taste like with every breath;

like the place might slant suddenly, geotectonically, and Africa might suddenly collide with South America while swallowing the Atlantic Ocean, and so where would all that seawater go but onto the land, and what would it bring but a million gulls, who are like crows—white crows—and so we'd all better learn to fly then.

I know, that last item is not a smell.

It's an everything.

Are you sure you want to admit me to your school? It could be a waste. It could be throwing away a perfectly good spot.

Did I tell you that I am student-body chair and that in the course of my duties my nose has turned purple?

How was it that a whole school could imagine the same play over and over—the arcing spiral, the swooping catch, hapless Wallin players running comically after a flying Pyke—yet the closer it got to game day, the easier it became to imagine it might not happen at all?

Pyke hadn't been to practice.

He had said he would—to all of his friends in Human Geography, to his Spanish buddies, his bandmates, to Shiels's brother, Jonathan, who at her insistence had cornered Pyke in the cafeteria and then later outside the library. Pyke clicked his beak, he smiled, he said, "Za! Za!" whenever anyone brought it up.

He caught anything anyone threw at him.

On the track, in the early morning, he showed up only

one more time to accompany Jocelyne Legault, who lapped Shiels time and again while Pyke circled above the champion, keeping pace.

"He knows about the game," Jocelyne said to her when they—Shiels—was catching her breath at the end of the workout. "He'll be there."

Melanie Mull was a whirlwind organizer. She reminded Shiels of herself last year getting Vhub vibrating on all cylinders. Ticket sales were brisk; the buses ordered; the cheer team prepped; megaphones procured, tested, assigned. Shiels, master delegator, was left to ponder the enormity of the failure if Pyke in fact did not show. Late in the afternoon of the day before the game, she found Pyke behind the auto shop hanging out with the smokers. She approached them with her jacket pulled tight. He looked like any other juvenile delinquent slouching against the wall, puffing away.

"Who gave him that?" Shiels demanded.

Randy Eggles, with his pimply face and his hooded eyes, said, "He's a musician. Of course he smokes!"

Shiels wanted to snatch the butt out of Pyke's mouth, but she guessed she could never move fast enough. He seemed to be smiling at her. His crest was flaming.

"Mebbee zu try?" he said.

Shiels glanced around at the empty parking lot, the blank wall. Then she reached out and took the thing from his beak.

It seemed like a deeply intimate gesture. She thought she was going to toss the cigarette into the can but found herself pulling it to her own lips, taking a drag, closing her eyes.

She would not . . . cough.

"Oh—hey!" Lionel Catching said. He was a tall boy who was all Adam's apple. "Shiels Krane hanging with the low-lifers!"

She blew smoke into his face. Filthy, wretched habit. But she stood with the thing in her fingers. Now that she had their attention, she turned her full gaze on Pyke. "You need to show up for that football game tomorrow. You're part of this school. A lot of people have stuck their necks out for you. You can't let us down." She took another drag. Totally disgusting. She tried to make her face look like maybe it was all right.

Randy Eggles suddenly cried, "Pyke!" and flicked his burning butt into the air. Pyke leapt at it, swallowed it down triumphantly.

"Oh my God!" Shiels yelled. She wanted to whap Randy right on his smirking face, but he was too far away. Instead she said, "Pyke—cough it up! Cough it—"

Instead, Pyke twirled his beak and produced the cigarette, still burning, for all to see.

"Stop it! You—" She slapped him across the beak. The cigarette went flying and skittered across the cold pavement.

Everyone looked at her in amazement. She tossed away the other cigarette, the one she was still holding. Pyke's grin flickered for a moment.

"Gotta give a beast some lead on the leash," Randy said finally. "Especially if you're that hot for him!"

There was no time to react. A news van turned the corner and headed toward them. Shiels screamed at Pyke, "Get out of here! Go! Go!"

Pyke took off like an explosion. Shiels felt herself blown back against the wall. When she looked again, he was gone, disappeared around the corner of the building.

The van screeched to a halt. Two men scrambled out, one with a TV camera on his shoulder.

"Is this your lead?" Shiels asked calmly. "A bunch of kids in the smoking area?"

But she wasn't calm. On game day, when the buses were late because a windstorm had knocked out power to half a dozen stoplights in the downtown core, strangulating traffic everywhere, she raged against Melanie Mull's haphazard organizational effort in front of half the council — the half that had drifted somewhat back into Shiels's orbit—until Rebecca Sterzl finally said, "Shiels, enough!"

Enough.

(Rebecca Sterzl! Telling her!)

But it was enough.

Shiels's nerves were frayed. She was working herself into a state the way she had before Autumn Whirl. Why? Why did she operate this way?

She seemed to know, more than anyone else, what was at stake, how huge the failure would be if Pyke dropped the ball, or couldn't play, or didn't show up in the first place.

It was all on her. *All of it!*

"I'm sorry, Melanie. I'm sorry!" Shiels said, in front of everybody. "Of course it's not your fault. You've been terrific, all throughout this. The buses will come. Of course they will! It's all going to be fine."

And Melanie Mull accepted her embrace, wiped her tears, seemed to soak up this late praise from Shiels.

Later, on one of the buses, with a megaphone now in her hand, while Shiels called out the war cries of the Vista View Vikings, a strange part of herself seemed to drift above her body, like a spirit self looking down at the proceedings, at the strident young woman with the megaphone.

Hard left, hard right,

Cut, slash, Valiant Vikes!

It was as if the sound had leaked out of the picture, as if she were seeing things from the security camera mounted high above her life.

Inside, outside, crush 'em, fight!

Hurry hard, Valiant Vikes!

The bus hit a bump, and the red-faced, purple-nosed

girl with the megaphone grabbed a seat back to steady herself, while her spirit self looked on, unmoving, and thought: *What if this is all a dream?*

Kick 'em hard, trounce 'em, fight!

Stride to victory, Valiant Vikes!

A niggling memory: Mrs. Tron's world religions class last year. Some religions—Buddhism?—consider the entire world to be a construct, a mental fabrication (was that the right term?) . . . a dream. We take things in through our senses, we seehearsmelltouchtaste them, and reorder them in our minds, construct reality like a film on-screen.

We become fascinated by our own constructions.

Our dreams.

Walloping Wallin might be a dream, she thought.

Tear their jerseys, struggle, bite!

Fight forever, Valiant Vikes!

The bus felt real; the students' faces looked as real as in any dream. Shiels could stand and shout and feel her hip against the side of the aisle seat, and it was all as real as any flying Pyke dream she'd had in the last several weeks.

(Swallowing burning cigarettes, and then regurgitating them, still lit! How could she fall for such a, for such a . . . She wanted to say "clown," but he wasn't that. He was more like a god, and girls never got gods, did they? And if they did, it was always trouble.)

Who was that girl screaming into the megaphone? What

was she yelling about? For all this public display of volume and spirit, why did this feel like a descent into sadness?

The wind blew, cold and hard, in the stands, and Shiels was not dressed for it. She hadn't thought this through. Normally she was three steps ahead of events; she was used to cracking the whip on life and watching the wave turn into a snap. But Pyke was not there at the start of the game, and now she sat on the metal bleacher in her cotton pants and felt the chill of new-November settle into her tissues. She was clutching her megaphone still and every so often would stand and let loose a rallying call that rattled inside her as if her bones had turned into aluminum.

The cheers of the Vista View crowd sank into the cold air.

A lumbering player for Wallin knocked down four Valiant Vikes, stepping on three of them, to score a touchdown on the very first play. They scored again just a few minutes later when Jeremy Jeffreys threw the ball directly into a stiff wind, only to have the sickly pass curve into the arms of a Wallin defender who'd been standing alone away from the play.

Pyke did not show up.

Pyke did not show.

The wind flung blankets off huddled knees and at the end of the first quarter sailed away with the referee's hat. Programs flew off, only to be pressed hard against the chain-link fence at the end of the sports field, and everyone on the Vista View side looked to the birdless sky with draining hope.

It was too windy for Pyke to fly.

Pyke was not going to save the game.

Robbie Lewis, who played somewhere on defense—that much Shiels could understand—knocked the ball out of a Wallin player's hands and then ran down the sidelines the wrong way, into his own team's end zone, and threw the ball down in deluded triumph, only to have a Wallin player fall on it for yet another touchdown.

It was that kind of game.

If Sheldon had been there—Sheldon had a nose for important events, and was not at this one, which only added to the building dread in Shiels's gut—he would have delighted in the cascading incompetence of the Valiant Vikes under the pressure of playing a large, ferocious, talented team. He would have videoed and posted the Robbie Lewis debacle; he would have perversely gloried in the way the Vikes' passing game went haywire in the wind; he would have found new adjectives for the sound of the Vikes' bodies hitting the ground after colliding with such superbly conditioned monsters.

Manniberg had skipped out. Jocelyne Legault was not there either. Too late, Shiels realized that Jocelyne's absence was a clue. Pyke never had intended to come.

This was all part of the dream, obviously. You could not summon someone like Pyke. Gods do not come when called.

At halftime the score was 31–0. The eight visitors' buses left with most of the Vista View crowd and almost all the media. But Shiels stayed because she was student-body chair, and felt responsible, and was clinging to appearances. When the teams ran back onto the field for the second half, Coach glared at her as if he'd known all along her central role. From seventy-five yards away she felt his accusatory malice hardening the roots of her hair.

Could she even return to the school with this utter failure hanging around her neck? Somehow the image stuck in her mind that the doors would not even open for her. That she would be prevented from stepping foot in the place.

But then, with Wallin about to score again late in the third quarter—when there was still time for a comeback!— Shiels spotted a speck in the eastern sky. Then not just one speck, a series of them, gathering force: crows. By the thousands. Heading their way.

She grabbed her megaphone and yelled out, "Hold that line, Vikes!" so loudly that the players on the field turned to see what she was on about.

Or, rather, the crowd was so quiet, so sparse at that point, her amplified voice, even caught in the wind, surprised them. "Hold on! Hold on!" she cried, and pointed, so that many of the players turned to look at the gathering storm of crows.

Wallin ran their toughest player against the Valiant Vikes' front line . . . which drove him back two yards.

"Hold that line!" Shiels yelled again. She thought she could see one larger speck in the distant swirl of crows. It looked like Pyke was fighting the wind, trying to make it to the field.

The Wallin quarterback kept the ball himself and ran around the Vikes' stumbling defenders but was forced out of bounds. Close to scoring, but not quite.

Shiels moved down to the mostly abandoned front row of the bleachers. A girl sat huddled under a frayed blanket. Jocelyne Legault! She'd been there all the time. "Is he coming?" Shiels asked her. "Is that him?"

"Yes. I think so. I told him," Jocelyne said. So Shiels yelled into the megaphone, "One more time! Hold that line!" and Jocelyne stood with her, shoulder to shoulder, and joined in the chant.

The Wallin quarterback faked a pass, then ran around the Vike's defenders. He had a clear route into the end zone. But at about the two-yard line, something black came out of nowhere. A crow! Who pecked at the quarterback's hand and forced a fumble.

Vikes' ball! Coach called a time-out, and then everyone watched the mighty pterodactyl circle, circle, and finally crash-land near enough to the Vikes' bench that he was immediately mobbed by cheering players. Yet the players were nothing compared to the crescendo of crows now swarming the bleachers, the fences, any railing or tower or other surface that would have them. They blackened the screen so that it was suddenly difficult to know the score or the time left.

It was 45 to nothing, but that score would be changing. Shiels felt a sudden slide of something, that worm perhaps that had stirred to life the very first time she had glimpsed Pyke in the sky.

There was still time. Who could stop a player who could fly? There was still —

"He's going to win the game," Jocelyne Legault said. "That's what you want, isn't it?"

It was an odd thing to say, as if Shiels might want more than that, or something different.

"I'm sorry our whole crowd has gone home," Shiels said. She held her phone out and captured video of the masses of crows blackening the bleachers, of the Valiant Vikes huddling around the very first football-playing pterodactyl.

The teams took the field again. Vikes' ball on their own two-yard line. Behind the suddenly energized gray-and-gold front line, Pyke hopped, looking naked almost, without a jersey, without pads. When he opened his wings, the wind blew him off balance like he was a kite on the ground. So he hopped and shifted, fluttered, scrambled to stay on his feet.

Jeffreys took the snap. He faded back, deep, deep in his own end.

"Fly!" Shiels yelled. "Pyke! Take off!"

But Pyke didn't seem to know what to do. Wallin players surged after him even though he didn't have the ball. He dodged, ducked, fluttered.

"Fly!"

Jeffreys ran the ball to him. What was this called? A broken play.

A Wallin player now had a meaty paw on Pyke's wing. It was hard to see what happened. Pyke turned a little bit, and then it's possible he moved too fast for the eye to follow. The Wallin player backed off suddenly, holding his blood-drenched arm.

The other Wallin players stopped running for Pyke and instead stood gaping, stunned.

Pyke opened his wings and, rearing up, became monstrously large. The Wallin players fell back. One of the Vikes threw a terrific block then and flattened two of the Wallin defenders, who rolled on the ground, possibly hurt.

Pyke took off awkwardly, the ball in his feet. He climbed above the heads of the other players and headed downfield. Not straight—a sort of zigzag pattern, dealing with the wind. It were as if he were running downfield, avoiding tacklers. But no one could follow him up there. He climbed, and climbed, and circled the Wallin end zone, but did not touch down.

He didn't seem to understand what a touchdown was.

He flew off with the ball, thousands of crows now blackening the sky after him. A siren in the distance turned into a red flashing light, and then an ambulance was pulling up right at the side of the football field. That Wallin player really was bleeding badly.

Shiels didn't know what to say. For the longest time she and Jocelyne Legault stood at the side of the field looking at the black dots receding in the cold, gray sky.

XX

"I believe I have already told you a number of times about the importance of early application for Stockard College," Shiels's mother said, in a clipped, overly patient tone. It was evening. They were standing in the kitchen, the night outside already dark. Shiels was emptying the dishwasher, her mind stuck on the image of Pyke flying away with the football, getting smaller and smaller in the sky.

She had the feeling he was gone for good. That she would never see him again.

"Are you even listening to me?" Shiels's mother said.

"I'm working on it," Shiels said distractedly.

Her mother closed the refrigerator door with too much force. "How is your personal essay coming? I was going to look over the draft when it's ready."

"I have a few paragraphs," Shiels said. Where was her

student-body chair voice? She sounded to herself like a little girl from grade two who'd forgotten where she'd put her pencil case.

"What's the problem? You write these kinds of things constantly for the various causes and events you get involved in. You could write a knockout piece for Stockard in your sleep."

Shiels summoned a weary smile. Did her mother even know what she was saying? Shiels felt like she was just waking up, like she'd been asleep too much of the time to focus on all these mounting heartaches and uncertainties and things too harsh to gaze at directly.

Jonathan came in then with his phone ready to hit Shiels with it. With whatever news it contained.

"Pyke has been arrested!" he announced.

Shiels felt herself slump against the granite top of the kitchen counter.

"What?"

"He slashed that Wallin guy in the game. You were there. You must've seen it. Blood spurting everywhere!"

The video was even grainier than the footage of Shiels's wrangle dance. It was taken from the Wallin side of the stands, from quite a distance off. The frame shook in the wind. Shiels could see herself and Jocelyne Legault standing on the sidelines, near the end zone, screaming at Pyke to take off. The Wallin guy was coming for Pyke, laid his hand on Pyke's shoulder, on his wing. The video was actually in slow motion. Blur, blur, the Wallin player slumped back. Black blur—blood? All the other players stepped back, and Pyke screamed—why had Shiels not remembered the scream?—and took off. The camera followed him but then returned to the player who was down. And bleeding.

"Was that the football game you were so worried about?" Shiels's mother said. Shiels had said nothing upon returning home. As if silence might mean the whole game had never happened.

"What do you mean 'arrested'?" Shiels said. "Where did they find him? Did he turn himself in? Are they saying he assaulted that Wallin player?"

"The boy looks pretty hurt," Shiels's mother said. She was wearing her doctor gaze now. Her eyes were unwavering, the motherly nagging temporarily put aside.

"He's down at the jail right now!" Jonathan said.

Shiels's first thought was to fly to Pyke's side—metaphorically— to rush to the city jail and demand to see and talk with him one human to another. She had never been inside the jail, but she had a vague notion that Pyke would be on one side of a glass booth, that they would have to speak through a telephone, that the authorities might even have buckled his beak to his body to prevent him from slashing anyone else.

She wouldn't know what to say. She would just be with

him. She would throw herself at the police constable standing guard over him and demand Pyke's release.

All of that in a first thought. But this was more than a first-thought sort of problem. This would require planning, coordination, leadership, spine. She might have lost all standing and credibility over the wrangle dance, over her purple nose, over Pyke's disastrous performance in the football game, but she was precisely the right person now to spearhead the effort to free Pyke from unjust incarceration.

Spearhead—perfect pun. Shiels called Sheldon right away. "What do we know?" she asked. Of course he understood what she was talking about. They were on the same wavelength.

"Jocelyne talked him into giving himself up," Sheldon said. "The police got her alone. They pressed her. He doesn't have an attorney."

"Slimebuckets!" Shiels said. All she knew of the law came from crime dramas, but it was enough for her to imagine burly cops pressuring Jocelyne in a tiny, dark, airless room, alternately telling her what trouble she was in for aiding and abetting—she hadn't, she'd been on the sidelines!—and reassuring her that it would all be for the best, they just wanted to talk to Pyke, nothing bad would come of it.

"Is he charged?"

"With assault," Sheldon said. "People are saying Coach

should step down for putting a wild animal in the game."

"He's not a wild animal!" Shiels said. "He's a boy, just like anyone. Has Manniberg said anything?" But Shiels knew already that Manniberg would be the last to comment on something like this. He might not even have heard what had happened.

He would blame Shiels, no matter what.

"Here's what we're going to do," Shiels said. "We need a rally. Right now. The whole student body outside the jail. Everyone with video, everyone broadcasting. We need the world to know it was a terrible accident, there was no ill intent. It was football, for God's sake. People get hurt all the time. I have the megaphone still from the game, I'll bring that. How soon do you think—"

"*Shiels*," Sheldon said. It was the tone of voice he used when she was in full stride, when he had to get a word in.

"What?"

"You convinced Jeremy Jeffreys to throw that football in the assembly so Pyke would get into that game."

"I'm dealing with now," she said. "Not the past."

"He didn't know the rules," Sheldon shot back. "He never practiced. They would've killed him if they'd hit him. He didn't know he wasn't allowed to nearly take off somebody's arm."

"What are you saying?" But it was all right for Sheldon to practically accuse Shiels of causing the entire disaster all by herself. He was playing devil's advocate. He was her reality check. That was how they functioned together.

He didn't have to try so hard, though.

"I'm saying," he said slowly, with something dangerous in his voice, "yes, he might well be guilty. Maybe you, too. I don't know the law."

Shiels caught her breath. "Me?"

"You." Underneath the usual Sheldon calm, his voice sounded angry. "You get these ideas. You think that because they're yours, they must be worthwhile. Sometimes they are, but sometimes they aren't. This is pretty much a disaster, Shiels."

Well.

Shiels stood very still, eyes closed, holding the phone to her ear. She could hear Sheldon's breathing on the other end of the line. But she couldn't hear her own.

He might as well have said that Shiels had tried to maim that Wallin boy herself and turn Pyke into a dangerous criminal.

He might as well have said he thought she was somehow deranged and power-hungry and out of control.

That he didn't respect her anymore.

That he didn't love her.

That he couldn't even work with her.

That he thought she was somehow mentally or emotionally or psychologically incompetent yet at the same time arrogant and so full of herself as to be a danger to others.

He might as well have been saying that someone else should be spearheading—that word again—the effort to defend Pyke and make the case that he had acted out of pure self-defense.

He might as well have been saying that she ought to go to the police herself and take all the blame and maybe risk a criminal conviction of her own when she had done nothing except try to make a hugely unfair football match more of an even fight.

Or, further, he might as well have been saying that she was, in fact, the only person who could save the situation, not by rallying masses of students to make a huge public noise, but by telling the authorities her role in the whole affair.

Another unfortunate word choice—*affair*.

He might as well have been saying that she could yet find a way out of this disaster by putting herself not onstage, but on the line.

Sheldon might as well have been saying that he would respect her then, that she might truly redeem herself then, that if she did love Pyke in any way, explaining her own role quietly, fully, and honestly to the authorities would be the very best way of showing it.

A painful, pregnant pause. Shiels exhaled just to hear herself.

"How did you ever get so smart?" she said softly.

"I'm sorry?"

"I will do everything you're suggesting," she said.

Shiels would do everything, yet . . . there at the front door her father stood, looking ashen. "What's wrong?" she asked. She was sitting on the stairs tying her yellow shoes. She was going to run all the way downtown to the jail to give herself up to the authorities and tell all that she knew so that they would realize her central part in the disaster and Pyke's essential innocence.

But the disaster was still unfolding.

"He almost lost his arm," her father said.

His own arms hung loosely at his sides, hands open, empty of instruments. Shiels grasped that he had been the surgeon on call; he had been the doctor forced to save the poor Wallin player's arm.

"The site was terribly infected," he said. "It was like he'd been both slashed and injected with poison or something." His eyes focused finally on her. "Where are you going?"

Shiels finished tying her shoes. Her mother approached from the kitchen then. "The boy was poisoned?" she said.

"The tissue was purple, desiccating in front of my eyes," Shiels's father said. And then both parents turned to Shiels, whose hand went up to her nose, as if she could feel its hue.

Her father kneeled to examine her, the way he had so many times when she was young and some infection had found its way in. Despite his weariness, his fingers did not tremble, but were warm and gentle on the base of her nose, along the ridge. "It's still healthy tissue," he murmured.

Still. As if it might turn rancid any moment and kill her.

"He didn't poison *me*, Daddy," Shiels said.

"Where are you going?" her mother asked then.

The PD, the parental dynamo, had her surrounded.

"I have to clear my head. I'm just going for a little run," she said. But besides her shoes she wasn't wearing jogging pants or a sweat top or leggings. She was in her black jeans and a rose shirt and burgundy sweater. Her warm coat was on the floor beside her.

They saw through her. She had no power against them.

Shiels said, "I believe I am responsible in large part for what happened today. For both tragedies. That boy who got hurt. The other boy in jail."

"The one in jail is not a boy," her mother replied. "He's a pterodactyl. And you're in love with him. You're trying to go save him."

The three of them in the foyer made a sharp-edged triangle. Shiels had a sense she would cut herself no matter what she said, what she tried to do.

"If Daddy were alone in jail because of something you'd done," she said to her mother, "wouldn't you try to save him?"

"But what's your part in this?" her father asked.

"I got him into the game. It was my idea. I didn't know

what I was doing. When all those Wallin players came at him, Pyke just reacted instinctively. He thought they were trying to kill him. I should've known. If it weren't for me, he wouldn't have been there in the first place."

"And where was Sheldon?" her mother said. "He should've known. He bears some responsibility, surely!"

"Oh"—Shiels could feel the clay of her insides turn wobbly—"Oh, Mom!" she said, before the sobs came burbling out, hot and bitter, seeping between her fingers as she held her face in her hands.

What to do? What to do now?

At her desk in her bedroom, with her mother sitting by her side, Shiels worked on her entrance application for Stockard College. As if nothing else in the world mattered at this particular moment. Her phone sat on her bed, turned off, as her mother had insisted. No distractions until they had a presentable draft.

As if they lived in a bubble protected from the chaos out there.

"If you're going to be a doctor, you will have to learn how to focus no matter what else is going on around you," her mother said.

So Shiels sat still, her fingers poised at the keyboard.

Pyke is in jail in part because of me, she thought. *He is trapped in a steel and concrete cave while I write off for early acceptance to an elite college I don't even want to attend.*

"What is it you have always dreamed of doing with your life?" Shiels's mother asked.

"I have that," Shiels said, meaning those sentiments. She showed her mother the opening paragraphs she had written some days before.

"But you have the whole essay here already!" her mother said. "Let's have a look!"

Shiels closed the file and then deleted it.

Her mother grasped Shiels's wrists. "What are you doing? What—" Shiels became limp, like a doll. "You've never behaved like this before," her mother said.

Shiels sat staring at her wrists until her mother removed her hands.

"I don't want to be a doctor," Shiels whispered.

"You're too young to make that decision," her mother said quickly. "Once you get to the college, once you're surrounded by like-minded people, you'll realize how much you fit in, and how much you have to contribute. You have gifts, Shiels. You have a razor-sharp mind and formidable will. Don't let your quite natural rebellion against me cloud your judgment!"

"I don't want to be a doctor," Shiels said again. She looked at the strain lines in her mother's face—those etches bracketing her downward mouth. She looked into her mother's incredulous eyes.

"You've never expressed this before," her mother said.

Shiels glanced at her silent phone on the bed. Things were happening out there in the world. Someone she loved was this instant trapped and surrounded by hostile forces. And she was doing nothing. Nothing!

"I'm expressing myself now." Somehow Shiels stayed small despite the collision of emotions inside. Her mother wanted her to crack again, to spill her guts, to become malleable like she always did.

She wouldn't.

Not this time.

"I have thought about this," Shiels said. "I'm sorry I didn't tell you. I didn't want to disappoint . . . disappoint you both. Maybe Jonathan could become a doctor."

Her mother's eyes briefly doubled in circumference. Shiels wanted to smile, to make a joke of it. Jonathan didn't have the grades. He wasn't, as far as anybody knew, anywhere near doctor material.

"We're not talking about Jonathan here," her mother said. "We're talking about you."

"Well, here's my dream," Shiels said. "Lorraine Miens teaches in the graduate studies program, political anthropology, at Chesford University. You know I have been reading her, like, forever. She has lived an epic life. Her mind is molten. And she takes a handful of undergraduates each year. I'd like to be one of them. I want to study men and women as political animals. I want to know how things get done in society. Really, at a human, personal level, what goes into political decision-making? How do ideas and events change nations? How does the unexpected, the unbelievable even, change all of us? Lorraine Miens has dedicated her life—"

"I thought you had gotten over your fixation with Lorraine Miens," her mother said. "Honestly—that woman is a complete radical head case!"

"She's a freethinker," Shiels said. "On so many issues she sees clear to the core of—"

"She's been divorced half a dozen times! The *New York Times* did a feature on her last month. The leading program in political anthropology in the country right now is being run by one of her former students who can't stand her anymore. Are you sure—"

Shiels knew all about the former protégé. What did Lorraine Miens call him in *Depression's Laughter*? "An intellectual earthworm."

"I would rather be Lorraine Miens's lapdog than fixating on my own daughter's menstrual cycle. I will not turn into you, no matter how hard you try!" Shiels slammed her laptop shut and bit her tongue—literally, by mistake, a pain she almost relished. Is this what growing up was all about? Shouting out the unforgiveable until your parents screamed for you to move away?

For once, her mother was speechless.

Shiels would not apologize. She wouldn't say anything else just to unstrangulate this moment.

Finally her mother stood. "I don't want you to be me. Of course not," she said with quiet severity. "But I can see that you and Lorraine Miens could well deserve each other."

XXI

Down the stairs in her yellow shoes, her mother trailing.

"Where are you going? Shiels—"

Shiels did not pick up her warm coat, which was still lying on the floor.

"You're not leaving the house tonight, young lady! You are not—"

Shiels lurched for the door, her mother's hand on her arm. For a second Shiels thought of Pyke with that Wallin player grabbing his wing. Trying to tear it off.

She almost, almost turned to wrench her arm free. Instead she stopped and stared at her mother's hand. "Just let me go," she said, her voice burning the back of her throat.

Her father now was standing by them. "Let's talk this out," he said. And Jonathan, suddenly, was there as well, his phone out. "You won't believe what's going on! There's a rally at the police station—"

Shiels's mother dropped her hand for a moment. Shiels flung the door open and sprinted into the cold night. Her mother screamed at her, but she did not stop. She cut across the yard, then climbed the fence the way she used to as a girl, not so long ago, and jumped down like someone in an action movie. Maybe adrenaline was kicking in. She felt no pain on landing. She ran across the ditch, then into the Willmers' and past their swimming pool, covered now for the season. Their dog started barking, but she scrambled over another fence and into somebody else's backyard. Through two more yards then, before she stopped in the cover of a shadowed hedge. Her heart was hammering, but she wasn't breathing hard. If someone was following her— her father maybe, under orders from her mother—she'd lost him for the time being.

A rally? Without her? Who the hell was organizing it?

She would stay off the major roads. Probably her father would be out in the car, trolling around, looking for her in her yellow shoes.

He wouldn't find her.

Not until she was ready to be found.

Clip-clip, clip-clip. Arms working, legs steady, huh, huh, huh, huh, breathing like a machine. Does a machine breathe?

A balanced body. Purpose built. Shiels felt her focus merge into one task—step upon step, balanced and precise: deliver herself to the authorities.

Sheldon was right. He was right, right, right. She could have nothing to do with any rally. It was time to turn herself in, to take responsibility for her own actions. She was the cause of the entire debacle. She had set into motion a chain of events. She might as well have slashed that Wallin boy herself.

And until she made a clean breast of it—her breasts bounced roughly, reminding her with every step that she was no Jocelyne Legault—until she owned up to her leadership role, she would never amount to anything as a human being.

She cut across the Winglefield neighborhood, not a direct route at all. Her father would never suspect her of going that way.

I want to amount to something as a human being, she thought.

I haven't been doing such a good job of it so far.

I take credit for things other people do.

I follow my own urges and then can't even remember what I've done.

I use people. I put them in danger.

I am confused about whom to love.

The wind had died down, but a deep chill had settled

into the air. Her lungs ached with cold. Good. It felt good to ache this way.

She was going to turn herself in.

Down through Winglefield, then across to Bairnesly and onto the eastern edge of downtown, essentially approaching from behind. She felt as calm, as true, as right as she had ever felt in her life. It helped that it was all downhill, that the neighborhood of Vista View had been aptly named and everything else was below it. She was not running quickly. But her mind was set, her will firm.

Her mother was right. Shiels had a formidable will. When she knew what she wanted.

When she knew the right thing to do.

Shiels heard the shouting before she could see the police station. There was no public entrance in the shadows where the off-duty police cruisers were parked. She had to go around front, and that was when she saw them, hundreds of Vista View students gathered together with signs:

FREE OUR PYKE!
ACCIDENT OF THE GAME!
IF YOU CAN'T TAKE A HIT, DON'T SUIT UP!

"We all know what happens in the clutches of the police!" a voice said, over a speaker system—a girl's voice. There she was, on the steps leading to the public entrance: Melanie Mull. Shiels stopped for a moment, had to adjust her eyes. The same girl as always: blond, small, pretty enough. Next year's student-body chair. Stepping in, publicly, at precisely the moment when Shiels vacated the podium . . .

"Pyke was just defending himself in a dangerous game. Don't punish the pterodactyl! Don't punish Pyke!"

Melanie's calls turned into a chant:

"Free our Pyke! Free our Pyke!

Don't you hold him overnight!"

The crowd screamed it. Melanie Mull seemed to be a natural. Shiels was looking at herself replaced and forgotten in the space of a few hours.

In the dark, in the bustle, Shiels could've been anyone, a freshman even. She could've been unassuming Melanie Mull from just yesterday.

She spied Sheldon standing near the back, not chanting, not holding any sign, just watching. But he was leaning into Rachel Wyngate and she was leaning into him, his arms around her. They looked natural and happy together. They looked like lovers.

Shiels imagined Sheldon's parents at Sunday morning pancakes saying, "Good morning!" to Rachel Wyngate as she came down the stairs and brushed her hair, still damp from the shower, away from her forehead.

It was like seeing a dream of her life going on without her.

She felt strangely removed, even happy. Was that possible?

Sheldon had his phone out. He was texting someone. Probably Shiels. Probably telling her to get herself down to the police station, that a rally was happening without her, that she might want to be part of it after all.

She didn't even have her phone with her. She didn't want to be part of this organized confusion.

But she had to get past the speaker on the stairs if she wanted to turn herself in to the authorities.

And so she pushed through, calmly. At first it was a struggle, but then people saw who she was and made way. Quiet infected the rally. Even Melanie Mull stopped talking. When Shiels reached the steps, Melanie motioned to the microphone, ceding her place.

It was just because no one else was speaking up, Melanie Mull's eyes seemed to say.

Shiels was sure her feet were going to continue to bring her into the station. That she would pass up the chance to say anything—what would she say, anyway?

But she found herself heading for the spotlight. Maybe her father was here? He would have guessed where she was going. But she couldn't see him. The microphone was suddenly in her hand.

She glimpsed Sheldon. His arms still around Rachel Wyngate. His eyes big. Worried for her. She felt the wave of it from across all those bodies. And: he was going to have a good life. She felt that in an instant too. A happy, loving life.

Without her.

She fiddled for a moment with the switch on the microphone. Was it on? Off?

Someone in the crowd—Robbie Lewis, enormous in the back—yelled out, "Free Pyke! Free Pyke!" But the chant died soon after, when Shiels stayed silent.

They were all waiting to hear what she had to say.

On.

Off.

On. A little red light on the microphone handle. Proceed with caution!

"I'm sorry," she said simply. "I'm sorry for everything I've done."

And then she walked into the station to give herself up.

XXII

Inspector Brady, Shiels's interrogator, had the hands of a cement factory worker: thick fingers, stuffed tight like sausage flesh. She imagined him reaching across the little table in the airless room she now shared with him, those hands around her neck, how small her own hands would feel, gripping his meaty wrists while the life drained out of her.

She imagined Pyke bursting through the shut door, freeing her with one swipe of his deadly beak, and then the two of them flying off . . . somewhere. Somehow.

But she was here to save Pyke, not the other way around. And Inspector Brady was staying on his side of the table, scratching his biceps stuffed into the rumpled gray suit that looked as though he'd been wearing it since early in the week.

"I just want to be clear with you that you have waived your right to have a lawyer present, or a parent, for that matter. And if you do so agree, then please sign here to that effect." He pushed across a single sheet of paper filled with writing. Shiels felt like she was signing away permission for doctors to take whatever organ they thought necessary.

But she was doing this to save Pyke.

"You will let me see him after I give my testimony," she said, pen poised.

They had already agreed on all of these details.

"In all likelihood," Brady said. His sad eyes were red-rimmed. Shiels had a sense of him toiling around small print and hardened criminals for years upon years.

"Right after we talk," Shiels said. "You'll take me to see Pyke right after this."

"Sign first. Tell me what you know. I'll do my utmost after that." He had loosened his tie, yet she still wondered if enough oxygen was reaching his brain through his thick, bulging neck.

"You told me just a few moments ago that I would definitely be able to see him."

"And you will. Definitely! I haven't been a cop for twenty-two years without having people trust me." He widened his eyes at her, flexed his fingers, opened his palms.

Shiels signed the paper.

"It was all my fault," she said. "Pyke is in no way to blame for what happened. I am the one who—"

"Just a second, please, Ms. Krane. Shiels, is that your name?"

She nodded impatiently. If she wasn't able to confess soon, she might lose her nerve.

"Is it a short form? I've never heard of it before."

"It's short for Sheila Marie. Which I hate."

"Then Shiels it is." Inspector Brady placed a digital recording device on the table between them. When the red light came on, he said his name and hers, the date, and read into the record the fact that Shiels had waived her right to have either legal counsel or her parents present for the testimony. It was as if he were rubbing it in. So Shiels said loudly into the recorder, "And Inspector Brady has promised that I will be able to meet with Pyke right after this interview!"

Brady blinked wearily. "What is the nature of your relationship with the pterodactyl-boy who goes by the name of Pyke, Ms. Krane?"

Shiels examined her fingernails—short and serviceable. "I don't see what relevance any of that would have—"

"Just answer the question, please." He was smiling, but his voice weighed upon her.

"I'm his elected representative at the school. I am indirectly responsible for his being in the game. I was the one who got our quarterback, Jeremy Jeffreys, to throw a football to him during a public assembly, knowing that the principal, Mr. Manniberg, would take advantage of Pyke's phenomenal ability to catch just about anything, to change the tenor of the meeting, which I have to say was going badly at the time—"

Brady cut her off. "Are you aware of the existence of a video showing you apparently engaged in an intimate, sexual form of dancing with the pterodactyl-boy?"

Shiels felt like bricks were being stacked, quickly and efficiently, around her as she sat trying to do the right thing.

"I knew that Pyke would catch the ball. I knew that Manniberg would use the moment to—"

"What about this dance video?"

"It's called a wrangle dance. It was part of the school's Autumn Whirl festivities. As I said, I am the student-body chair—"

"That colored nose of yours—isn't it true it's only worn by women who have been sexually taken by the pterodactyl-boy in question?"

Shiels stood suddenly and lurched for the door. "I'm sorry, this is a mistake," she said. "I don't believe you're interested in hearing my actual testimony at all!"

She gripped the doorknob, but it wouldn't turn. They were locked in. "Please let me out!" she called, and pounded twice on the metal door.

Brady did not get up, but he softened his voice. "I have to ask these preliminary questions so your story can be evaluated in the proper light. No one is judging you. But it would make a difference if you were intimate with Mr. Pyke. You're not the only young woman I've had in here in love with this character."

Jocelyne Legault. Who had persuaded Pyke to give himself up. Probably she was being held in a room similar to this one, with its soul-sucking gray walls, its dangerous shadows.

"We're not intimate," Shiels said. "We danced at an event. I have spoken with him on fewer than a dozen occasions."

Pitiless eyes. "Could you sit down again, please, so I can record your testimony properly?" He leaned toward the device. "Subject has moved away from the microphone."

Warily Shiels returned to her seat.

"You dream about him constantly, don't you?" Brady said. He flipped back some pages in his yellow-lined notebook. "Just a few days ago you wrote on something called the *Leghorn Review* . . ."

"All right, all right, yes!" she said. "I didn't realize dreaming is a crime. Or that the police have such ready access to Vhub. Are you sure you have enough prisons to hold everyone who ever lusted after somebody else?"

Blink, blink. "I just want to tack down the nature of your relationship," Brady said.

"I am a friend. He is a pterodactyl in my school. I don't know why my nose has turned purple. But I'm still a virgin. I thought I was pregnant by my boyfriend of the time—" She'd almost started to name Sheldon! "But we didn't actually . . ."

Brady wrote furiously. "So would you say that the sexual fantasies you have about Mr. Pyke are so far unfulfilled?"

"I wouldn't say any of that!" she declared. Why had she ever agreed to submit to this questioning? She was never going to see Pyke. She knew that now. She had a wild idea that she could gouge out Brady's eyes—or at least confuse him greatly, somehow, with her short fingernails—then grab the key from inside his pocket and dash for the door. But probably he didn't have the key in his pocket. Probably he had to knock on the door himself to be let out.

"This line of questioning will never hold up in court!" she said. Hadn't she seen something like this sort of blatant harassment on a crime show recently? Sheldon would remember.

Sheldon—

"We're not in court, Ms. Krane," Brady said in a tired voice. "I'm just trying to figure out who you are, and then we'll get to what happened."

He pressed his eyes shut with his enormous fingers. Part of him seemed exhausted.

Part of him was taking a prurient interest in the supposed love life of the teenager opposite him.

"I'm the one who dreamed up the scheme of putting Pyke on the football team for the game against Wallin," Shiels said. "It came to me quickly, in the heat of a situation. I thought it might even up the game. I should've tried harder to prepare him, make sure that he went to practice. I'm responsible. It was my fault that boy hurt his arm so badly."

"You told the pterodactyl to slash anyone who came near?"

"No."

"You told him to poison his opponents?"

"No, of course not."

"So he did it on his own?"

"No. No. He's just a pterodactyl. He reacted—"

"He had no such order from you, student-body chair of Vista View High?"

"I wanted him to win the game for us. But I was blind to what he might do—"

"Because of your infatuation with him. You and every other girl he seemed to know."

"He's a pterodactyl, he just was himself. It was my duty to know better. I put a lot of people in harm's way."

Why was he taking so many notes when he was recording the interview anyway?

"All right," he said finally. He put down his pen and stopped the recorder.

"All right, you're taking me in? You're letting Pyke go?"

"No—all right, we're done. I'll call you if I need any more."

"But—"

"You're not the coach of the team, Ms. Krane, or the principal of the school. You didn't put that ball into the pterodactyl's hands. And you didn't cause him to slash the other boy's arm. I watched the video. You and his other girlfriend were just cheering from the sidelines. He probably couldn't even hear you because of the wind."

"But—"

"You know what?" Brady said. "I've had a really long day. And I promised you you'd be able to see the poor bastard before you go."

They walked down the hall to a dark and narrow side room. Though Brady seemed to get puffed even in that short distance, he also looked impressively solid. Shield imagined herself bouncing off him like a crow flying into a pile of cannonballs. Brady pulled open a screen, and Shiels was able to see through a two-way mirror into a cheerless, fluorescently lit room with a bunk, a sink, a toilet, and something bundled in the corner, in the darkest spot. At first Shiels could not make out what she was seeing in that corner. It looked flattened, like the contents of a parcel that has fallen off a truck and then been run over several hundred times in the ensuing traffic. There was a wing, oddly pale, stretched at a strange angle over bits of rib and bone; there was a beak, bent back, headed in the wrong direction.

"You've murdered him!" Shiels cried.

"No, we haven't." Brady's voice was neutral, stony. "He's perfectly fine. That's just the way he folded himself when we brought him in."

Like a fossil, Shiels realized. Pressed cruelly into the rock wall of the cell.

"Let me talk to him," Shiels said. It was hard to tear her eyes from the pitiful sight of her flattened Pyke, but she knew she had to address Brady full on. "You told me I could see him!"

"And you're seeing him," Brady replied. "But I can't let you get closer than this. He's a risk to anyone he comes in contact with. Even you."

Shiels threw herself at the mirror. "Pyke! Pyke! It's me!" she screamed. "We're going to get you out!"

Her hands did not shake the heavy glass. Her voice echoed off the many hard surfaces, and Pyke did not stir. He didn't seem to hear.

"If you kill him, if you kill him in custody—" Shiels yelled. "I swear, I will train the rest of my life in the law and will come back and prosecute you to your grave!"

Brady's face folded into a lopsided grin. "Be careful about threatening an officer of the peace, Ms. Krane," he said quietly. "And are you sure you want to add to the world's growing surfeit of lawyers? Why don't you do something worthwhile with your life instead?"

The rally had broken up. Downtown felt deserted. She had not brought her phone. If she had, she could've taken a photo of the miserable conditions in which Pyke was being held. She could've broadcast to the world how crushed he was in the grip of the state. There would've been an outcry, a massive movement from every corner of the wired planet to free him.

Outside a corner store, in perhaps the last phone booth in the city, she called home. Four rings. Five. The answering service kicked in, her father's voice, calm, reassuring. He would get back to the caller as soon as he could.

"Daddy," she said, "I need you to come pick me up. I'm sorry for all the trouble I made. But Pyke is dying; he's being held in barbaric conditions at the police station right now. I've seen him—" And then her father was on the line.

"Baby," he said, "are you all right?"

Shiels hadn't been "baby" to her father since Jonathan had been born. She started to tear up just at the word.

"No," she said. "I'm not all right. I've screwed up everything a hundred times over. I'm sorry. I'm so sorry!"

She thought she heard him crying too, and that was disconcerting. He was her father, a surgeon, for God's sake. He was professionally calm. "Did they charge you with something?" he asked finally. "Is this your one phone call?"

It took a long time for Shiels to set him straight. "I'm outside," she said. "They aren't interested in me. But we need to free Pyke as soon as possible. Oh, Daddy, if you'd seen him—"

She described it all for him, the grim room, the flattened, beaten being lying in the dark corner. "I know . . . I know Mom is going to kill me," Shiels said. "But I'm glad I went. I had to see him. We have to get him out!"

"Your mother really is going to kill you, because you broke her foot when you smashed the door on it," her father said.

"*What?*"

"On your way out of the house. Didn't you hear us yelling at you? You didn't even stop. I had to take her to the hospital."

Shiels suddenly noticed just where she was—the cracked glass of the booth, the scratchings on the black metallic side of the ancient phone box, the blinking pink and red fluorescent lights of the corner store illuminating her black pant legs, the way her breath seemed to be clogging in her throat.

"*I broke Mom's foot?*"

She had a glimpse of herself flinging the door open right on her mother's foot like some Godzilla toppling buildings with every unthinking swish of her tail. It was a heavy door too, and her mother had cried out. Shiels remembered it now. She thought it had been just to keep Shiels from turning herself in.

The imagined pain of it now crackled through her body.

"I didn't . . . I'm so sorry!" Shiels said. "I wasn't thinking."

"Don't go anywhere!" her father said. "I'm coming to get you."

She could not call Sheldon from the pay phone. It felt wrong somehow, desperate. But if she had had her phone with her, she would have told him everything. Just out of habit. That was the way they worked. The cement mixer fingers, Pyke flattened against the wall, smashing her mother's foot.

That she was fracturing everything she touched. At least they would have talked about it.

And somehow the sound of Sheldon's voice would've calmed her. What would he say exactly? She couldn't think—she couldn't think, except that if she were talking with Sheldon, she wouldn't have felt so completely alone standing by the ragged phone booth in a sorry part of town in the blinking lights of a convenience store.

A car approached, a beat-up boxy thing, not her father's gray Mercedes. She let her eyes drop. She thought: *I am all alone standing here without a coat in the cold, and I do not even have my phone.*

The window opened. She saw a narrow face, a balding head. *Tell me this isn't happening*, she thought.

I am just a block away from the police station, she thought.

Probably they wouldn't even hear—

"I thought I recognized those yellow shoes," the man said. "Are you all right? Do you need a lift?"

It was the old guy from the running-shoe store. He looked concerned.

"No. Thank you. My father's coming to pick me up. He's on his way. I just called him. Really."

He looked like he didn't believe her. His engine was idling. She could smell the exhaust. And God, it was cold. If she hadn't just talked with her dad, she would've gone with the running-shoe man. He seemed harmless enough.

She imagined herself in his car saying, "Any ideas how to spring a pterodactyl from prison?"

"How are the shoes?" he asked finally.

"Good. Great! I would run home now but I am exhausted. And it's uphill. I broke my mother's foot."

"How did you do that?" he asked, and she told him a bit of it without going into details.

"That stockroom you cleaned up is a hundred times better than it was," he said. "If you ever want to come work at the store, I'll find a place for you."

She thanked him and thought if she didn't end up

studying with Lorraine Miens, if she didn't become a doctor, if she didn't go to law school, she could see herself happily stacking running shoes, keeping at least that corner of
the world in order.

"I know a thing or two about running," the old guy said.

"I'll keep it in mind," Shiels replied.

The ride home with her father was quiet. What could Shiels
do about her mother's foot now? Nothing. Other plans
whirred in her head, forming and dissolving and reforming
like clouds on a riotous day. They absolutely had to free
Pyke. If Melanie Mull now was the one to rally students,
then maybe Shiels could rally the crows, and together they
could sow confusion amongst the police, and in the meantime . . .

"Your mother is in a state," Shiels's father said quietly
from behind the wheel.

Shiels imagined the crows descending upon the police
station like something out of Hitchcock.

"You're going to have to be careful how you handle
her," Shiels's father said.

In a state. What did he mean by *in a state*?

"It's not just her foot. She's really worried about you and
your future. She asked me to talk to you—"

"I am so sorry about her foot. You know I didn't mean
it. But, Dad, a pterodactyl is dying in a jail cell right now

because of something else I did. If there were any justice in the world, I would be the one kept in solitary confinement like . . . like a beast in a zoo!"

"I know, baby. You're concerned," her father said. "You get wound up in your causes. It's admirable. So many adults are past caring, or they have no idea what they can do to help. But I'm giving you a heads-up about your mom."

Her father had curly hair, too brown still for a dad his age. And he was doing what he always did—he was taking his wife's side against his daughter, as if his wife were not the perpetual champion of everything in the family, now and forever.

"I didn't know her foot was there," Shiels said. "I just ran and shoved the door behind me. I will apologize to Mom. But about Stockard—I really have been thinking. I've been thinking for a long time now. I'm not—" How to frame it so he would understand? "I'm not doctor material."

Her father snorted, the way he did whenever something unbelievable was happening on the television news. His hands were strong and relaxed on the steering wheel, his fingers long and tapered. *Like Sheldon's hands*, she thought. "I changed your diapers long before you knew what a doctor was," he said. "I know all about your force of will, your focus, how smart you are. Believe me, Shiels, you could be a terrific doctor if you wanted to be. But that's not the issue here. The issue—"

"That's just it!" she said. "I don't want to be a doctor. That's the whole issue!"

"The issue is that your mother is in a state," he said again, slowly and carefully. "I'm fine with you not being a doctor. Really I am. And your mother will be too. But right now she thinks you're out of your mind in love with a pterodactyl. She thinks that you don't need her, that you don't love her. She thinks you broke her foot on purpose."

"I didn't break her foot on purpose," Shiels said.

But maybe she had wanted to bring the whole house down?

"You're going to have to tell her yourself," her father said. "Carefully. You know your mother is a lot more fragile than you are."

Now it was Shiels's turn to snort. Her father glanced at her, his face naked with surprise. "She has always felt threatened by your strength," he said. "And so you have to be very gentle with her. You know you're going to win."

"I have no such thought in my head!" she blurted. "Win what? I lose every time it comes to Mom!"

The car hummed ever homeward in the dark.

"You're young, just coming up. You don't know your own strength," he said.

Her father had tried to warn her, but still Shiels was unprepared when she got home. She tiptoed into her mother's room ready to say the right words, to ask for forgiveness, to set things as right as she could before turning her attention to the larger problem of saving Pyke. But who was this pale, withdrawn creature propped up on pillows, her foot enormous in a black plastic cast that looked like a ski boot, her eyes pilled-up and dopey?

Who was this woman who did not seem to see her?

Shiels approached cautiously. "Mom?" It was her little-girl voice, still living somewhere inside her.

Her mother stirred. She looked a decade older. Had Shiels really done all this to her just by rushing out the door?

"Baby." Her mother's voice was groggy. She lifted her hand slightly. Shiels took it and squeezed. She had a sudden feeling of someday years from now, decades away surely. The day her mother would die.

"I'm sorry, Mom," Shiels said. "I wasn't thinking. I'm sorry."

Her mother seemed to both see Shiels and not see her at the same time. Obviously she was heavily drugged. Shiels remembered something about foot pain being amongst the worst a body might suffer. Wasn't that a torture method, beating people's feet?

Shiels sat still, holding her mother's hand, until her mother seemed to be fast asleep. The more Shiels thought about it, the more dreadful the whole thing seemed—the weight of the door (which she could remember now feeling in her hand as she'd fled), what a relief it had been to throw that weight behind her as she'd run. How shocked her mother must've been when the heavy metal had swung so hard into her instep.

Normally Shiels would have stopped to see what was the matter.

She hadn't *tried* to injure her mother.

Had she?

She hadn't been trying to defeat her so utterly as to send her into a medicated stupor like this.

Had she?

Shiels retreated down the hall to her own room. At last, reunited with her phone, she saw that indeed Sheldon had been texting her during Melanie Mull's rally for Pyke outside the police station. One text even included the word "sori," as in, *sori i doubted u. huge crowd. portant 2B here.*

And then: *what r u doing?*

And then: *cant bleve u just did that.*

And then, much later: *where r u? have u seen Pyke? whats the word?*

She phoned him, and he picked up even before the ring—which used to happen, a lot, before things fell apart.

Why had they fallen apart? Because, she realized, she had not been paying attention. Just flinging doors on her way out.

"The word is bad," she said, by way of greeting. "I saw

him, but I didn't get a chance to talk to him. Oh, Sheldon, he's broken, he just looks folded and stepped on. We have to do something right away. I don't know that he'll last the night. It's that bad!"

"Where are you now?" he asked. She imagined where he was: in the arms of Rachel Wyngate. She almost blurted, "That was pretty fast moving there, mister!" She almost said, "Glad to know I can be replaced in about fifteen minutes." She almost yelled, "I saw you with her! At the rally you practically told me not to go to!"

And the voices in her head argued—He already told you he was going with Rachel. . . . But it makes a difference when you actually see people together. It isn't real until you see it.

It was real all right. Shiels felt the sadness tighten like a shrinking ball in the shell of her rib cage.

"I'm at home," she said. "The police didn't want me. Except to know about my sex life."

"What?"

She told him about the questioning by Inspector Brady.

"So—you fantasize about Pyke?" Sheldon said.

Oh, for God's sake!

"I told you already," she said. "I've had dreams. We all have. It isn't real. What's real is that we have to get him out of there. But I don't know how to do it. I'd like to rally the crows somehow, but the cops are keeping him in a window-less room—"

"You are practically raving right now," he said. "Rally the crows?"

And she remembered: He hadn't been running at the track in the early morning when the crows had come en masse and lined the fence to watch her; he hadn't been in the gymnasium to clean up after Autumn Whirl, when the crows had rescued her and Pyke from hours and hours of thankless toil; he hadn't even been at the football game when the crows had swarmed the stands in the sucking wind.

"It won't work anyway," Shiels said. "I'm not crazy. I've just seen some things you haven't."

And in saying this, she realized they had been inseparable, one mind practically, two bodies, and now they were ordinary again. Separate and alone.

Well, Sheldon wasn't alone.

"The media have picked up on the rally," Sheldon said. "It's a pretty unusual story, a pterodactyl football player ending up in jail. Maybe if we can raise enough of a stink—"

"Yes," Shiels said. They talked about it, the stink, the attention they might be able to garner in a short time, if they caught the world's attention, if the right people became aware. And as they talked, she thought about that night she had spent with Sheldon, after the wrangle dance. In his room, in his bed, skin to skin. How he hadn't tried to take advantage, yet . . . They had simply held each other, and breathed together. He must have held her while she was sleeping.

Oh, how she liked the idea of that, falling asleep in someone's arms tonight, if somehow sleep were even possible. Yet most of her yearned to burst out of the house and do something superhuman to free Pyke immediately!

But even if she could have flown, she couldn't penetrate the walls of the city jail.

Even if she had had all the strength in the world, she was not going to be able to put Pyke back together. Not quickly. Not in one magnificent gesture the way she longed to.

This night, at this moment, there was nothing she could do but surrender herself to the slow crawl of time and fate. What was going to happen was going to happen.

Still, it was a comfort to talk to Sheldon, to hear his voice.

Shiels did not think she would sleep, yet the moment her head hit the pillow, she was back in that dark little observation room, Inspector Brady beside her in his rumpled suit with his garlicky breath. (Why had she not noticed his breath when she'd been so close to him for real? His breath now stank up her dream.)

Pyke was folded, fossilized in the corner, but she could see now that he was still breathing. His little broken chest expanded and fell, somehow discernible despite the smudging of the glass (she had to strain to see, as if through fog).

His dark eyes rolled open, but he couldn't see her, she was trapped in her other reality. (Was that what it was?)

She placed her hands on the glass. All her yearning seeped through her arms and out her palms into the dark prison room where Pyke was being held. *Drip, drip* went the leaky faucet. There seemed to be a flood in the room above. Water now was streaming down the walls.

She yearned at him, and yearned, and he stirred.

He looked at where she was in her separate reality.

Could he see through the mirror somehow?

The water rose around him. It was cold, and stank, too—sewage water, she came to understand. A hundred times worse than the reek from Brady.

Sewage water was rising up from the caverns below the city jail, and it was only a matter of time before Pyke was drowned. She started to swim—she was in one of the caverns now, trying to follow the signs, but sediment in the water was slowing her down. LIBRARY, one of the signs said. STADIUM. Where was the jail?

Where was Pyke's cell?

The water rose, and it was warm now with sludge, and she was able to breathe somehow, to look around. But no openings appeared. It was as if she were under the sea ice now, strangely warm, looking up, looking for the hole . . . but instead of rising to the light, she sank farther, into the mud at the bottom.

And then she needed to fold herself, to become quite small, so she wouldn't be found. Brady was looking for her. He had a clipboard full of unasked questions. So she tucked her head under her arm, she wrapped herself with her wing, she pulled the mud over her and burrowed down, down, ever deeper, so she would blend in.

XXIII

Shiels awoke before the sun. She seemed to know that the thing to do was to don her yellow shoes, to bundle up and go to the track. She wasn't sure why, exactly. When she slipped out the front door—the very one she'd unwittingly jammed against her mother's foot—she had a sense of passing from one part of her life to the next.

But it was just a door. She closed it silently.

A thin coating of ice had formed overnight, slickening the pavement. It would probably melt by midmorning, but she wanted to feel her body in motion, her blood surging with warmth, her feet on the ground traveling some distance, even if in circles.

Maybe the crows would be there, maybe there would be a council of crows, maybe, somehow, the crows would know what to do, how to pry Pyke from the clutches of an uncaring law. Or maybe . . . Shiels would see Jocelyne Legault. The blur of yellow feet, the bouncing ponytail. The reminder of how this had all begun.

Shiels had to be careful of where she placed her feet. She had to keep her mind on what exactly she was doing as she ran.

Now, she thought.

Be here now.

Be aware of the slope of the road. Of how much weight sank on what part of the foot, of where to keep her eyes. She had to get there in one piece.

It was enough, for now, to place one foot after the other.

The cold air stung her cheeks. But it felt good to be moving. The illusion of progress, she thought.

No—one foot after the other. Don't race ahead. Her legs were tired, they did not want to run. But they could, just through will. The fatigue would go away.

Tree branches fingered blackly into the sky. The light of morning was coming on. The ice clung better to the piles of leaves on the side of the road than to the black pavement.

She crossed into the school grounds. No Jocelyne Legault circling the track. No crows anywhere. The world was quiet, still, except for Shiels's own breathing, and the *clump, clump* of her feet hitting the earth.

She would like to be lighter of foot, she thought. Jocelyne Legault, when she ran, almost seemed to float above the ground. You couldn't hear her unless you were terribly close. No wasted energy.

I waste a lot of energy, Shiels thought.

But it felt good to be alone, to circle the track slowly, on her own terms, to feel her body steaming in the cold morning air.

Then, on her way home, Shiels saw Jocelyne Legault standing at the corner of Roseview and Vine just the way Sheldon used to before everything fell apart. She was in a turquoise ski jacket with a scarf pulled around the lower part of her face. Shiels stopped jogging as she came upon her.

"My uncle is a lawyer. He is representing Pyke," Jocelyne said. "But the judge has set bail at ninety thousand dollars."

The champion runner's white hands were ungloved, balled into small fists. Her face looked rumpled, pulled from the bottom of a drawer.

"You've already met with the judge?" Shiels said.

"It was my fault," Jocelyne said. "I told Pyke to talk to the police. He should have just flown home and been done with all of us. But I wanted him to stay."

Jocelyne's eyes looked like the tired blue of a bright day leaking into cloud.

"Where . . . where is home for Pyke?" Shiels asked.

"Somewhere they'll never reach him," Jocelyne said. "I don't know where. It was his choice to come here. He wanted to make contact. After all these years. My family doesn't have enough money."

For the bail. Shiels completed the thought. Jocelyne was talking to her now because her family did have the money.

"You love him," Jocelyne said sadly. She was standing unnaturally still, as if her words could not come out otherwise. "Everyone knows that. Pyke . . . has feelings for you, too. You could help him. You have to help him, Shiels!"

Jocelyne had never said her name before. Shiels was aware of the sharp wind on her face now that her body was cooling down. She stopped herself from shuffling from foot to foot. Pyke too would have stayed extremely still.

"I saw him in the jail last night," Shiels said. "I thought he was dead. He was squished into the corner like . . ."

The thought hung. Jocelyne Legault did not blink, and Shiels knew that she, too, had been brought into the spying room by Inspector Brady. Probably Brady had interrogated her on her sex life with the pterodactyl too.

Shiels didn't like to think about that.

"Let me see," Shiels said. "Maybe I can get the money together."

Shiels's father was in his study riding his exercise bike. He had his tablet open. He was listening to something on his earbuds. Maybe Brahms. He often retreated with Brahms on the weekends.

Shiels did not wait for him to completely unplug.

"I would like to use my education fund to save some-one's life," she said.

The strains of something classical—Mozart, perhaps, not Brahms?—leaked weakly from the tiny speakers now dangling near the spinning wheel of the bike. "Save who?" her father said. "The pterodactyl? That wrecked that boy's arm?"

"Pyke is a living link to a world that existed millions of years ago. He chose to come here, to make contact with us. Without bail he'll die in a soulless cell being watched over by sadistic guards. We have to save him."

Her father slowly stopped cycling.

"You know this—how?"

"He has touched a number of us directly, so we know. We just know it. Dad—how many pterodactyls are we going to meet in our lives? This is important!"

He mopped his face with the sleeve of his sweatshirt. "It's your education money, Shiels. You can't throw that away. You can't trade your future for some . . . killer who is just going to fly off anyway."

"He's not a killer!" Shiels had to move now, to throw her hands in the air. "It's my fault. I practically put him in that game. He just defended himself. And he won't fly off. For one thing his wings are broken. I saw him in the jail. He could no more fly away than some fossil you chipped off a rock."

Her father's eyes wavered. He could never deny her any-thing, not really. He loved her. This she knew.

"He is the most precious ambassador we have ever had from the distant past. You can't turn your back on him. We need to save his life now, bring him home, where he can be cared for . . . by two physicians. You are a doctor, Dad. You took an oath!"

His expression softened. She did respect what he did, what a doctor could do and be. Maybe . . . maybe she even gave him the impression that she might after all pursue medical studies, that she was having a change of heart.

She wouldn't rule it out. Whatever it took to get Pyke free from that jail.

"Your mother—" he began to say, in his old weak away.

"Mom will be fine with this," Shiels said quietly. "You will be too. Pyke is an extraordinary person. We might not see his like again for a million years. We have to do this, Dad. We have to," she breathed.

"Absolutely not," Shiels's mother said. She was standing in the kitchen in her black plastic foot cast, making a cup of tea. Hardened snowflakes—they almost looked like hail—pecked against the back picture window.

Shiels shifted her stance, braced herself.

"You will not use your education money for anything other than school," Shiels's mother said. "Don't even think of it. Your father and I have signing authority. He would never agree to it."

Until I turn eighteen, Shiels thought. *In February. You have signing authority until then.*

Her mother kept talking. "*I* will never agree to it." She thumped her broken foot against the floor, then winced, in case Shiels had not gotten the message.

"They are killing him in prison," Shiels said softly.

"You do not risk your future," her mother said. "Not for a boy. Certainly not for a pterodactyl. Not now. Not ever. As a parent I will not let you."

Shiels's mother pulled tight the collars of her bathrobe.

"There is very little risk," Shiels said. "We will get the money back. Pyke is not going anywhere. His wings are broken."

"No." Her mother's dark eyes did not waver.

"We can nurse him back to health here," Shiels said. "You're both doctors. This will be the perfect environment."

"No."

"What are you so afraid of?" Shiels felt calm inside, as if somehow every *no* was going to turn into a *yes* eventually.

The snow rapped harder against the window. Winter was starting, the real thing. Despite the furnace burning downstairs, despite her warm clothing, Shiels felt the grip of the cold slipping under her skin.

"I'm afraid of you butting your head against the world,"

her mother said. "You move so fast, your eyes are fixed to the ground, you have no idea what you're walking into. That's what I'm afraid of."

They looked made for each other, somehow, sitting in the coffee shop booth, squeezed together: Sheldon and Rachel Wyngate. Shiels would not have been able to imagine having such a thought just weeks ago. Yet here she was sitting opposite the adorable couple. Sheldon looked rumpled, unshaven, sleepy-eyed, vibrating almost. The same old mismatched clothes, his trench coat and his blue cable-knit French intellectual sweater and the bright pink shirt underneath. He had an extra crackle to him.

And Rachel was rounded in the way she cuddled against him. Had they just slept together? It was possible.

Her eyes were sunny-morning blue. And she had taken no care whatsoever with her hair. It was simply perfect in a soft-focus-magazine-ad sort of way. She looked like she'd been lying in a cornfield in her blue jeans with a shirtless perfumed wonder boy feeding her strawberries.

Anything was possible, Shiels thought. That was how wild the world was.

"Thank you for agreeing to meet me," Shiels said, somewhat formally. She would never have said that just to Sheldon. But this was Sheldon and Rachel, a different beast altogether. "We have a small window of time. A couple of days at the most, I would think. If we're going to crowd-source, it has to happen in a heartbeat."

She said it to Sheldon, had her eyes fixed on him. It was hard not to think of all the many projects they had worked on together, those memories fused together into one hot lump of feeling. But Rachel was the one who answered.

"He's the only pterodactyl student to ever be sent to jail," she said. "So we have novelty on our side. This could reach contagion, and if we just got one, two, five dollars from every person . . ." Shiels could tell by their postures that they were holding hands under the table.

They had fused together. It had happened in an eye-blink.

"We need a video for that," Shiels said. "If it's going to go viral." She had already run through the possibilities in her head—Vhub footage of Pyke first arriving at Vista View, of the famous wrangle dance with Shiels herself, of some parts of the football game. It was all supposed to stay private, but certainly the police had seen it. The regular media was hungering for content. Sometimes the rules could be broken judiciously for a good cause. "But we have a problem," she said.

Did she have to spell it out? Sheldon knew already where this was going, but Rachel Wyngate, with her perfect skin, her athletic shoulders, her wide-eyed look, was still miles behind.

"As soon as we ask for money," Sheldon said, "all anyone is going to see will be Pyke slashing that guy's arm."

Sheldon was already leaning toward the solution. Newspaper coverage so far had not been particularly favorable. What was a pterodactyl doing in high school anyway?

"Crowdsourcing might not work," Shiels said. "It might not work in time. We have to get our hands on the money right away and for certain." She let the words sink in. She had not tasted her coffee yet, and now it was growing cold on the table in front of her. She forced herself to take a sip. Snow was piling up outside, not the hard pellets anymore but large flakes, settling in for the duration.

"I have a college fund," she said. "My parents started saving before I was born. I get full access to it in a few months. I'll pay everyone back. But I'm not eighteen yet, and my parents are against me."

Her eyes had not moved from Sheldon's. Of course he understood. The way they sat across the table locked in one gaze, there might as well have been no one else in the whole place.

Sheldon was eighteen already. He had his own fund he could draw on.

"Wait a minute," Rachel said. "You're not suggesting—"

"I don't have anywhere near ninety thousand dollars," Sheldon said. But calmly.

"You shouldn't even be asking—" Rachel said. "Ninety thousand dollars is just such a crazy stupid amount of money!"

"How much do you have?" Shiels asked. "Sixty? Pyke is not going to fly off. I don't imagine he can even walk now. He's going to die in there. And I will be good for every penny in February after my birthday. You know that. You know I am true to you."

She said it as if Rachel Wyngate weren't sitting right there, glued to the young man Shiels used to be glued to, in her own way. It didn't matter. Truth was truth.

Shiels and Sheldon would be true to each other through this life until neither one drew breath anymore, no matter who they married or what fortunes and abuses life sent their way. Their bond was their bond.

"Sheldon!" Rachel was holding his arm now, trying to get him to look away from Shiels's gaze.

"You're going to get a scholarship anyway," Shiels said. "Everyone knows that. And Pyke should be a rock star, or something. He should get that chance. We're holding his life right now in our hands."

"I have sixty-five," Sheldon said finally. "That's not enough anyway. Where are you going to get the rest?"

Oh, she loved him. And she wasn't going to have him, not anymore. He was welded now to Rachel Wyngate and her simple beauty, her feet-on-the-ground good sense.

Shiels suddenly saw them surrounded by children, stupidly happy.

"I have an idea for who else to ask," she said.

A text might do it, actually. Or, Jocelyne Legault was so stuck on Pyke, so anxious to get him out of harm's way, Shiels imagined she could have sent a crow with the request, and Jocelyne would have transferred money.

If she had money. That was a question. There might not be family resources.

Jocelyne lived in Delside, the low-income housing complex in the neighborhood adjacent to Vista View. Below the ridge, leading toward the river that snaked through town. She was a cross-boundary transfer, allowed in part because even in elementary school she'd been able to run faster than most of the rest of the world.

Shiels got her address from the electronic school roll, which she had access to as a student-body chair who had watched Principal Manniberg type in his password a number of times when they'd been discussing student activity outreach in light of emerging fiscal restraint.

2313 Lundlass Lane, unit 31B. Shiels followed the directions on her phone through Delside's warren of "lanes" and "courts" and "boulevards." No one was out, not in the new, serious snow slowly burying doorsteps and vehicles, walkways and postage-stamp lawns. Even a playground basketball hoop, bent and drooping, supported a growing ring of white. The backboard had gunshot holes in it.

Running was Jocelyne's ticket out of this place. She would pull in a scholarship, she had to. But had the family been saving too? Jocelyne had said the family didn't have *enough* money. But did they have some?

Shiels followed her phone's instructions to the graying aluminum storm door of unit 31B. She pressed the bell and wondered if perhaps it didn't work. Maybe she should knock? Or text Jocelyne that she was standing outside her door.

She wanted to see where the girl lived.

The girl who had so captured Pyke's heart.

A pause. Shiels pulled open the storm door and raised her knuckled fist to knock. But the wooden front door was already opening. Jocelyne Legault's face looked chalky against the purple of her nose. Could it be darkening?

"Can I come in?"

They walked along an entrance corridor that made Shiels think of the word "downtrodden." It was the carpet, really, that attached to itself all the sad meaning of that word—the brown, filthy, threadbare carpet that should have been ripped up years ago, but what was underneath? The town house looked like it was made of sawdust and glue.

"Do you have any news?" Jocelyne asked when they were in the back room, the one that got a modicum of sun and that overlooked a patio space piled with old furniture: a rickety table, some broken plastic chairs, a loveseat with stuffing bursting from inside, visible even with snowfall.

Shiels filled her in. Jocelyne sat unnaturally straight, similar to her running posture. Her body seemed to be swimming in old clothes.

"I will pay back the money to everyone in February, as soon as I get access," Shiels explained. "I think it makes sense to bring Pyke to my house for rehab. Both my parents are doctors. Of course you could come and see him whenever you want."

But he will be under my roof, Shiels thought. *I will see him whenever I want too.*

"How . . . how much do you need?" Jocelyne could not seem to keep herself from looking around at her sorry surroundings. The dull blue walls probably had not been painted in thirty years. A pressboard shelf sagged improbably under the slight weight of miniature porcelain figurines of cats and elves and chubby-cheeked ballerinas.

Jocelyne's trophies and medals must be elsewhere, Shiels thought. In her room, maybe.

Shiels told her the number. When Jocelyne's eyes widened, Shiels realized how preposterous she was being. It looked like Jocelyne's family hardly had enough for groceries. They would not be bailing out the pterodactyl boyfriend.

Shiels rose. "Look, I'm sorry. We can try other ways. We might be able to crowdsource this and—"

Someone else entered then. Shiels turned to see a slight woman walking stiffly. Jocelyne bounced to her feet. "Ma, I want you to meet Shiels Krane. She's the student-body chair. We're just working together to get Pyke out. I think . . . I think we might need to dip into the buffer."

The woman held herself unusually straight. Her skin looked strangely tight, unhealthy, almost translucent. "Are you?"—her voice was breathless—"a friend of Jocelyne's?"

"We know each other from school, Ma," Jocelyne said quickly.

Ma looked Shiels up and down. "Your nose has gone purple too. It's that pterodactyl boy, isn't it?" She was shaking slightly, older perhaps than her years.

"He has affected us all," Shiels said simply. "I'm raising funds for his bail. No doubt Jocelyne told you what we saw in prison—"

"We don't have enough for the whole bail," Ma said. "We can give some."

"Ma—" Jocelyne said.

"It's all right. We can talk about this."

Jocelyne seemed uncertain. Shiels wasn't sure what to do. Finally she said, "Should we sit down?"

"If I do that, I'll just have to get up again," Ma said. "I have a blood disorder. But there's insurance. I want to do what's right."

Shiels had a vague sense that Jocelyne's father did not live here and that Ma probably didn't work, that Jocelyne and her mother had been living thin for many years. Yet Jocelyne had mentioned a buffer. It might be all that stood between the two of them and complete disaster.

Nonetheless, Shiels laid out the plan. She looked Ma and Jocelyne steadily in the eye, one after the other, and kept her body still. A life was at stake. Today was Sunday. They could perhaps get Pyke out Monday or Tuesday.

If he lasted that long.

"I don't want anyone else's money at risk here," Shiels said. "I will pay back all the creditors myself, no matter what happens. But I won't have access to those funds right away. And Pyke needs us now."

Ma's eyes too shifted between Shiels and her daughter. Shiels had a sense that this woman was watching her child grow up before her eyes. Crime, prison, punishment, bail—it was all in the realm of adults. Pyke, too, was technically an adult by age, although the football game had been played with boys.

"Those players break arms and legs all the time on the field," Shiels said. "No one gets hauled up in front of a judge. It was an accident of play. It wasn't Pyke's fault he has a razor-sharp beak."

"Exactly!" Jocelyne said. "He's just a boy with a beak . . ."

"And if he's not a person," Shiels said, "he's a pterodactyl, so all laws are null and void, they're only for humans. If a cougar wanders into town and slashes someone's arm, you don't throw him in jail."

"No, you shoot him," Ma said. She looked exhausted, yet Shiels could see something of Jocelyne's steel there too.

"So he must be a boy," Shiels said. "And we need the bail right away." She almost said, "How much can you spare?" but the words would not come out. What was she doing? Jocelyne's mother was terribly ill, and no matter what she said about insurance, this family had no business funding bail for some pterodactyl, no matter whose boyfriend he was.

Shiels stood quickly, before the feeling passed. "I'm sorry. I can find the money elsewhere, I'm sure. Don't worry about—"

"We're not worried," Jocelyne said quickly. "It's not like we're spending anything here. It's an investment, right? To save a life." She was looking at her mother, who smiled finally, perhaps to see such fire in her daughter's eyes.

Eleven thousand dollars. That was what Jocelyne and her mother could come up with. Shiels felt humbled, in awe. But she was still fourteen thousand short. She had no money of her own, nothing to speak of. She got an allowance, but she had never worked a paying job, had always simply had to ask to use her parents' credit card, which was never unreasonably withheld.

She had not needed a lot. Until now.

As she walked away from Jocelyne's house, she was already texting Sheldon to get him to send her the money as soon as possible. She and Jocelyne would meet with Jocelyne's uncle, the lawyer. Monday morning.

It would happen. The money would come together somehow.

Sheldon texted back that Melanie Mull was going ahead with a crowdsourcing drive to raise Pyke's bail. *Good luck with that*, Shiels thought. But maybe they could raise some part of the missing fourteen thousand?

Maybe it would be possible.

Certainly something would happen. The feeling was too strong to deny now. Pyke was in her gut. He had been growing there all along. She felt his energy in her limbs, her heart. Her body was full of the possibility of him—the muscles in his shoulders, the darkness of his eyes, the slope of his beak.

As she walked, she felt like she was carrying his wings for him.

XXIV

Monday morning breakfast. Shiels's mother was preparing to go back to work despite her broken foot. She clumped about the kitchen in her tailored jacket and slacks and her plastic ski boot cast. "The radio says it's icy out, of course," her mother said.

"You could take a taxi," Shiels said.

"Of course I'm going to take a taxi. But I still have to get out the door to the driveway!"

Shiels's father had left already, but Jonathan was available, and he never fought with his mother. It was silently arranged that Jonathan would help her down the walkway. Also silently understood: Her mother didn't trust Shiels. Not on ice. Not with a lot of things.

Shiels was terribly aware that her parents' spare credit card was sitting where it always sat in the little bowl on the kitchen island. It was good for pizza, for take-out Greek, for taxis and such. The credit limit, she happened to know, was fifteen thousand dollars.

Her parents would freak, of course they would, but that would be down the road. They could absorb a hit like that, and no one would go hungry. It was just a number to them.

All right, a large number, but still . . .

Her mother settled at the door with her purse, her brief-case, her tablet, her shoe bag, while Jonathan stood by, the obedient son. Maybe this was a good change, Shiels thought, this journey she was taking into disobedience. "Have a great day, Mom!" she called. "I'm sorry again about your foot. I'll make it up to you!"

She could be a good daughter and a delinquent at the same time.

Purse, briefcase, the shoe bag, the coat, the scarf, the tablet. Her mother checked her face again in the hall mir-ror. "You will make it up to me," she said. "Come give me a kiss for now."

Shiels reported as requested.

"What's happening with the pterodactyl?"

Shiels looked at her mother's socked toes sticking out of the cast. "There's a crowdsourcing thing," she said. "For the bail."

"Melanie Mull is leading it," Jonathan said helpfully.

"Is that on the Internet?" her mother asked. Then—"Do

not use your own money. Do not gamble your education. Do not let your head be turned by a boy."

Shiels felt her face baking. "We'll get him out somehow," she said.

Her mother kissed her. "You have a good heart," she said. "That's so impressive. Just keep your perspective. That's all I ask."

Shiels wasn't sure of the process, but it seemed to her that after the meeting with Jocelyne Legault's uncle, they might be able to go directly to the jail with the funds and bring Pyke home. She might see him later that day. She might be the one carrying him out of prison, cradling him in her arms. She could practically feel him against her chest, the weight of him and the lightness.

So she wore her yellow shoes. In case she saw him. In case he saw her.

She wore them despite the snow that had fallen, and the ice that had formed on top of it overnight. Those yellow shoes might as well have been ballerina slippers — they gave so little traction. She should have worn ice skates. And carried ski poles. She slipped and slid all along the roadway on the sidewalk, creeping like an eighty-year-old.

I'm not doing this for a boy, she told herself.

She was almost all the way to school before she looked up enough to notice them, the hundreds of crows lined along the telephone lines. Looking down. At first she thought they were frozen, they seemed so still.

Watching her.

And then it seemed to her they were mourning—that Pyke might already have died, that in their silence and stillness they were letting her know she was too late, that all this slipping and sliding came in vain.

She stopped to look at them. "What is it? *What?*" she called finally.

The crows did not move, did not squawk and bicker amongst themselves, did not acknowledge her in any way.

They were supposed to meet the lawyer at eleven o'clock in his office downtown, but Shiels felt she could not wait, and she certainly could not sit through biology lab with her head spinning in such different directions. She hunted down Jocelyne Legault in anthropology, and stood quite shamefacedly at the front of the class to tell Mr. Pinkle that Jocelyne was needed on an urgent matter of school council business. As she was saying the words, Shiels felt their truth; as she walked away with Jocelyne down the hall, she wondered if she wasn't simply accessing mankind's deep and ancient reserve of brazen self-deception.

I say it and feel it, so it must be.

"We're way too early," Jocelyne whispered.

"I think we need to be there now," Shiels said.

Sheldon had not yet texted her to confirm that he had transferred his education fund to her bank account, the meager one she did have access to, so she brought Jocelyne to communication science and rapped on the door. Mrs. Keele opened it impatiently. Shiels said, as importantly as she could, "There's an emergency meeting of the school council to work on the Pyke issue. Sheldon Myers is needed right away."

Mrs. Keele's eyebrows knit together. "Do you have a principal's note?"

"Principal Manniberg has called the meeting," Shiels replied. "You won't be able to reach him on the office phone. He's in the library, where the meeting is being held. Sheldon's late. That's why we're here to get him."

Mrs. Keele was barring the doorway with her heavy arm. Under it Shiels could see Sheldon in the far corner, reading something, lost in thought.

Mrs. Keele said, "I didn't think Sheldon Myers was even on the school council." At this mention of his name, Sheldon finally looked up.

"He's a friend of the council," Shiels said immediately. "We need his input. He knows Pyke better than most of us."

Mrs. Keele stared pointedly first at Shiels's nose and then at Jocelyne's. "I doubt that could possibly be the case," she said.

If only Shiels could push the woman out of the way! If

only she had a beak, Shiels thought, she'd slash the woman's arm from that doorframe.

"Please, Mrs. Keele," Shiels said quietly. "A life is at stake. Believe me, Sheldon can help."

But Sheldon could not help. In the school parking lot, when they were waiting for the taxi to arrive, Sheldon blurted out that his parents had forbidden him to use his education money to bail out a violent pterodactyl.

"He's not violent!" Shiels said. "He reacted in self-defense. And you promised me the money." Sheldon could not look at her. "Why did you wait until we got all the way out here before telling me?"

The boy stared down at his own running shoes, hopelessly inadequate against the ice and snow, before finally raising his eyes again. "You didn't give me time, Shiels." His ears were red. He looked like he might blow up, but his voice stayed quiet. "You're just a tornado. You carry everything in your path, and you don't stop to think about anyone but yourself."

"I'm thinking about Pyke! That boy is close to death. When I saw him on Friday night—" Her fists were balled, her voice filled her neck, oh she wanted to just blast at him!

But his quietness somehow got through to her. Maybe too it was that Jocelyne was also standing quietly, looking at the both of them.

"I know he's in rough shape," Sheldon said. "You told me. But even if I get a scholarship, college is still going to be expensive. We don't have a lot put by. I just can't risk it."

Shiels bit her lip. The jab about the tornado—well, of course it was true. That was who she was. That was how she got things done. If Sheldon didn't love her for that—

If Sheldon—

(Sheldon kissed her on the cheek then, unexpectedly, as she was standing. The taxi entered the curving driveway of the school.)

If Sheldon—

"I'm going back inside," Sheldon said. "Sorry."

He walked away.

The taxi smoothed to a stop in front of the girls. The driver kept the engine idling while he lowered the window. Maybe it was too icy for him to get out? "Where to?" he said. He was blurry until Shiels wiped her eyes. Then he was a Middle Eastern man who looked like he had been up all night, driving around, waiting for calls.

The school door closed, and Sheldon really was gone.

"I think maybe we don't need you after all," Jocelyne Legault said uncomfortably.

"Yes. Yes we do!" Shiels said suddenly. She opened the door and forced herself inside. To hell with him. To hell with Sheldon. "Haven Heights Hospital!" she said.

• • •

A young woman had been hit by a bus. She'd been riding her bicycle in the ice and snow, and obviously the
bus driver had assumed no one was out on skinny tires in
such weather, and had cut across the poorly designed bike
lane. . . . It was a cascading disaster of bad choices, accord-
ing to the nurse in surgery, who explained this all to Shiels
and Jocelyne, presumably because Shiels was, after all, the
surgeon's daughter. The nurse had a blood spot showing on
her left elbow, just below her pink short sleeve, and was formidable in a down-to-earth way. Any thoughts Shiels might
have had about barging into the operating room to plead
with her father one last time to bail out a young pterodactyl
melted into the same puddle that was forming on the floor
below her soaked yellow shoes.

"How . . . how long do you suppose he'll be?" Shiels asked.

"The leg is broken in four places. It could be hours," the
nurse said. "Do you want me to tell him you're here?"

Shiels hesitated, then said no. But where else to go?
Time was running out! They needed to just stop for a while
and think things through. She and Jocelyne took seats in the
small waiting room. A thick-necked man with white curly
hairs heading down into his collar sat staring at the floor, his
huge hand clasping that of the birdlike woman beside him
with a clenched jaw—the parents, presumably, of the cyclist.

On impulse Shiels leaned over and touched the man
on the knee. "You couldn't have a better surgeon working

on her in there," she said. The man stiffened, and then his eyes narrowed when he saw her face. Her nose.

"Please take your hand away," he said coldly.

"I'm sorry. I—"

The mother, too, looked at Shiels in alarm.

"It's our *son*," the man said finally. Jocelyne pulled on Shiels's arm. But Shiels still didn't understand . . . until she glimpsed the boy through the partially opened door of exam room A, with her father's assistant, Kelly Brogue.

The boy with the bandaged, limp arm that Pyke had slashed and poisoned.

"Oh!" Shiels felt sick suddenly, roasting from within. "I'm so sorry!"

"What have you done to your faces?" the mother said to both of them. "Shame on you. You're supporting that . . . that . . ."

"Mary—" the father said.

"That beast attacked our boy!" the mother said. Shiels sat like a statue, unable to move. "We'll never be able to afford the physical therapy. He can hardly move his fingers now. His muscles are wilted."

Jocelyne pulled Shiels to her feet. "We're terribly sorry, ma'am, sir. We're just leaving. Please excuse us. Please."

The man squinted. "You're those girls we saw on the video. You were cheering on that damn bird!"

"I'm sorry!" Shiels sputtered, over and over, on her way out.

• • •

Shiels allowed Jocelyne to pull her to the hospital cafeteria. On the way ghostly patients in drab blue gowns wandered by wheeling IV stands, or shuffled with walkers, or looked up from their tilted beds to see who was passing by.

A menace, that's who, Shiels thought.

A young woman cavalierly setting plans into motion with no idea what the actual outcome might be. And for what?

To salvage her own standing.

To appear a certain way to others.

To "win," whatever that meant.

What did anything mean?

At a table, in front of a plate of french fries, her chest constricting, Shiels flipped through the world on her phone. Melanie Mull's crowdsourcing effort had raised $117 so far. "She'll never get there," Shiels said. "And we have to raise money for the Wallin boy, too. For his rehab."

"Why are you doing this?" Jocelyne asked quietly.

She was such a slight girl when she was not outrunning everyone. With her winter coat resting on the chair behind her, she looked like she was twelve.

She had no trouble downing french fries, though.

A simple question, but the usual constant flood of answers was not available. The cafeteria was a sorry excuse for a refuge: dismal plastic trays, muted colors, gloom-stricken faces of relatives and friends masticating mediocre food in a windowless prefabricated room trapped in the depths of a massive edifice of illness.

This felt like the culmination of many things. Shiels hadn't had to touch that father on the knee and try to say something genuine and human. But she had, just as an instinct, with the best of intentions. She had tried. And even that had gone terribly wrong.

Why was Shiels doing this?

"I don't know what's happening to me," Shiels said. "I'm not the same person at all since Pyke arrived. I don't know who I am anymore. I think I love him. Whatever that is. I think I love him profoundly. But I don't know why. And I know you love him too, I know he is fixated on you. I know I have no right or expectation. I just feel he's cracking me open, and I can't do anything about it. I don't want to. I want to see so much who I might become after all. And I absolutely don't want to see him suffer and die in prison. I don't think I could bear it."

Jocelyne had left only two french fries on the plate. Shiels ate one of them, Jocelyne took the last. "You scare me," Jocelyne said. "You always have. Everything is perfect with you, and if it isn't perfect, you make it so, no matter what."

"That's not who I am. That's who I used to be. Right now I am out of ideas. I don't know how to save Pyke."

"I used to be afraid of a lot of things," Jocelyne said. "I

was so afraid of losing a race, I would run through my own puke to win. But when Pyke arrived, all that fear just fell away. Now I just run to feel like I'm flying."

"Yes." In her own pokey way that was how Shiels felt too.

"So we're sisters, you and me," Jocelyne said. "We'll leave it at that. Pyke is big enough for a lot of ways to love him." She checked her phone. Her eyes flattened in disappointment.

"What?"

"The fund is at $243. They're never going to get there."

Shiels took out her parents' credit card and tapped it, nervously, on the table.

XXV

"The movement spreads like a virus," Lorraine Miens had written in *Animal Man*. "It doesn't even have to be a good idea, it just has to be infectious. We are built to mimic our neighbors—to covet their lawns, their cars, their hula hoops. One in a million of us sees the world fresh; the rest watch with cow eyes and then copy as if our lives depend upon it."

And an infusion of cash usually doesn't hurt to start the ball rolling. Anonymously—she needed to buy the time from her parents' wrath—Shiels sent a good round number, ten thousand dollars, which she would pay back in February. Her parents would forgive her. Maybe. Possibly. Shiels imagined Melanie Mull staring at her screen in shock when the huge donation came in. Minutes later Melanie purpled her own nose and sent round a selfie with news of the groundswell. By the time Shiels and Jocelyne were heading back to Vista View in a taxi, the Free Pyke crowdsourcing fund was at more than twelve thousand dollars. And the number kept climbing as the pictures rolled in from across the city and all over—kids, mostly, sending in a few dollars and purpling their own noses now with markers, with paint, some even getting themselves tattooed.

He's the sexiest pterodactyl high school student ever, one girl wrote from somewhere. *We can't let him die in jail just because of some stupid football game.*

The fund hit seventeen thousand dollars as the taxi was pulling into the school drive. A dark-skinned boy painted his nose white. *Just because he has wings doesn't mean he can't be real!* the boy wrote. That issue became an odd part of the debate. A whole contingent of people sent in money apparently to prove that Pyke really did exist, because another contingent insisted he was a hoax and that people were investing in a fiction.

He is not the Loch Ness monster, Melanie Mull wrote. *He is not the yeti or the Sasquatch. His name is Pyke, and he will die soon if you do not help!*

It was twenty-two thousand dollars as Shiels and Jocelyne pushed through the large front door of the school. A handful of students were sporting purple noses—no, more than that, everywhere Shiels looked she saw dark noses.

Don't just color yourself in! Melanie Mull wrote. *Five dollars will save a unique life, so do it!*

Jonathan glided by on his longboard, his nose darker than Shiels's. Even Sheldon had joined in. Shiels saw him by his locker, looking stupidly at Rachel Wyngate. They were sporting couples' purple noses. How much had they given? After Sheldon had pulled out of his agreement with Shiels?

"Can you believe this?" Shiels said to Jocelyne.

The fund hit forty-eight thousand dollars by the start of the first afternoon class.

What was the feeling all through Postlethwaite's distracted discussion about the decline of literature in the digital age? We don't read the same on-screen, he was trying to say; we flit about following one idea and the next, using a residue of brainpower while the rest of our minds anticipates or yearns for the next fillip of entertainment. No one knew the word "fillip" except for Shiels, who did not raise her hand. She quietly felt as if one flick of the finger from Melanie Mull, and her insides would shatter into fragments.

Why so suddenly brittle? It was *her* ten thousand dollars—her parents'—at just the right moment that had given the fund liftoff. Yet all anyone could talk about was what Melanie Mull was doing, what *she* was achieving in the fight for Pyke.

But no, it wasn't simply Melanie Mull having usurped her—effortlessly, it seemed—as the prime mover in the Vista View galaxy. Shiels would be graduating in a matter of months; it was (theoretically) good to know someone was poised to fill her shoes.

How quickly Shiels felt left behind in the pull of events. That was it. She had marshaled significant forces, but in an instant it was all beyond her. Melanie Mull's movement was going to free Pyke—what was left of Pyke to free—if not in the next few hours, then soon. Pyke would not stay with the Kranes for rehab. Despite all her donated parental money, he would go wherever Melanie Mull wanted, that much was clear.

Shiels would not be near him.

That was the thing, she realized as she sat taking in nothing of what Postlethwaite was saying. (Her pen dashed notes quite independent of her brain.) Some important part of her had been longing to be close to Pyke, day in and day out. To be at his bedside in the morning with hot tea (if that was what he wanted). To sit with him at night while he rested and healed— perhaps reading to him excerpts from the works of Lorraine Miens. How much would he care about or even understand? Somehow she felt it would be enough for him to hear the sound of her voice. It would be enough for her to sit close by, to wipe his brow, change his dressings. (Would he have dressings? Would they need changing?) To soak up his energy.

He had energy. He radiated. She had quietly been hoping to have him to herself for a time, and now she knew it wouldn't happen.

Why hadn't Shiels tried crowdsourcing herself? She knew that if she had asked kids to purple their noses for Pyke, she would have been the butt of countless jokes. But Melanie Mull was making the most of the money that came in. She was purpling noses all over the place, using Shiels and Jocelyne as examples, and people couldn't join in fast enough.

At dinner that night Jonathan could barely stay seated. "You should've seen it! You should've seen it! One minute she had two dollars in there. Then suddenly everybody was doing their noses. There was, like, one purple marker in the whole school, but it got passed around."

Shiels's mother shuddered, possibly at the gross lack of hygiene.

"There was a big donation," Shiels said carefully, chewing her bean salad.

"No, it was everybody!" Jonathan said. "Kids everywhere sending in a couple of dollars."

"What donation?" Shiels's mother asked sharply.

"I just heard it was large," Shiels said in a neutral tone. "Maybe some thousands of dollars. I heard it made a big difference."

"But you weren't behind this stunt," her father said. He was leaning forward in his chair, paying too much attention.

"It was all Melanie!" Jonathan said.

Shiels chewed quietly. She wondered: *Is this what they call soft power? Achieving results without leaving finger-prints?*

She was good at this at least, she thought. At starting things off.

Her mother was staring at her. This was all going to explode as soon as the credit card bill came due.

But hopefully Pyke would be free by then. And still alive.

"It *was* mostly Melanie," Shiels said quietly. "And every-body else who chipped in. Amazing to watch, really."

She chewed, chewed, had a drink of lemon water.

"How great that you didn't have to be involved," her mother said finally.

In bed that night, in her sleep, Shiels found herself wander-ing a dark cobblestone alley. The water was dripping down rock walls, soaking and chilling her bare feet, which had outgrown her boots. She had to keep an eye on every foot-fall. The stones were rounded and slippery, and she had to grip with her toes. It was like being blind. She ran her right hand along the wet rock wall, which was just as soaked as the cobblestone but rougher. It hadn't had thousands of years of feet wearing its surface smooth.

Soon she would look up, and see what cross street she'd arrived at. She would know where to go.

Wings would be nice, she thought. *Wings would let me straight out of this state.*

It might be one of those obsidian-black nights when the stars pricked the velvet by the billions. She'd heard about those nights, had seen the photos on nature programs.

But for now she was feeling her way along.

In the morning: sun. More glorious than had been seen in many days. Light sparkled off the new snow like a prettied-up calendar photograph, and Pyke was at the door, unexpectedly.

Shiels had wandered into the front room, breakfast toast in hand, to look at the snow on the windowsill in the eastern light, when the doorbell rang and there he was, standing on his own, wrapped in a cloak of sorts, with galoshes on—galumphing brown curiosities keeping his toes from the ice. His eyes shone as ever, but he looked wilted beneath his cloak, and at first Shiels saw no one else, only him.

He wore a strange, fluorescent synthetic thing—it looked like a security bracelet that had been modified to fit around his neck.

Melanie Mull stood behind him, her nose still purple, her hands out as if he might fall, and some paces behind her stood Jocelyne Legault—was her nose even more beak-like?—looking concerned. And on the drive was a police cruiser, with Inspector Brady slouching by the open door. He didn't look like he was going to approach.

No photographers, no reporters. Somehow the media had been duped.

"We sprung him early this morning," Melanie said. "He's eighteen, legally responsible. He asked for you. I hope that's all right."

Shiels's mouth opened, but nothing came out. For a moment her teeth felt unnaturally sharp; her tongue faltered in forming words.

"He's not allowed to leave your house," Melanie said, "except for court dates and such. That's a locator ring that can't be taken off. Your parents are doctors, right? They said they would take care of him?"

Pyke was trembling in the cold; Shiels felt like she should engulf him in an embrace, but could not make herself move.

"You're going to have to say something, Shiels," Melanie Mull said.

"He asked for me?" Shiels blurted finally.

"Yes."

Melanie Mull was going to make a tremendous student-body chair. Shiels could see it all clearly. The example of the younger woman helped her regain a semblance of balance. "When the bail is returned," Shiels said, "when Pyke is freed for good, that money needs to go to the Wallin boy who hurt his arm. For rehab, for whatever he needs. Understood?"

XXVI

So Shiels did get to carry the pterodactyl-boy up the stairs in her arms. She was alone in the house. Both her parents had left for work, and Jonathan was already on his way to school. She had been thinking of perhaps just taking the morning off anyway. She worked so hard, normally. School could wait.

The place could get along just fine without her for a day.

And now this!

She cradled him, afraid to break something. His wings did seem to fold properly, but his beak drooped, his neck chafed in the security bracelet, there seemed little left of him. Where were those glowing pecs? His eyes were teary. He felt like he was made of kindling.

"Are you hurting somewhere?"

He rubbed his beak against her arm in reply, like a

dolphin nudging her. His breathing sounded squeaky, shallow.

"I'm just going to put you to bed. Have they fed you? Are you famished?"

His eyes brightened. She couldn't tell if it was by accident or in reply to her mention of food. What did they have? Smoked salmon in the fridge. Her father's disgusting store of kipper snacks. Some frozen fish sticks for Jonathan.

She carried him down the hall. He was light, light in her arms, but he felt warm—feverish?—and Shiels breathed in the deep, rich, seaside smell of him. Was he used to flying all the way to the ocean to feed? He seemed happy to snuggle into her chest and to close his eyes. Maybe he was reveling in her smell too? What did she smell like?

Bed. Fitful sleep. Cellular-level exhaustion.

What did she have to feel tired about? Nothing. Pyke was here in her arms. It was like a dream, but there were her actual feet on the hardwood floor, that was her physical toe nudging open the guest room door. She carried him in and bent over as gracefully as she could to pull back the blankets and sheets before setting him down and soothing him between the covers.

His wings were fine. They were just . . . weak. He needed rest. It was a good thing she had decided to stay home today.

"Water?" she asked. A noncommittal wiggle-dip of his head. His sunken chest quivered with the shivering of his heart. His crest had faded to the barest smudge of brown-ish red.

If it ever got to court, she thought, no jury would con-vict this boy of a vicious assault. He didn't look like he could hurt a beetle, in his current condition.

She got a glass of water from the bathroom, then trooped downstairs to the kitchen to find a straw in case that might make it easier to drink. But what would his lips do with a straw?

He didn't really have lips.

He had that long, sleek, almost polished beak.

She imagined trying to pour the water down his throat, what a mess that would make. So—not a glass. Instead she found a cooking bowl—a big steel basin—and filled it with water so that he could dip his beak.

By the time she carried it up the stairs, he was fast asleep in the guest bed, sunlight slanting through the window straight onto his pillow. She set down the basin, drew the drapes, then just sat on the edge of the bed and watched the fascinating creature as his breathing slowed, his chest rose and fell, his presence filled the room like a warm, sweet, barely visible spectrum of light.

One of his wings had slipped out from under the cov-ers. She lightly touched the three long fingers—so cold at first, then warmer, warmer—and sat as still as she could, just watching.

• • •

Really, she thought, as she sat on the living room floor now, on a patch of white carpet that got the most sun in the morning, she should call the PD. They were going to find out anyway, as soon as they got home. Better to lay the groundwork now. Lay it all out: the donation, her reasons, how she would pay for it, how Pyke had come to be upstairs. There would be a battle no matter what. She shouldn't appear to be hiding anything.

She was in her floppy clothes still, she hadn't even taken a shower. She was, however, wearing her yellow running shoes for when Pyke woke up and saw her again.

He liked her as a runner. As if she might be a Jocelyne Legault! Maybe he couldn't tell the difference—any girl who wore yellow shoes and ran around a track was devastatingly beautiful to him.

That would be all right, she thought. *To be devastatingly beautiful.*

Lorraine Miens spoke up in her head. (*Oh, Lorraine!* Shiels thought. *For once just let me enjoy this.*) "A woman with great beauty is like a man who has inherited too much money—crippled by the apparent gifts of birth."

Thank you, Lorraine, she thought. Ms. Killjoy, who had been, by the way, strikingly beautiful in her own youth. It hadn't hurt her career. How many female academics get on the cover of national magazines in their twenties? The beautiful ones. Who do bold things.

I'm doing a bold thing, Shiels thought. *I have brought a pterodactyl into our guest room, and this is the calm before the storm.*

She wondered (the Sheldon part of her brain kicking in now) who the first person had been to throw shit into a spinning fan. Or had some genius imagined the phrase, like Einstein with a thought experiment, and left the world to do the actual testing?

She wanted to text Sheldon right now to tell him that Pyke was sleeping just upstairs, that she had held him in her arms, that he smelled like the seaside. But even when they were at their closest, she realized, this would not be a share-with-Sheldon sort of thing. She had feelings for Pyke.

Non-Sheldon-like stirrings.

But now, at least, Sheldon was not hers to betray.

At least she could feel good about that.

She showered and changed into a black, body-hugging running outfit, as if she were going out for a jog, but of course she stayed in, glancing into the guest room from time to time. Pyke slept soundly—clearly he felt safe here, away from the clutches of the uncaring law. Shiels fussed unusually with her hair, and then she changed outfits entirely, into a black skirt and leggings and a slashing, purple top that still went with her yellow shoes. Somehow deep red lipstick seemed to complement her purple nose—or at least it gave her face an unusual severity, which she thought perhaps a pterodactyl would like. But just as she applied the finishing touches, she remembered how, early on, Pyke had blithely walked past her when she'd been all made up in her short dress and zebra leggings. Maybe he didn't like provocative women. Maybe the casual jogging look really was what turned his crank.

So she scrubbed her face and changed again, into her running shorts and black sports bra, which could be a top, too. It was cold in the house, so she turned up the heat— better for Pyke's recovery, surely—and she looked in on him again.

Still sleeping.

But he wasn't as peaceful as he had been. His leg trembled under the covers, he tossed from side to side, his beak opened and closed, sometimes slowly, sometimes in a snappish way that would illustrate to juries in an eyeblink how easily this pterodactyl could harm someone else. That security bracelet could not be comfortable. What dream was he having? Was he replaying his deplorable treatment in prison? Slashing out again at the Wallin players trying to kill him? Hunting in his home grounds, wherever they might be?

She thought again about calling her parents. Her father

first—she would leave a message. If he got back to her, it would be later in the afternoon, his head somewhere else, still mentally performing surgery. Her mother would call back sooner. Shiels would have to pull the phone from her ear, and wait for the waves to stop crashing quite so shriekingly. But better to start the battle by phone than to wait for the full in-person opera.

She knew it, she thought it through, but she couldn't pull her phone into her hand. She couldn't compose the number. The hours began to leak.

What a strange thing, time. When you are used to juggling a thousand things, traveling at warp speed, now to suddenly have a whole day at home to listen to the tap drip. Shiels sat in the guest room in the comfy chair by the window, wrapped in a blanket, listening to the faint *tap-tap* from all the way down in the kitchen. That faucet didn't even drip, usually—she had simply failed to shut it completely when she'd filled the basin with water. A quick trip downstairs could bring silence, but she didn't move.

She watched the light change slowly as the sun moved across the windowsill.

She was overdue on an English assignment. She needed to write a critique of David Foster Wallace's famous speech to the graduating class at Kenyon College in which he went into excruciating detail about the suffocating disappointments of adult life, and then showed how to embrace them, love them even. He even gave a glimpse of living in sunlight, unburied by the blankets of the faulty and deceiving perceptions under which we usually hide. She had watched the video, she thought she knew what she might say about it, she had hours and hours to write it up, but her computer was in her bedroom, she was here, and what did it matter?

What did any of it matter? The expanding or shrinking universe, the qualities of a cell, social strategies in the digital age, the rise over the run, the infinite approach to zero? It all took effort, and she was already where she wanted to be. She could hear her pterodactyl breathing on the bed.

Her pterodactyl.

Jocelyne Legault will want to visit him, she thought.

Shiels would have to be gracious.

Her parents would be home in a matter of hours, and the house would shake and the heavens tremble.

Of all of that, what was real?

This moment, sitting by the window, her body in running gear but for now at rest, wrapped in the brown blanket she used to drag into this room when she was very young and would park her nose in an open book and let the rest of the world slide on by.

"Clozzer," he said when he woke up, and he moved his beak slightly, beckoning. His eyes were lit, how? In a kindly, intense way. Shiels felt her whole body smiling, and the few steps across the floor to his bed were like those steps onto the stage had been at Autumn Whirl.

She remembered those steps now, that stage. The whole movie of it seemed to be playing in her body.

But she was here, now, too. Here.

"How are you feeling?" she asked.

"Clozzer," he murmured again, and he tickled her with his eyes, his expression. He seemed to be laughing inside, unusually joyful.

She sat very close to him and let him put his hand—his wing fingers—on the bare skin of her leg. She was in shorts still. It wasn't cold in the room, not at all.

"Can I get you anything now?" she asked. "Smoked salmon? Water? Do you have to"—the thought just occurred to her—"go to the bathroom?"

He had been in this bed now for hours. The afternoon was draining, the light slanting away.

"Clozzer," he murmured again.

He rubbed his beak against her cheek, she stopped breathing. Really, she thought, she shouldn't let him do that.

Why not? she wondered.

His beak was smooth and hard, and all of him, it seemed, pulsed with heat, even in his diminished condition. He was half in and half out of the blanket. What was that along the edge of his wing? It looked like . . . a fourth finger! How had she not seen it before? It didn't look like a finger. It stretched on and on like a flexible tent pole supporting the membrane of his wing. And under the blanket, parts of him were poking up in ways she couldn't quite sort out. Was one of those other prodding tent poles . . . something else? Not a wing part or tail tip or elbow . . .

He rubbed her, so gently, his beak against her cheek. He seemed to be breathing her in, and so she breathed him in as well. It felt like one of her dreams, like soaring over the treetops and leaning into the bareness of light. Like out-winging the clouds. Like the hot, damp embrace of earth as well, rooted, like pulling life from the black soil.

Her hand fell naturally to his chest. He was more animated, she could see it clearly. He wasn't quite the same beaten animal he'd been when she'd carried him up the stairs some hours before. Already the bed rest had done him good. She loved the silky feel of his fur.

She snuggled closer, his beak now between her breasts.

She kissed, so gently, the sleek edge of his crest, which looked, even now, slightly more crimson than before.

She fingered the cool smoothness of his locator ring.

Jonathan clumped through the front door downstairs, his longboard rattling on the tile floor of the main entrance to the house.

Shiels pulled herself back.

Pyke implored her with his impossibly large eyes. She caught her breath. "Oh," she moaned, "later?"

Was that her voice, wrung-out and limp?

It was not time for surrendering to whatever it was she wanted.

Oh . . . but she wanted to!

XXVII

Through sheer force of will Shiels returned to her bedroom and pulled on her warm clothes. She hurried downstairs and caught Jonathan with his body half in the refrigerator.

"I need you to be more advanced than you're probably capable of right now," she said.

"What?" When he turned to her, his mouth was full of chilly pizza.

"I need you to not be your adolescent self for the next while. I want you to pretend to be a reasonable and mature and even sophisticated human being."

"Hello to you, too," he said, chewing. "You weren't at school today."

"I need you to listen and to understand, because Mom and Dad are going to be home soon and the roof is going to blow off this place for a time."

"Pyke got out on bail today. Melanie's crowdsourcing campaign worked. Nobody knows where he's been holed up." Jonathan stood by the still-open door, chewing but not otherwise moving. Shiels pushed the door shut, and only at the last moment did Jonathan turn to get out of the way. "What's your problem?" he said. "Just because Melanie did what you couldn't manage to do."

"Are you finished?"

Congealed tomato sauce clung to his chin.

"She's going to be student-body chair next year," he said. "She's going to be way better than you. People actually like her."

"Pyke is upstairs in the guest bedroom," she said quietly.

He smiled as if she had just said something deranged.

She spoke slowly and deliberately. "Don't go in there. Don't bother him. If you want to say something in support of his convalescing here when the PD get home, fine, but let me do most of the talking. Do you understand?"

A chunk of pepperoni fell onto the floor at the boy's feet. "Pyke is here?"

"In the guest bedroom. Tell no one. It's much better if—"

"But how?"

"He asked for me. He wanted to stay here. Your mouth is hanging open, Jonathan."

"And Mom and Dad agreed? How did you ever—"

"They don't know. Are you even listening to me?"

"Why didn't you tell them? They're going to—"

"Shut up. Just pretend you are a support post holding up the wall. Do you want Pyke to stay here or not?"

It took a while, but finally his body seemed capable of motion again. He threw the remaining pizza crust into the sink. "Do you mind if I video what happens?" he said.

At about eight thirty in the evening there was a pause in the action, as if all parties recognized at the same time that stomachs were rumbling, that nothing had been done about dinner, that despite the dramatic circumstances unfolding under their own large and comfortable roof, it had been a long day for all of them and they could not keep repeating the same accusations and countercharges, and at such a volume, indefinitely.

They were in the living room, where battles tended to happen. Shiels's mother clumped around the perimeter of the oriental rug, her black plastic walking cast occasionally pounding on certain words for emphasis, heightening the pain on her face. "I don't know what else there is to say," she said, in that moment when the air seemed ready to run out of the storm. "We are deeply, deeply disappointed with you, Shiels. I can't express how, how . . . *monumentally* upset I feel right now. You do understand that much?"

Shiels's father sat in his reading chair, but perched forward, and he nodded in his way, in agreement with everything his wife was saying. As if all these thoughts sprang fully agreed-upon from the same two-headed brain.

Shiels's mother stopped pacing and held her temples. "Tell me, please, that you understand how utterly *betrayed* we feel that you essentially *stole* a large sum of money—don't tell me again how you're going to pay this back, that isn't the point—and brought this . . . *predator* into our house, have offered him our *protection*, without the slightest consultation or clue as to what you are up to. Just tell me . . . tell me that you do not *hate us*, and that you have not gone *completely insane*."

Shiels was seated, unmoving, on the sofa by the window, her back straight, her eyes never leaving her mother. Jonathan stayed standing by the doorframe, in apparent imitation of a support post after all. His hands seemed to be itching to pull out his phone.

"I understand, Mother," Shiels said. "And I apologize. Again. I felt a life was at stake. I wanted to talk to you in person. Not on the phone. You do understand *me* when I say that?"

Her mother's mouth was set. "He is not staying. I hope I am being entirely clear on that. He will not stay here, he cannot stay here. I'm sorry if he misrepresented the situation to the court. We can take no responsibility for his care or security. I will not have him in the house. You do understand that as well?"

Her father nodded, nodded. Jonathan had said nothing all along.

"At least have the decency to meet him," Shiels said. "Go upstairs, see what he is like. Your money helped save him! You can't just throw him out on the street."

"Oh, for God's sake, we're not throwing him out on the street!" her mother erupted. But it was only a shadow of her anger before. They were all getting hungry.

Pyke must be starving, Shiels thought.

He must have heard every word hurled and screamed.

"He is not some pet you can buy and drag in here and imagine we're all going to fall in love," her mother said. "That's not how this works. You will tell him yourself and you will get him out of here before bedtime. I don't care if he goes back to jail or if he stays with Sheldon or with any-one else in your school. Do you understand me?"

It was time to stop talking—that much Shiels under-stood. Her mother was going to be angry for hours, maybe days.

(That much Shiels understood.)

Her mother would develop a migraine soon, if it had not already started.

"I do understand, Mother," Shiels said.

Something clumped upstairs. Her mother's face freeze-dried in panic. "Is it . . . Is he moving around?"

One of the upstairs toilets flushed.

"He had to go to the bathroom. That's all," Shiels said. "Even in prison they let him do that."

Enough. They all needed to eat. To get past this firestorm.

Noise now on the stairs. No! Shiels vaulted from her seat, but already Pyke was halfway down and in plain view of her parents.

"You need to rest! I'll help you—"

"Mizzer," he said. He leaned hard on Shiels and on the banister. His momentum kept him moving down.

"Oh, man!" Jonathan blurted. He hop-hipped in imitation of the way Pyke used to move when he was healthy. "Look at those wings!"

Pyke hadn't even extended his wings, except around Shiels's shoulder.

"Jonathan!" Shiels's mother said. "Don't get too close!"

Even Shiels's father was standing now, fists balled up.

"He's harmless!" Shiels cried.

"Mizzes, Mizzes," Pyke muttered. At the bottom of the stairs he freed himself from Shiels and hop-hipped gingerly, as if in imitation of Jonathan imitating him.

Shiels's mother stepped back when Pyke approached her, but her father touched her arm and said, "I think it's all right."

The pterodactyl looked a fraction of his former self. The security bracelet drooped, as if made for someone several sizes larger. He would have to eat something soon if he wasn't going to fade away completely. "Mizzes," he said again, and extended his hand to Shiels's mother. His eyes were moist, tired, imploring.

Doubtfully, Shiels's mother took the three fingers in her own hands.

"Pleez you mede me," Pyke said, bowing. His crest came close to caressing her cheek.

Shiels could not seem to exhale.

Her mother was blushing.

(Her mother was blushing!)

"Why don't I make us all some dinner?" Shiels said quietly.

There was the soup in the freezer—Shiels set it in the microwave immediately. The smoked salmon would all go to Pyke, as would the fish sticks (in the oven), and she found sushi, too. Who knew how old it was? But it smelled all right to her. Her mother had brought home artisanal bread—twelve-grain, organic, produced entirely within thirty miles of their house—and premixed salad. Would Pyke eat salad? Jonathan wouldn't, but Jonathan was always happy with more leftover pizza.

It wasn't brilliant but it was food, ready, on the table in twelve minutes.

They converged in the dining room. Now that Pyke was

real, a person, not just the name of someone out of sight upstairs, Shiels's mother was her warm, graceful, public self. She lit the candles. She deplored the lack of flowers for the centerpiece—why hadn't she picked some up on her way home? She knocked her foot cast against the table leg as she was setting out the cutlery and laughed like a little girl who has done something silly. "I'm so clumsy with this thing!" she said.

They were not yet seated. Pyke stood to the side, a thread of pterodactyl drool suspended from the corner of his beak, as he eyed the smoked salmon.

"Sit! Sit, please!" Shiels said.

Pyke had trouble with the chair—Shiels wasn't sure if the problem was his weakened condition, or if he still was not used to sitting, despite all his practice in school—so she helped him into place. Pyke slurped up the smoked salmon in one quicksilvery motion. When Shiels turned fully to look, the plate was clean.

He raised his beak, and the lump of fish slid down his throat.

But Shiels's mother missed it all. "Aren't you serving anything to our guest?" she asked.

"There's more," Shiels said. "Just sit."

Pyke speared the pizza off Jonathan's plate and gulped that down too. "Hey!" Jonathan said. His hand had been on the edge of the table, just inches from the spearing.

Pyke darted three times into the salad bowl before Shiels snatched it away from him. "Pyke!"

Shiels's father pulled her back from the table by her shoulders. "Just give him all the food!" he said. "I'm calling the police."

"No! No!" Shiels said. "I can feed him separately."

Pyke slashed at the five varieties of lettuce with oil and vinegar and a touch of lemon seasoning. He looked around at his hosts, at Shiels, with guilty eyes. "Zorry," he said.

Shiels's father had his phone out. But Shiels pulled on his arm the way she'd done when she used to drag him to the back garden to admire her mud-pie concoctions.

"I've seen what that beak can do," her father said.

"I'm sure it's because he was starved in prison."

"It's okay," Jonathan said, and pushed more pizza toward Pyke, who plucked it from his hand with a knife-like motion.

"You step back too, Jonathan!" Shiels's mother said.

"He eats everything," Jonathan said. "Don't you, Pyke? Everyone feeds him in the caf."

Shiels prayed that Jonathan would not throw food for him in the air now. "Are you starving, Pyke?" she asked. He just grinned. So Shiels headed back into the kitchen, and there, hiding in the fridge behind a jar of bacon fat, was a half-opened tin of oysters. When she brought it out, Pyke could barely stay in his seat. Before she even made it to the table, he stretched toward her and plucked the tin from her hand.

"Well, you certainly love those!" Shiels's mother said.

"There's more!" Jonathan hurried back into the kitchen pantry, and returned with three more tins. Pyke slurped as if he had not eaten in a week.

"Zorry, zorry," the pterodactyl-boy said when the gorging was done. When he grinned—it was a disarming gesture—slimes of oyster juice hung from his pointy beak. "Me mebbe bed-zleep gain."

"Are you exhausted?" Shiels asked.

Her father was still standing by his seat at the head of the table with his phone out.

Pyke eyed the empty tins as if he might have missed something. Shiels could bring him the fish sticks later. She bent over and lifted him. Cradled in her arms, he felt like a big, bony baby. "Please don't call anyone," she said to her father. "I can feed him in his room. He's really not dangerous. *Dad!*"

She stood in front of her father with Pyke draped across her.

"Jesus Christ," her father said.

Shiels hurried him back into bed before there could be any changing of minds.

In the night, when Pyke had been put down and the house had settled finally into an anxious stillness, Shiels lay awake just a few rooms from where Pyke was sleeping. They were under the same roof now, breathing the same air. His piquant odor, that raw physical fishiness, became more apparent as darkness descended and other senses shut down for the night. Was that his snoring she could hear, a fine-toothed saw slowly cutting through the hold this household had on her life?

She would be leaving this place soon, she thought, no matter what happened. She would be out of her mother's grip. Jonathan would be on his own under the PD's yoke, but he was a boy, they treated him differently. He was managing to keep their expectations low, low.

And she . . . she was causing such a stink that her parents were going to fire her out of the house in a cannon before too long.

The application for Chesford was due soon. She couldn't keep putting it off. She'd had too long to think about how to impress Lorraine Miens, but surely this most recent development could be turned to her favor. "As student-body chair of Vista View High, I fought to integrate the first pterodactyl-student in school history into regular student life, and even sheltered him in my own home against the oppressive machinery of a state system bent on prosecuting difference and stifling individuality."

Sheldon would have phrased it better.

Sheldon—

Would she ever get into Chesford without Sheldon?

• • •

Late in the evening—or early in the morning—in a dazed sort of half sleep, Shiels thought she heard something moving down the hall. Was it Pyke? Was he up, wandering around, had he forgotten where he was and that he was safe for now, freed from his cell?

The footsteps sounded both soft and thudding.

Shiels crept to her door and listened. Nothing. A tree branch outside complained of the cold. A slow wind rested against a tired fence. Insomniac traffic moaned far away.

Another few steps soft-thudded in the hall.

"Pyke?" Shiels whispered. She opened her door. In the dark she looked for his muted form, for the hop-hipping gait headed to the bathroom perhaps.

It took the longest time to see her mother despite her bright white housecoat. In her cast still, she was slowly step-hopping down the hall . . . toward Pyke's room.

"What are you doing?" Shiels asked.

Her mother was slow to turn around. "Just go back to sleep, baby," she whispered finally.

Why was she heading to Pyke's room now? "Is he all right?" Shiels asked.

Shiels, in her pajamas, pushed into Pyke's room right behind her mother.

The pterodactyl-boy lay wrapped in the bedsheets, his

gorgeous beak lolling to one side, toward the window, snoring gently.

Mother and daughter stood side by side in the doorway staring at their sleeping guest. The prisoner ring around his neck glowed slightly in the gloom, like the fluorescent hands of a wristwatch.

He's beautiful, Shiels thought.

Her mother murmured something Shiels could not hear—a coo almost. A sound you might make around a newborn.

"Shall we let him sleep?" Shiels said, and then she turned and stepped back into the hallway, and waited until her mother joined her and returned to her own bed.

XXVIII

"I think I need to stay home today," Shiels's mother said at breakfast, calmly, as if she were commenting on the weather. "I need to make sure Pyke is healing properly." She glanced across the granola box at Shiels. "And you need to get back to your classes, young lady. First semester marks are crucial for college acceptances, as you know."

Her mother was dressed as if going to work, yet the tone of her voice suggested she had had it in mind for some time to stay with Pyke today.

"It would probably be good to stay off your feet anyway," Shiels's father said. As usual he was hurrying out the door. "The clinic can cover your load?"

"I hardly ever miss a day," Shiels's mother said. "I'm due."

She had mentioned nothing about the episode from

last night—the both of them visiting the boy in his bedroom. It was as if it had never happened.

"You must be anxious to get back to Sheldon and all your . . . organizing," Shiels's mother said to her.

Jonathan blurted, "Shiels split from Sheldon, like, forever ago! He's totally in love with Rachel Wyngate now!"

"Oh," Shiels's mother said. Her eyes said, *These high school romances. Half-life of a fruit fly.*

She did clump over to her husband to kiss him goodbye for the day. "The sooner Pyke gets better, the sooner he'll be out of here," she said, but in a gentle, almost mocking tone, as if in fact she meant the opposite.

It felt wrong, wrong for Shiels to be walking to school when Pyke was at her house, in a weakened state, being attended to by her mother. Her mother—who had never taken time away from her own work of healing others to stay home with Shiels when she was young and stricken by flu or chicken pox or an ear infection. It was *Stay in Bed.* Then, *Read a Book. I'll call you at lunchtime.*

It was definitely cold outside, the steel gray sky offering no relief, just promises of winter, long and slow. Shiels had only missed a day and a half of classes, yet it felt like she'd been away much longer, that somehow she had outgrown the place in the meantime. Her English assignment was still incomplete—she would have to watch the David

Foster Wallace video again to refresh her mind—and no doubt other assignments had been piled on in her absence. Normally Sheldon would have kept her in the loop. And normally she would've met with him at Roseview and Vine. They would've walked together, strategized about the day.

What was there to strategize about now? The day was going to happen no matter what she did.

As she walked along, the bitter wind smarting her cheeks, the grayness of the sky sinking into her, she thought about how dreamlike her life had become. She was still Shiels, Vista View High still loomed ahead of her like a city unto itself. Her family was still her family, her mother still Mom. Yet, some dial had been turned. She felt like a different person almost.

Instead of walking across the street and entering those cold institutional doors with all the others flooding in for morning bell, she turned right and followed the contour of the hill, like water heading toward the path of least resistance. What path was that exactly? It was meandering, but settled downward. She shoved her hands into her pockets and let her feet slap against the pavement, avoiding the ice. November. Not winter yet, but the ground was frozen; snow lay in patchwork clumps as if undecided yet to stay or to go. It was cold on the feet. She should have worn her boots, not her yellow runners.

She began to run. Slowly, slowly she found a bit of a

rhythm: feet slapping, arms pumping, lungs working. Cold breath, blowing out, eyes on the sidewalk directly ahead. Away from the school, from Sheldon, and Manniberg, from Melanie Mull and Jocelyne Legault and the eight million questions about Pyke.

"I have left Pyke with my mother," she said aloud, to no one, as she ran along.

The running-shoe shop looked closed, almost mournfully so: cloudy windows, dullness inside, no lights, no people. Shiels gazed along the street—cars were inching their way downtown. It was definitely a weekday morning in the life of the city.

What now? She could go to a coffee shop and sit in the window nursing a hot drink like some homeless person with nothing to do, no other way to fit in. She could wander around, running some more until she couldn't, and watch the faces of the office workers and the retail clerks as they began their day. One man was going store to store with a bucket in his hand, cleaning the windows of the shops opening for business. Did he have a contract, or did he just do it on spec, one step above a beggar, hoping to get paid?

A woman opened the door of the florist's shop across the street and spoke to the man, who nodded his head, grimaced while smiling, and kept cleaning the big picture window.

Why wasn't the running-shoe shop open yet? The front window was filthy. They needed her to call across the street to the window washer guy to get him to spruce up their business just as soon as he was done with the florist's window.

Shiels checked in her pocket. Would the window guy be insulted if she offered him five dollars to clean the shoe shop window?

Someone approached her from behind. "It's you again," said the old guy, the running-shoe man. He had his keys in his hand.

"You really should get your window cleaned," Shiels said. "And you're kind of late. I bet the mall stores are already open by now. If somebody wanted to pick up a pair of shoes before work so they could go out running at lunchtime . . ."

Her words dribbled to a stop. The man stared at her with windy blue eyes. He unlocked the door and said, "I used to open at eight, but nobody ever came. Why are you here?"

He held the door for her, in a gentle way, and she stepped into the gloom of the store. Really, there was so much he could do to make this place more attractive. "I think maybe you need to hire me," she said. "Nobody's here because, frankly, the place is a dump."

He flicked on the lights, but it didn't seem to make much difference.

"It's like you're caught in a time warp. You need new lighting, wall posters from this century, fresh carpets. My God, how old are these benches?"

He neither smiled nor moved. "The last time I saw you," he said, "you told me you'd started running." It was an obvious statement. She'd run most of the way here, was sweating still from the effort. She pulled out a tissue and wiped her nose.

"I can start without a salary," she said. "Sort of an internship. After a while you could see whether it's been worthwhile having me around or not. I'm sort of a natural organizer. I'm currently the student-body chair at Vista View High School." As the words came out, she hated how needy they seemed.

Needing to have him acknowledge her worth.

"Why aren't you at school now?" he asked.

"I have a flexible arrangement." The lie came so easily, it was a shock, and she amended herself at once. "I'm thinking of taking a break, actually. Things have been fraught with me. At school. And in general." Was she saying too much now? Those eyes on her did not waver.

"I think you wanted to learn how to run better," he said.

"Well, actually," she blurted, "you wouldn't believe how much I've improved since I bought these shoes from you! The first time I tried, I ran back to the school. I was late for this event I was organizing—and I almost died. I swear to

God. I had this, like, out-of-body experience. I practically collapsed at the end of it. But this morning, you know, I just ran here, and it was like I was running . . ."

She was going to say "downhill," but in fact it had been downhill. That probably accounted for more of the difference than she cared to say.

"If I'm going to teach you how to run," the old guy said, "you're going to have to start by learning how to breathe."

Shiels chortled, it was such an odd idea. "I already know how to breathe."

"You're using your chest and nose and even throat muscles to get air down to your lungs. Completely wrong." He stepped closer to her and grabbed her abdomen with his large hands. "Engage your diaphragm. Let your belly spill out."

She held her breath, reflexively, and then blew out, and found herself gasping for air.

"Move my hands to breathe in. Use your diaphragm and your stomach muscles."

She did it, she moved his thick fingers.

"Fine, but that was exhaling. Reverse it now. Engage your diaphragm to breathe in."

It was ridiculous to be standing in the dust and disarray of the shoe shop being groped by an old guy who clearly hadn't the slightest idea how to run his business. Yet she did it—she found the large muscles below her rib cage and inhaled.

"Now relax, use your low chest muscles to release the air. Let it slide out. Good."

Someone could walk in and see them.

"Again. Move my hands. You have to keep breathing."

Obviously he was doing this to get her to go back to school. And she would, she would. But part of her also really wanted to keep moving his hands, to show him that she could do it.

"How's it feel?" he asked after a time.

She didn't know. She was just breathing.

"Relax your throat, your jaw. Don't engage your shoulders. Just let them rise and fall naturally with the movement." He took his hands away, like her father releasing her bicycle all those years ago, when he'd first taught her to ride and she had managed a precarious balance.

"Keep thinking about it. You'll go back to your old habits if you don't keep it in your conscious mind for a while."

Honestly, she couldn't tell the difference. It was just breathing a different way. She had never run out of air.

"This is how you were born breathing," he said. "You learned to breathe shallow when you started to stress out. Just use your body the way it was designed. The large muscles for the large actions. Breathing affects everything else. When you get really good at it, it will become a whole body movement. Are you following me?"

She was feeling better. Maybe it was just because she

liked being around him for some reason. Maybe she was calming down after her run.

"My name is Shiels," she said, thrusting out her hand.

"Linton," he said, grasping it. "I'd be happy to have some of your help around this place. Just . . . be patient."

Patient! She could be as patient as the next person, but really. The place had not been cleaned—really cleaned up—in years. The silly excuse of a broom just moved the dust around, the mop was a health hazard, there was no vacuum. She sorted that out, took Linton's credit card—with his permission—and went down three blocks to Vacuum City and did not buy the most expensive model but didn't get the cheapest, either. She had to empty the vacuum three times in the course of cleaning just the main display areas. By the time she was finished, the window washing guy was long gone but he'd be back tomorrow morning, she felt confident. People go about their lives in patterns.

She was breaking hers. She did not miss school. She didn't miss it! She felt, actually, a huge relief to not be hurtling down those hallways, cramming other people's agendas into her head, or her agendas into theirs. She could be herself here, she could be simple, she could . . .

. . . breathe.

She could breathe here.

Her whole body was feeling better.

She hadn't even known it wasn't feeling well.

At one point her phone vibrated and she realized she'd forgotten all about it. Someone with a strange accent was calling from far, far away asking her if she would like to have her ducts cleaned. They were having a huge sale in her area.

"I like the idea of it," she said, almost gleefully. "But I'd really like to try doing it myself."

And then, oddly, in the middle of the afternoon, in the middle of rearranging the soccer cleats display, it was as if Shiels woke up to her larger reality.

She had abandoned the boy she was supposed to be protecting.

Pyke was alone with her mother, the least motherly person on the planet. Probably her mother had been putting on a display. Probably as soon as Shiels had left the house, her mother had sent the pterodactyl back to the authorities. And Shiels had trusted her!

"That's enough for today," she said to Linton. The poor man was on his own. No extra staff had come in to relieve him, and hardly any customers had visited. How long could he manage like that and still stay in business?

No matter.

"I have to get home now," she said.

Outside, she ran despite the stiff breeze, the uncomfortable chill in the air. Of course she did. It was uphill, and at first she felt almost as wretched as she had the afternoon of Autumn Whirl—but not to the point of puking. Not that drastic.

She was a better runner than that, now.

She was breathing better. When she lost the feeling of the thing, she gripped her midsection with her own hands and ran a few awkward strides like that, pushing their fingers out with her diaphragm and her belly muscles. It did seem she could get a lungful of air now. It did feel better.

Somewhat.

As always, she ran slowly, chugging up the hill.

Had her mother sent Pyke back to jail while Shiels had been away?

If not, what had they been doing together all day?

Chug, chug, step by step, the distance slowly shrank.

No sign of crows.

No sign of what she was going to find.

Her mother. In an apron, stirring things in a big bowl, a recipe book open on the counter. A smudge of white flour on her cheek.

Her flushed cheek.

"Hello, sweetie," her mother said. "How are you? Did you run somewhere?"

"Where's Pyke?" Shiels blurted.

"Upstairs. Resting. How was school?"

Shiels hurried up the stairs, her body still throbbing from her run. Pyke's door was slightly ajar. She burst in.

Jonathan's head jerked guiltily toward her. He sat on the corner of the bed, showing Pyke something on his phone, which he snapped into his pocket. "Where were you today? You didn't come to school," he said.

"Mind your own business," Shiels replied. "Don't say anything to the PD."

Pyke was looking at her in his way. Steam heat rushed through her, curled her toes.

"Manniberg was asking for you," Jonathan said. "I said you were having your period."

How could this juvenile idiot be her brother?

"Thank you," she said. "I will offer a similar level of sibling support to you someday."

Jonathan wiggled into his usual knuckleheaded laugh. But Pyke kept gazing at her, long and steady, as if he knew, understood, nothing else.

Wanted nothing else but her.

Shiels stepped toward the bed. "Why don't you go do your homework?" she said to Jonathan.

"I finished it in Healthy Society. We weren't doing anything else anyway."

"Why don't you go play with your skateboard boys," Shiels said, looking always at Pyke.

"It's too cold out there, nobody's into it," Jonathan said.

Shiels turned her gaze on him until finally he squirmed away.

"Close the door, will you?"

Jonathan left the door open. She breathed quietly—in the belly, deep and deeper—then walked to the door and shut it. Oh, how her chest filled! "How was it all alone with my mother all day?"

Pyke smiled crookedly. He wasn't saying, he was just looking. Looking at her.

She approached the bed again. She supposed she should ask him all sorts of questions about his defense—was there a trial date? Had he had time to meet with Jocelyne's uncle, the lawyer? What were they going to argue? Had they entered a plea yet?

He must have, to have been released on bail. It must have been not guilty.

A raft of questions floated into and out of her brain. Details. To be sorted out later. Now . . . now was for leaning onto the bed beside him and stroking, very lightly, his lovely beak. He seemed to like that. He closed his eyes and let out a deep, animal, purring sound—not a cat's, really, or at least not any small domestic cat's that she knew. Something stronger, wilder. Subdued for now.

He looked small but felt immensely strong still. She imagined he could fly anytime he wanted to, except for the surveillance ring around his neck.

She imagined he could take her with him.

He smelled . . . of oysters. "Did you get enough to eat?" she murmured. "Did my mother go by the fish store?" She stroked a little more firmly now. "Is there anything you are . . . craving?"

She couldn't help it, she leaned closer to him until her chest, sweating and hot still from the run, pressed against the side of his folded wing.

He nuzzled his beak harder against her hand.

This wasn't . . . at all . . . like being in the janitorial closet with Sheldon, which had felt like . . . practice somehow. This was . . . well, she wasn't controlling her own breathing particularly well. Her mouth was very close to . . .

"Shiels!" her mother said, striding into the room. "Maybe you should have a shower, dear!"

A strange smile. Her mother was bearing a large tray of oysters on crackers.

"He just loves these," her mother said, and practically pushed Shiels off the bed. "And he needs building up. While you . . . You must have a lot of organizing you need to do."

Shiels stumbled upright. Her legs felt liquidy.

"How are your applications coming, dear?" Her mother held a cracker poised just inches from the pterodactyl's spear-like beak.

But Pyke did not snatch anything. He waited, patient, subdued even, while she fed him like a child.

• • •

Shiels's Chesford application was due now, if she wanted to be considered for early acceptance. Lorraine Miens would look at the first of the thousands of files coming in, Shiels felt sure—she would read them with a fresher mind, more hopefully.

But was that what Shiels wanted now? She couldn't even seem to bring herself to go to class anymore. If she didn't finish her senior year, then the whole question of college applications was moot.

Yet—she was happy cleaning an old running-shoe shop. She liked hanging around Linton, improving his business. She liked running, as slow as she was. She liked feeling her body. Learning to breathe.

It did feel better dealing with a lungful of air.

I am challenging all my old assumptions, she wrote on her laptop. *So much is changing, every day, I can hardly imagine how much I will learn under the tutelage of one of the great thinkers of our age.*

Blatant flattery. Probably Lorraine Miens threw out those applications without reading any further.

I feel like every movement is strangely bursting with life, she wrote.

In her dream that night she was on the pterodactyl's back, clinging, her arms around his muscled neck, her legs dragging behind. It was morning, chilly, she should have worn gloves, she thought, but where she was now, above the clouds, it felt warm, almost watery. Blue sky. As Pyke pumped his gorgeous wings, she could feel the depth of his breathing—his whole body seemed to turn into a long, magnificent, organic oxygen processor.

But that wasn't it.

She was breathing with him. In time. His rhythm was her own. As he moved his body—the arc of the wings, the undulations of his core—she moved too. She was mounted on him, after all; she would have to move with him or else they'd crash back to earth.

Where were they going? It didn't matter. The wind was warm and wet upon her face. She felt herself intertwined, pulsing . . .

That was enough.

She awoke clutching her pillow with a layer of sweat between her body and the bed. It was still dark, the house seemed cold. For a moment she closed her eyes again and willed herself onto the pterodactyl's back once more. But she couldn't quite make it happen.

The house was still. Her feet slid coldly onto the floor. She went down the hall to the bathroom, peed quietly, then sat still, feeling her breath. She was using her abdomen, as Linton had suggested; in less than a day she had changed something as fundamental as the way she nourished herself with oxygen. It did feel calmer, more peaceful. Almost entertaining—to listen to herself breathe!

She got up, wondering which way her feet would turn her body—right, back to her bed, or left, toward Pyke's room?

She decided not to make a decision, to let her feet dictate, if that was possible. Just as an experiment. She would simply breathe, and her feet . . .

Went straight, almost into the wall.

She smiled, turned left. Opened the door quietly and stepped in. Her mother was not there, this time. Only Pyke, sleeping quietly. She just wanted to look. She liked being near him. Where was the crime in that? It felt almost like she was floating to his bedside, that all of this was an extension of her Pyke flying dream.

Maybe it was?

She sidled onto his bed. Her body felt the chill of the night. His beak was tilted away from her. There was no reason to reach for it, but if this was a dream—it was starting to feel more and more like a dream—then there was no reason not to reach for it either.

She just liked to stroke it. She liked having its power in her hands. He didn't wake up, not at first, but he seemed to settle into her hands as if this were exactly what he wanted.

Her feet were so cold from the floor, it only made sense

to draw them up, to snuggle inside the sheets. Since this was . . . this could have been . . . a dream.

Then she was wrapped in his wings. She couldn't believe how quickly it happened, yet it was completely tender and caring. The movement was enveloping, not painful. She was wearing her old pajamas. Nothing could . . .

Well, she had thought she was wearing them, but—she couldn't feel them. The world seemed to have turned skin to skin, (skin to fur!) and Pyke's heat was urgent now. She was on top of him but wrapped inside him too, inside his wings. It wasn't the same as flying on his back—as the feeling from the dream—but it wasn't terribly different, either.

He started to rock. She felt . . . intertwined. She breathed deeply. Everything seemed to be happening with her whole body. She thought she should stay quiet, but it was difficult to hold herself in. It was just a dream, after all. It was—

She woke, or at least she opened her eyes. Pyke's rigid beak was rubbing gently against the side of her neck. His eyes were closed. He seemed to be in another world, about to—

She pushed herself free. "God!" she said, as if a deity might have been in the room, might have been responsible for hypnotizing her and leading her into the beast's bed. Maybe some ancient god, responsible for duping mortal beings.

She bolted from Pyke's side.

She couldn't speak, couldn't look at him. She stumbled

into the dark hallway. Where were her pajamas? She gathered them quickly. Where was her room?

"Shiels—are you all right?" Her mother was standing in the gloom by the door to the master bedroom, her own robe pulled tight.

"Just—I had to pee!" Shiels said.

In a moment she was back in her own room, back in her bed, shivering in the cold.

XXIX

At breakfast the next morning the silence was crushing. Even Jonathan seemed to be soothing his spoon along the edge of his cereal bowl in an effort to make no noise. Shiels's mother gazed into her tablet screen with the intensity of a cat waiting for movement in the shadows. She was dressed as if made up for work. Her face, especially, seemed overly prepared, perfected.

"So what's on the agenda for today at school, Shiels?" her father finally said.

Shiels took her eyes from her mother's composed figure. "Just an ordinary day, I think," she said.

"What's next on the social calendar? What's the council working on?" he pressed.

The council seemed like a piece of clothing she used to wear.

"Shiels really needs to focus on her college applications," her mother said. "And getting every ounce out of this semester's grades." She turned to her daughter. "You've done enough on the social and political front, dear."

Jonathan left the table and clattered his bowl in the sink. Shiels's mother snapped her head to look at the boy and said, "Could you please rinse and put it in the dishwasher, honey?" Shiels saw in profile what she hadn't noticed before in the slightly different light. Her mother's nose seemed . . . more prominent than before. Slightly, slightly darker than the rest of her skin.

"I'm going to stay home with our guest again today," Shiels's mother said. When Shiels's father raised his eyebrows, she said, "He's making a lot of progress, so this won't be forever. I know I have a practice to sustain." She glanced back at her tablet screen again, and her nose looked perfectly normal.

Just heavily made-up.

Shiels finished her bowl of grapefruit pieces sliced into yogurt and sprinkled with granola. When she gazed up again, her mother was looking directly at her. "Tell me you will have a draft of your personal essay done by tonight so your father and I can read it over."

Blink, blink. "I'll do my best, Mother," she said.

On her way to the running-shoe shop (and away from the high school she now seemed allergic to), Shiels tried to breathe from deep within her, in time with the *slap-slap* of her feet on the chilly pavement. Though bright, it was cold enough to snow again. It felt like winter's army had quietly surrounded the city, was bunkered down not yet attacking but preparing for a long siege.

Her mother and Pyke?

Unimaginable! And yet . . .

Makeup or not, you cannot hide a purple nose for long.

The window washer agreed to wash the front window of the running-shoe shop for ten dollars not five, because it hadn't been cleaned in decades, probably. Shiels paid, since Linton was not yet there. When Linton did arrive, the front glass gleamed in the sun. He stared at it for a moment but did not seem to recognize exactly what the change might have been.

He did notice once again that Shiels was in her yellow runners, that she was sweating from her exertions. He asked about her breathing.

"Better," she said. "I have to think about it, but when I do, I seem to be feeding myself more oxygen."

"'Feed' is a good word." He did not seem to be in a hurry to open the door and get out of the chilly air. "Everybody thinks about fuel from food, but most of our energy actually comes from breathing. The better you breathe, the less food energy you need to burn. Show me how you run." His hands were on his hips now. He stood like a coach, although he was old and it was hard to imagine him running anywhere for himself. "Just go up the block and come back. Pretend I'm not watching."

Shiels felt self-conscious about every footfall. She wasn't very good, she knew that. She wasn't Jocelyne Legault and never would be. But she tried to be sleek and smooth, to move quickly, to hold herself straight and land softly and pump her arms. She was out of breath before she turned around, so she tried to inhale deeply on her way back, to blow out hard. It didn't work. She was pretending, trying to be some runner she was not.

She stood gasping in front of Linton again. "I'm sorry," she said. "I was terrible. I can do it better."

"Don't fight gravity so much," he said simply. "Watch." He ran to the end of the block and back, and while he was running, he wasn't old anymore. He seemed to move inevitably, like a freight train wheeling across the center of town. He covered the ground much more quickly than Shiels had, she felt sure of that, but he wasn't breathing hard. His face was slightly flushed.

She didn't know what to say.

"Start by standing straight," he said. "Engage your core. The same muscles you breathe with. Tuck in your chin a little bit. Lean forward slightly. Not from your waist, from your ankles."

Shiels tried to do it, but she stumbled forward instead.

"What just happened?" Linton asked.

"I don't know. I was clumsy."

"When you leaned forward, gravity pulled you. Don't pick yourself up and carry yourself along like you're the dead weight of a refrigerator. Lean forward, cycle your legs easily, and keep yourself moving." He demonstrated by running loosely, easily again, a few paces, as if he were about to fall over. Shiels tried and stubbed her toe on an uneven bit of concrete in the sidewalk.

"Better!" he said. "You have to pick up your feet. But don't overstride. Don't reach with your legs and pull yourself along. Cycle your feet instead. Push back rather than reaching forward."

She tried it, she tried it, it was all very confusing. Running was so basic. How could she have been doing it wrong?

"You're going to have to think about it a lot, get it into your conscious mind, before the feel of it settles into your muscles," Linton said. "But there's no hurry. You're young."

She tried again. Office worker types passed them on the sidewalk, looking at their gadgets, not interested at all in what they were doing.

She was learning to breathe. Learning to run.

Why didn't they teach this in school?

"We'll add the arms in a moment," Linton yelled after her as she ran. "How's it feeling? Keep your stomach muscles engaged. Let the world pull you along."

She wasn't so good at that, Shiels thought. She pulled and pulled a lot herself, but she wasn't good at letting the world pull her.

What did that even mean? *Slap-slap*, her feet hit the pavement. This was like being a baby again, learning everything from scratch.

Why was everything so bloody difficult?

"Why aren't you going to school, anyway?" Linton asked when they were inside again. The store was as still as a mausoleum—significantly less dusty than it had been yesterday before Shiels's efforts, but Shiels still felt gripped with a certainty that no one would drop by that day to buy anything.

"I'm not there in my head anymore," she said. "So I'm taking a break. Figuring things out."

"Fair enough." He disappeared into the back room. When he came out again some minutes later, he handed her a cup of coffee and sat down with his own on one of the ancient customer benches. He leaned back and looked out at the street. "Did somebody clean this window?" he asked.

As Shiels told him about hiring the cleaner, he seemed to be viewing her with new admiration. She said, "Keep sprucing the place up, and more customers will come."

"Maybe," he replied, the word laced with doubt. Then— "It is a great thing to have more light."

He seemed happy to sit still and watch. Nothing in particular was happening outside—a woman walked past pushing a stroller, a bus stopped and let off a couple who held hands briefly, then parted.

"How did you learn all that stuff about breathing and running?" Shiels asked.

Linton paused before answering. "I was a mildly talented runner when I was young, but serious, and I made it my business to learn as much as possible from the people around me. If you keep doing that for a long, long time, then eventually you learn about even basic things like breathing and running."

"What else don't I know?" Shiels asked. It seemed a perfectly legitimate question, but it cracked him apart with laughter.

"That's lovely, lovely!" Tears shone on his cheeks. He spilled coffee onto his sleeve.

"No. I mean it. What other basic things don't I know? When you look at me, what do you see?"

He brushed away the spilled coffee. "I see someone who needs to open up."

The coffee tasted musty. "How do I do that?"

"Allow for the possibility, every day, with every breath if you can, that you might not know everything, that you might not be right, that you don't have to be hard."

She didn't like the direction this conversation was taking. This man owned an underachieving little running-shoe shop. Who did he think he was?

She took a deeper breath. "What do you mean 'hard'?"

"You walk around with a heavy shell on your back. Not just you, of course, we all do. But at some point you'll grow tired and put it down. It takes so much energy carrying it around. Maybe that's why you're here, you grew tired of school and family and whatever makes up your own personal shell. You're trying to put it down but you don't know how. Just recognize how tired you are, trying to keep up the pretense of having everything under control. You don't, of course not. Nobody does. Relax into yourself. Don't be so hard."

It was easy to say. She felt something shift in her, difficult to know just what, but she felt like blurting, "I'm in love with a pterodactyl and we don't even talk; it's all physical, but it's more than that. If anyone gets me to unload my shell, it's him, but there is a stupid outside possibility my mother might be upside down over him too, and I don't know where anything's going, probably he'll be shut away in jail if I don't start organizing his defense. . . ."

Instead she asked, "Do you have a family?" He wasn't wearing a wedding ring, and there were no pictures on his walls of anyone other than presumably famous runners of the distant past. She didn't know why she'd asked the question, just that she wanted to know.

"I have a wife and two children, a boy and a girl," he said. "*Had*. They were killed at a country crossroads at two o'clock in the afternoon by a drunk. He'd already lost his license. They were two and six, Don and Samantha. My wife was close to making the Olympic team in the 1500. She'd met the qualifying time in practice, and nationals were coming up. Every breath I take, I feel like I'm breathing for them, too."

Sunlight now was streaming through the window. He held his blue eyes on her unwaveringly—winter sky—and she did not feel like looking away. She didn't know what to say.

The door opened then—it was the woman with the stroller who had passed by earlier. "Do you have any broom hockey shoes?" she asked. "My husband's company is doing this charity event, and suddenly I need broom hockey shoes."

Linton was on his feet in a moment. "What size do you need?"

Seven. While Linton rooted through the back room, Shiels kneeled by the stroller and jiggled a colorful toy suspended above the baby's head.

Linton must have been decimated after that accident, she thought. How could someone recover from such a loss?

"I don't know how many times I've walked past this store," the woman said, "but I had no idea what it was till today. What did you do, clean the window?"

"Something like that," Shiels said.

• • •

Linton served her noodle soup from a package at lunch, and they sat by the side window now, where the sun had moved. Only a few other customers had come in, but it all seemed usual to him. Shiels wondered if perhaps when life has done its worst, then nothing else can touch you.

Or you become as brittle as an eggshell rolling in traffic.

"Do you mind talking about it?" she asked him.

"It was twenty-three years ago," he said. "For a long time I felt like I couldn't close my eyes. And then I could."

He didn't look at her as he spoke. It was none of her business, in a way, but he had noticed her, taken her in. If they couldn't talk about everything, then what was the point of being here?

"How did you find out?" she asked.

"I was at home, putting in fence posts because I was too cheap to hire a guy. I wanted to do it myself. Even though I didn't know how. And Alison wanted to take the kids to the beach. I stayed home with the fence posts. It was blazing hot. I was digging down through shaley rocks that took a lot of pounding to cut through. I didn't have the right digger. So I was going to go rent an auger, but I didn't have the car. And they were late getting home. I just kept pounding bit by bit with the wrong tool till my hands were raw. Finally, I went inside for some water, and there was a message on the machine. The hospital was calling. So I dialed in. I remember standing by the phone, and then I wasn't standing anymore, I was on the floor for some reason looking at my blistered hands, wishing I could feel them. Wishing I could feel anything, really. I was practically dead myself with the shock of it."

Somehow Linton had downed his entire bowl of noodle soup. Shiels had hardly touched hers.

"It was a T-bone at a country crossroads. The drunk was going more than a hundred miles an hour." Shiels could barely stand the intensity of his gaze, but she would not look away. He said, "She was a better driver than me. But I should have been at the wheel. I should have died with them." He wiped his eyes.

The front door opened—a customer came in, looked at them and said, "Does the number four go south when it gets to Cheasley, or north?"

"North," Linton said.

When they were alone again, Shiels said, "My mother sometimes drives me nuts, and sometimes she says wise things. One thing she said to me not long ago was, 'Just because a big wind blows, it doesn't mean a tree is going to fall on your house.' But sometimes, obviously, a tree does fall. It crushes everything. How . . . how do you survive that?"

"You don't," Linton said. "Not really. You might still be standing, but you won't be the same person. All of us . . . we all go through everything, pretty well. There are no short-cuts. But at some point you find yourself alone with a terrible beauty. I don't know what to call it. But it's naked, it's alive, it's all around us. The Brits have a word: gobsmacked. That's how I feel sometimes." He gazed off, then back at her in a piercing way. "This place might not seem like a sanctuary to you. But it is to me. From here I can look out my window, and every so often I come across some really remarkable person—she just walks right in here vibrating with life, and I think, *Maybe I can help this person.*"

It was almost too much to bear, that gaze. "You have, Linton," she said. "You have helped."

He got up, made a show of rearranging a small display of wrestling shoes.

"Anyway," he said, "after that big bloody wind, either you just keep hating the rest of your life, or you get on with it."

On the run home, up the hill, Shiels tried to lean from her ankles, to hold her stomach firm, to breathe from her belly, pump her arms. Her stride got shorter and shorter. It didn't feel easy, but she didn't stop, she didn't falter for lack of breath.

The crows didn't leave her alone. They flew high above her in increasing numbers, squawking amongst themselves some great news she wished she could understand. It was something about her, she thought—yet how could that be? How could crows know anything?

Anything about her and Pyke?

At Roseview and Vine, Jocelyne Legault now stood waiting for her. Were the crows behind that somehow? "Pretty good stride," Jocelyne said when Shiels was close enough to hear.

Was it? Or was Jocelyne just saying what Shiels was hoping to hear?

"I need to see Pyke." Jocelyne looked different somehow—bulky in her winter jacket, her shoulders broader, as if she'd been lifting weights for some reason, beefing up.

Shiels asked if everything was all right. "I've been thinking about the legal defense," she said. "Does your uncle need to—"

"I just need to see Pyke," Jocelyne said.

They fell into stride together, walking. It wasn't far to the house.

"When's the next court date?" Shiels asked.

"My uncle has all the details." Jocelyne's voice seemed tight, as if she were holding back, trying not to say too much.

"Jocelyne, what is it?"

"I just need to see him," the runner said.

In the kitchen, Shiels's mother was making bouillabaisse, the smell of which filled the entire house. Cut-up sections of weird-looking fish filled a large cutting board, waiting to be boiled, and two lobsters sat, sullen and twitching in the sink, their claws bound shut with thick elastics. Oysters, tins and tins of them, were spread across the counter.

"Jocelyne Legault is upstairs with Pyke," Shiels said to her mother's back. "She's Pyke's girlfriend. The one he really loves."

Shiels's mother did not turn, but in the counter mirror Shiels saw that her nose . . . her nose had gone purple. Just like her own, and like Jocelyne's.

"*What have you done, Mother?*"

"We need to feed him very, very well," her mother said.

"I mean your nose!"

Shiels's mother turned finally. "I'm just showing solidarity with his case." Her hands were sticky from fish guts. "We are harboring him, after all."

"*Is that all you're doing?*" From upstairs, Shiels thought she heard squawking, as if crows had somehow penetrated the house.

"Yes. That is all," she said calmly. "But clearly he affects me, too, maybe in some maternal way. I don't think he has a mother. Certainly not nearby. I think he feels quite alone in this world. Now, you tell me, young lady, where did you go today? And don't say school, because school called for you."

"I'm taking a break. I don't expect you to understand. I work at a running-shoe shop."

Daughter and mother eyed each other across the fishy

expanse of the kitchen. Steam from the bouillabaisse was beginning to fog the windows. Her mother looked ridiculous with a purple nose. But maybe . . . maybe no more ridiculous than did Shiels herself.

Shiels fled to her room, her sanctuary, but there was no peace. Her window vibrated with crows trumpeting something from their perches, cloaking all the neighborhood trees. And just down the hall Jocelyne and Pyke were involved in . . . well, who knows what they were involved in? They seemed to be squawking themselves, the floor vibrating with whatever they were doing. Shiels imagined that if she took those few steps, the door might not open to her. She imagined that if it did . . . she would not like what she saw.

How dare Jocelyne invite herself into Shiels's own home and then get up to whatever it was she was getting up to with Pyke? The old Jocelyne would never have . . . Well, none of this would've happened if she had simply remained a running champion. What was she turning into now?

Shiels could not help herself. Her feet took her into the hallway, where Jonathan was standing outside the guest room door, ready to burst in himself. "What are they doing?" he asked.

"Get out! Get out now!" Shiels screamed. There was so much baseball bat in her voice, the boy ran along the hall and downstairs.

Fleeing to their mother, no doubt.

Shiels burst through the door. It was freezing inside—the window was wide open. Outside, crows were dashing against themselves like paparazzi scrambling for a glimpse.

Of Pyke and Jocelyne Legault.

On the bed. And around the bed. And above the bed. And knocking into walls—a lampshade tilted crazily—and rolling on the floor, like two beasts wrapped in one covering, in Pyke's wings. At first they were moving so fast, Shiels couldn't tell exactly what was going on. Was he hurting her? Murdering her? Where did he stop and she begin?

Jocelyne's coat lay ripped open on the floor by Shiels's feet; one torn pant leg dangled from the bed. Should Shiels try to pry them apart? How could she? She couldn't even move. A crow suddenly broke into the room, flew around her head and exited.

The interruption startled her into action. "Jocelyne!" she cried. She grabbed a pillow and swatted at the pair of them, as if they were bats loose in the bedroom. "Let her go! Let her go!" But there was nothing to grab—wings were everywhere, and sharp claws, Pyke's beak, flashes of Jocelyne Legault's white flesh against Pyke's glistening purple hide.

The pillow ripped, foam and feathers spilled out, and Shiels had to step back. What were they doing? What could she do? Why had she thought—

Shiels backed up another step, then another. The roiling

couple stayed still for a moment. She caught a glimpse of Jocelyne's face, of her ecstasy, the flushed peace in the middle of what otherwise seemed to be mayhem.

Shiels didn't mean to stand staring. She turned finally, allowed her feet to take her from the room.

XXX

Shiels sat in a living room loveseat lump while her
mother held her. Where was her breathing? She didn't
know what she was doing. Somehow air went in and out,
though her lungs felt full of sand.

"I'm sorry I brought him into the house," Shiels said.

"You couldn't have stopped them from doing what they
did," her mother said, strangely calm, unalarmed. She certainly didn't feel this peaceful, this accepting, about the
dodgy conduct of any of her own children!

But it did feel good to be held like this. Shiels hated
being enemies, this ache as if she had to leave everything.

"I think they're done now," her mother said.

The crows were done, at any rate. Silence seemed to
have frozen the household.

Done what? Shiels wondered.

Jonathan was sitting on the loveseat opposite, holding himself, looking pale and stricken, as if a relative had died.

"How do you know what they were doing and if they're done yet?" Shiels whispered to her mother.

Her mother gripped her tighter. Shiels felt she couldn't be squeezed any further. "I just have a sense. I have spent the last couple of days getting to know him. I sang to him, I tickled his back, the way I used to tickle yours. Do remember, when you were very young?"

Shiels did remember. Her mother's warm fingers. Her soothing voice, the silly songs they made up together.

I built for you an igloo
of straw and glue and leather shoes
waiting for the snowfall . . .

"Did he tell you . . . what was going to happen?" Shiels asked.

"He's a force of nature. We can't really hold him much longer. Or Jocelyne. They are bound together. They always have been. You've known that, I think. Haven't you known that?"

"I don't know what I've known. About anything!" Shiels blurted.

Her lungs were full of sand. Her body ached for no reason, it just did, through and through. Yet she kept breathing. The house had not fallen down. Outside the front window, the yard looked as it always did this early in the winter.

The steam from the faraway kitchen bouillabaisse licked the edges of this window too.

"I wanted to have a feast, and a normal night, for when your father gets home," Shiels's mother said.

Shiels did not know when Jocelyne Legault left the house. It happened quietly, whenever it was—perhaps when Shiels was in the kitchen numbly chopping vegetables for the side dish for dinner, or when she sat by herself in the smallest main floor bathroom hugging her knees to her chest, trying to shake free from her thoughts.

When her father came home, no one said anything about what had gone on—not Jonathan, who retreated to his room, not Shiels's mother, who kissed her husband deeply at the door and poured him a glass of Palacios, the absurdly expensive Spanish wine he had bought at a charity auction. Shiels felt like she was six years old again, all eyes and ears, but not saying a word, not bringing any attention upon herself.

"I hope that comes off," her father said about the new darkness of his wife's nose.

"It's for a good cause," she replied serenely.

Shiels's father was full of the details of the shoulder reconstruction he had performed that afternoon, and while Shiels took in his words, she focused primarily on how animated he was, talking about the torn labrum, the ligaments.

How attentive her mother seemed. She was giving him what he needed at the end of a long work day, but also pretending that the world was still spinning on its right axis.

Maybe it was?

At some point Shiels was simply aware that Jocelyne had left the house, by some method or other, that there was no danger anymore of her father walking upstairs and stumbling in on . . . something fierce and wild and unnatural or perhaps all-too natural. Something unusual, at any rate, and disturbing. She did not glance again into Pyke's room, but she imagined the gashes in the wall, the ripped rug, the pillow guts everywhere.

When Pyke came down for dinner, he seemed himself: unruffled, gleamy-eyed, dignified, the same fierce smile spread all along his prominent beak. His crest was fully crimson again, almost throbbing with color. He moved with vigor. Clearly he had regained his strength after his days in prison. That beast roiling with Jocelyne around the guest room was not some invalid marshaling his meager resources. He rippled again. He lightly clutched a slice of fresh baguette and dipped it into the bouillabaisse with all the élan of a pterodactyl in his prime.

Pyke has entered his prime, Shiels thought.

The three small wing fingers gripped the soup spoon with surprising dexterity. He slumped, but not badly. He ate everything. He eyed Shiels's mother as if they had a bond going back half a million years.

Shiels supposed Pyke must have a real mother some-where, out there in the wild. But maybe she was half a world away.

"What's new on the court case?" Shiels's father asked, when all the compliments had been paid to the chef, and everything seemed so normal and sincere that Shiels was almost ready to rip herself from the table and run screaming from the room.

"I'm sure there will be a breakthrough soon," Shiels's mother said, "but you know how long these legalities take. Have some more wine, dear?"

He would, he did. Shiels noticed, in particular, how Jonathan watched the entire scene—their parents' almost scripted interactions, Shiels's growing discomfort, the ptero-dactyl's blossoming table manners—with hungry eyes.

Future psychologist?

Shiels left the table as soon as she could.

She noticed through the living room window, in the darkness, lights on the street, vans, people milling around. No, not just people, reporters!—with cameras. Keeping their distance but looking in on them. Shiels pulled the drapes quickly. "We've been found out!" she said. Her mother, father, and Jonathan rushed to the living room to look.

Pyke seemed happy to continue eating, oblivious.

"They can't come onto our property!" Shiels's mother said. "We don't have to talk to them!"

A cameraman seemed to be filming them as they looked out the window, and Shiels's father pulled them all back and let the drape fall. "How much longer are we supposed to shelter him?" he asked.

"As long as he needs our protection," her mother said.

The situation could not last much longer, and it didn't—much later, in bed, in the middle of a scorching dream of running barefoot in desert sand with Pyke circling above her, Shiels tried to cry out. She sat upright, and there was Pyke, hunched halfway on her bed, his huge eyes so close, his beak lodged impudently between her breasts against the outside of her pajama top.

Even in the shadows she could see that his crest was flaming red.

She tried to scream, but her throat cracked, she was so thirsty from the dream.

"Weez . . . weez go!" Pyke whispered in the darkness.

"Where? Go where? To the bathroom?"

"You zee. You zee."

She was still half-asleep. He nudged her out of bed. She threw on some clothes, including her yellow shoes—she still could feel a disappointment from her dream that she hadn't been wearing them.

"Do you need help?" It was dark but not the dead of night. The red digits of her alarm caught her eye. 5:17. "You can't go outside," she said. "The press are there now. The police will track you."

His security bracelet was glowing around his neck in the semi-gloom.

A cold wind worried the windowpane. And the crows were back, raising a racket from some nearby rooftop.

"You can't leave. You're under house arrest. If you disappear, we lose your bail money, which does not belong to you. It belongs to the Wallin boy whose arm you tore. Besides, they'll find you, they'll—"

He edged his beak under the window, levered it open.

"Pyke! You can't— "

But he could. In a heartbeat he slid out the opening. Somehow she felt like an accessory, but she could do nothing to stop him. She ran down the stairs, flung on her coat, threw open the door. Crows everywhere, God, and the wind was stupidly cold. Ghostly clouds lined the dark sky. She scanned the swirls of flying crows. Where was he? Gone already?

"You zeet! Zeet!" There he was by the garage, gesturing to her. "Zeet!"

The press vans were still parked on the street, as quiet as death. But they would wake up, photographers would soon be on them. The police would—

She had to stop him!

"Zeet!"

She ran at him, he raised his beak. He wouldn't slash her, would he?

"Zeet!"

She grabbed what she could—his neck, the security bracelet. He hopped, she flung herself along his body, straddling him to hold him down.

He would not stay down.

She thought she might crush him to the ground with her weight but he was strong—of course he was—and she was nothing to him, she realized. His back held her like she was made of balsa wood.

He exploded them both into the air, jumping upright with all four limbs then pumping, pumping his wings with everything he had. She was almost bucked off. A cloud of crows had to scatter to make way. She held on, held on.

Far below she caught a glimpse of someone stumbling out of one of the press vans, dropping his camera, slipping on the ice.

She thanked the skies she had thought to wear her winter coat. From the first rush of cold wind, upon liftoff, the freezing air screeched past her, hollowing her out, it seemed. How was Pyke even equipped to deal with such icy cold sucking the heat from his lithe body? He seemed to be a warm-climate sort of beast—hadn't his kind died out because of planetary cooling? Yet his wings brought them higher, above the trees, into the even cooler reaches, past the water tower. Shiels clamped her bare hands around the ring, lay still, tried not to pull too hard, which might choke him.

"Put me down! Pyke! I'm freezing!"

He didn't seem to hear.

Her mitts were in her coat pockets. She forced herself to release the fingers of her left hand . . . *Ow*, like chopping through ice. But her hand was the ice. Hanging on with just the right now, she found herself slapping the side of her coat absurdly. How could she even grab her mitten if she couldn't feel her fingers?

She could feel them a little bit. She clasped something, pulled it to her mouth—woolly. Jabbed her hand at it. Pyke screeched at her, wobbled midair. She shifted wildly, then righted herself and tried again to insert her left hand. Mitted!

She held on. She held on. She nearly dropped the other mitten on the way to her mouth but fought the thing onto her hand anyway. Then after a time her feet seemed the coldest. Those yellow shoes really were flimsy. She tried to curl and release her toes. . . .

"Put me down!" she yelled. "Where are we going? How much longer?"

Pyke's wings beat relentlessly. His back . . . began to warm up. He was like an electric blanket beneath her. He climbed, climbed. It took forever. Yet at some point he was not pumping his wings so often but just soaring on the air current. She had a sense of thousand-mile migrations, of circumnavigating the globe.

His body heated up in the effort, and she was warm wherever she could touch him, cold everywhere else. She pressed her hands alternately against his neck. It helped for a while, but her balance felt so precarious that she couldn't allow herself to ride one-handed for long. She wouldn't last, she couldn't—did he understand that?

"I'm freezing! You're going to have to put me down. I'm sorry! I'm sorry!"

Why—why was she sorry? For being weak. For not being able to stop him. For not having wings of her own. For being heavy, and cold, and clumsy, and slow to understand. Ever since his arrival she had failed to grasp fundamental things about who he was, what he was doing here. Yet now, with his wings spread so wide beneath her, his power to shrug off the weight of the world, she had a sense of something important . . . that would not fit into words.

She allowed herself to look down. The Earth was white and brown and both hugely solid—stretching everywhere but the sky—and insubstantial somehow. A rumor of firmness far, far away.

Something that could be leapt from, left behind.

Even in the mittens, her fingers were killing her!

"Pyke, please, I can't hang on!"

But she could. She did. She hung on so hard that she didn't know if it would be possible to let go. Her hands, her arms, her shoulders and back and legs were all clamped into place. Her heart might chill into a hard unbeating block, but she would still hang on.

She would hang on because, well, it was all becoming clear the longer they flew. Whatever had happened the day before with Jocelyne, whatever that was, he had chosen *her*. The knowledge of it spread through her against the cold.

Pyke had chosen her! So where were they going? His lair, then? Some giant nest of his on a mountaintop far from the midget hills of Shiels's hometown? Would others be there — brother and sister pterodactyls, squawking and squabbling like their cousins the crows? Mom and pop pterodactyls, babies? A valley full of lumbering, ancient beasts, like in some impossible movie?

What was that? She thought she saw one flash by in the distance, another pterodactyl. Lighter, smaller perhaps, it was hard to tell. As she strained to see, her left leg interfered with Pyke's wing — they stalled for a moment midair, before she was able to kick her legs painfully into place again and Pyke fought back into flight. His wing muscles were so strong, she could imagine herself crushed in the recovery effort.

But his body was warm. In her core now she bathed in the heat of him. (*He had chosen her!*) Some part of her remembered lying with Sheldon—this must have been something like that. Some part of her relaxed into a sort of loving embrace of this flying man-bird taking her . . . somewhere.

He felt strong, capable, as if he knew what he was doing. (Although as she gripped the security bracelet, it did occur to her the police would know he had escaped, there would be pursuit of some sort, cars with flashing lights, maybe even helicopters. Yet how remote that seemed! She pictured Inspector Brady looking up wearily from his stack of paperwork, exhausted at the prospect of chasing after a fly-away pterodactyl and his fangirl.)

She didn't see mountains. Below them was a tiny road, civilization still. Where was the other pterodactyl?

Shiels didn't dare look behind. *Just hang on, hang on,* she thought.

High up in the nest, that's where he's bringing me.

To his family and friends, who would look at her puny yellow shoes, her pathetic little darkened nose. What would they think? Probably they would shriek in their own secret language and peck out her liver.

"Pyke! Put me down!" she said, more whisper than a cry, since her jaw did not seem to be working anymore, her words were hard inside her.

How long was the flight? She did not have a good sense of it. Daylight leached into something else, not quite night. Tears froze on her face. It was hard to keep her eyes open to see. Pyke was warming parts of her just as other parts felt chilled beyond her command. She had to remember to hold on. She glimpsed a river below her, frozen white in the gray gloom. Trees, rocks, shoulder-like hills. The white of the ice and snow now seemed to be reaching to grab them . . . but Pyke pulled up, the frozen river was curving. A carpet of black appeared now on a new stretch of white. The carpet shimmered, then exploded into flight. It looked like black fireworks on a white backdrop blooming below.

The crows. A mass migration of them, a cacophony of crow song, or whatever it was. Whatever they were saying to one another.

Was real. It seemed to Shiels that everything in the last few impossible months had been leading up to this moment, with the ice screaming closer and closer, not a smooth surface either, not glassy, but frozen in chunks, some heaved up by the force of the water below, jagged and hard and . . .

Ow!

They hit something and bounced. Shiels felt the blow

in her shoulder, then they were rolling, rolling . . .

(*God!* Why had Pyke never learned to land properly?)

A bounce and something sharp again on her knees and then . . .

Still.

(The crows flapping all around them.)

Still.

On the ground.

Alive.

Her hands, her arms, would not move. Pyke seemed folded up beneath her, like that fossilized version of him she'd glimpsed in prison. He roused himself, struggled to his feet, but her fingers were still clamped to his neck choker (she couldn't let go, it would take a crowbar!).

It would take crows. A storm of them all around her, not pecking at her digits but prying them open. She thought her fingers might snap off like Popsicles twisted apart . . .

Ah! Ah!

She fought free and staggered to her feet.

"If you *ever* . . . do that . . ." Her voice cracked. She wasn't sure she could speak.

She was surrounded by a universe of crows.

"*Where the hell are we?*" she croaked.

On a frozen river somewhere in the backcountry, hemmed in by whitened hills pixelated with dark trees in the gloom. On the shore a few collapsed buildings, graying with age, were also cloaked in crows. The roar of them hit her full force—as if her hearing had been knocked out but now was online again.

Pyke stood unsteadily, his chest quivering with the effort.

Was this it? The honeymoon spot? How was she supposed to live here? Or were they just resting, were they actually heading somewhere even more remote, more private, more their own?

He did look, somehow, bravely heroic just at this moment. Obviously exhausted from the flight, his muscles spent, but he still sported that mischievous grin, and he was looking at her in naked love, starving with passion. It was true, what a romantic gesture to stage the breakout and fly her all the way here just for this moment when they—

Unless, of course, he wasn't quite looking at her. She glanced behind. Another pterodactyl, the one she'd glimpsed sometimes flying near them, now stood a distance away, wings folded, staring back at Pyke.

They were gigantic, these two, surrounded by the crows.

They pulled each other like planets entering mutual orbit.

She did not move, the female pterodactyl. She didn't have a crest. The back of her head was rounded. She was smaller. Her feet were yellow. She looked . . .

"Jocelyne?" Shiels cried out.

Jocelyne's gaze did not waver. It was Pyke who moved

first, stumbling toward her, while Jocelyne stayed where she was, quietly catching her breath the way she did when she had broken some record on yet another long-distance run. Pyke staggered to her on the uneven footing, hop-hipping, his wings spread but clearly too weak for any more flight, at least for now. Jocelyne flew at him—he leapt at her, more than anything else—and they collided and locked wings. They spun and fell together with the crows swarming around them, cushioning their fall.

"No way!" Shiels yelled, picking past the ice chunks as she stepped toward them. "No way do you get to fly me here to watch you have pterodactyl sex yet again!"

The crows scattered, the lovers looked at her like something they didn't understand.

"Why am I here? Am I supposed to become a pterodactyl too? Part of the harem? Where are my wings?"

The wind shrieked, her body was chilled through. The two pterodactyls were not talking . . . not talking to her.

"Because I'm not doing it. I'm not! I had a life . . . I *have a life!* I'm human. Do you understand that?"

It was like yelling at the wind. Pyke—he thought he was God's gift, he thought he could just scoop her up and fly her against her will . . . practically against her will . . . all the way to this frozen stretch of—

It felt like the spell broke, like the sudden cracking of ice, like those endless pictures of glaciers falling away into the ocean. (What was the word? Calving.) This wasn't her place. This wasn't her. She was *human*, she had to . . .

Get over this hallucination, this ridiculous romantic fascination that had so upended her life! Pyke didn't love her. He loved her shoes, for God's sake. He wanted her to grow wings and a beak, to repopulate the world with shrieking little baby pterodactyls! But she was human, she had a brain, a life, a plan to go to college. All right, it wasn't flying above the clouds for hours against the sun, but it was her life, *hers*.

"*I'm human!*" she screamed at him.

She had to act like a human, she had to . . . organize something.

Heat, for example. She wasn't some flying, writhing, shrieking beast. She was not equipped. Her teeth were rattling now, she had barely recovered control of her limbs, her gut was a chunk of ice. She had read about hypothermia. This was a crucial stage. She needed fire, she needed . . .

She thudded off to the nearest abandoned shack. What was this, a mining community of some sort, disappeared now back into the bush? The walls slouched, the roof was partially caved in. How old was it? No way to tell. The door was frozen shut.

For God's sake!

She kicked at it, the wood splintered, she fought her way through.

(How could she have fallen in love with a shrieking pterodactyl?)

She needed fire. It was truly black inside for a moment, but then her eyes adjusted. She hurried past the collapsed beams into the middle, to what used to be the kitchen. To a crumbling counter. To drawers . . . that would not open. The wood had jammed into place with the awful settling of the house. . . .

If Shiels ever survived this, what was she going to say to Jocelyne's mother? "It's all right, Mrs. Legault. They fly, hunt, and fish together. I'm sure Jocelyne will be wonderful at hatching the young."

Jocelyne's mother, who might not be alive too much longer anyway.

A rusted oil drum crowded everything. Shiels almost knocked it over, getting to another drawer, which did open—old, cold cutlery. And in the drawer below: paper napkins, still wrapped in crinkly plastic that fell off when she picked up the package.

She could use the drum to house the fire. The paper to grow it.

She had no matches.

Outside, the screaming of the crows, and now of Pyke and Jocelyne, reached new heights. The beasts and birds were all warm with their movements, she felt sure, but she was going to freeze senseless in the next few minutes.

Already her fingers, her hands were reacting spastically—
she wasn't sure she could light a match now even if she
were to find one.

The drum smelled oily. Maybe just a spark would do it.

She was no Girl Scout. Rub two sticks together? She
didn't have two sticks. She pushed the paper napkins into
the drum. They fell in a clump. In reaching down to spread
them out, she felt frozen chunks of old burned logs. So the
drum had been used for fire before.

There might be matches.

She would never have Pyke. Couldn't have him! Impossible. Not all for herself. Yet she'd fallen anyway.

In the cupboard above the sink—nothing.

She wanted to live.

She wanted to go to college. She wanted to pay back her
parents the lost bail money, and raise a hundred times that
for the boy who'd nearly lost his arm. All her fault! Because
of her infatuation with a freak of nature. Because of what
that freak had unleashed inside her.

She had things to do with her life!

Another cupboard near the rusted fridge. The blasted
thing opened finally. . . . A dead, frozen rat fell out and
bonked the counter.

"Ah!"

Right beside the glass jar of matches that had been in
front of Shiels's face all along.

What did Pyke think she wanted to be, anyway—a freaking pterodactyl?

Her fingers worked. Barely. The first two matches fizzled, but the third flamed long enough for her to drop it into the drum, which did indeed have the residue of something oily. It leapt into flame so suddenly, Shiels had to step back. Just as quickly, it seemed, the fire died down again and Shiels regretted, in a sudden shocking thought, having thrown all the paper napkins in at once. The half-burned frozen logs would not catch fire so easily. She ripped the cupboard door off its hinges—where did that strength come from?—and splintered the board against the counter. She spilled the kindling into the drum, hoping.

She grabbed a fistful of matches—all of them—then threw them into the drum and blew and blew.

She said to herself—"I'm sorry, Sheldon. I loved you, but I didn't know it. I didn't act it. Didn't treasure who you are."

She said, "Linton, if I see you again, I want to know about your wife and your boy and girl, Don and Samantha, not about the accident but about *them*, who they were."

A dull flicker of flame.

To her parents she said, "Forgive me. Forgive me! I forgive you."

She blew till she could hardly breathe anymore. The flames licked the edges of the kindling from the smashed cupboard. So she smashed some more. She tore up some of the floorboards, the ones that were sticking up anyway. She didn't care when she ripped her mitts and bloodied her hands.

Even Jonathan she wanted to see again. She missed that gleamy look in his eyes when he was chewing pizza and thinking about something ridiculous.

He wasn't ridiculous. Neither was she. She had things to do with her life.

The fire grew, and she knew she was not going to die.

She was not going to die. In the growing glare of the lovely warm fire the rest of the cabin disappeared into darkness. She could hear the uproar outside getting closer, closer, but she was so soothed by the hard-won heat that it took her a while to realize her fire was drawing the pterodactyls, Pyke and Jocelyne, back to her, and with them the crows. She fed the burning drum bigger and bigger boards. Soon the flames shot up to the cracked and slumping ceiling. Soon the beasts and birds began to spill in and out the broken-down door, much as they had in the gymnasium after Autumn Whirl, when Pyke had summoned them to help her out.

Flashing out of the darkness, Pyke glinted in the sharp light, shrieking as if onstage. She felt her blood coursing like the dark waters under the frozen river so close by. Maybe the spell was not broken?

Is this how it happened? A sort of animal madness grows within, and Jocelyne Legault presses her way into someone else's bedroom to mate and roil until she, too, becomes a winged thing? Was the darkened nose the start of it? Was Pyke trying to engulf Shiels in this fire now? Was this Autumn Whirl all over again?

The crows were feeding her cabin fire now, bringing twigs, branches, busted boards and scraps of faded clothing, long abandoned. Flames scratched the ceiling, leapt into the darkest corners, then retreated again, and the rising, roiling, shrieking dance of birds and beasts did not stop. Shiels remembered Jocelyne dressed in black, whirling herself, before the wrangle dance, which reinvented itself now within Shiels's kindling body.

(She did feel a flame, a burning from within. But she was awake now, she knew what was happening.)

What was happening?

Her body floated above the flames, almost (that was how it felt), she was lighter somehow, like ash dancing on the current.

(This was not a surrender. She was awake, wide awake! It was a dance.)

A current of air.

(Sweating now. In hypothermia you end up shedding your clothes. The last remaining heat has fled your core and so you feel hot, deluded.)

But she was sweating from the dance, from genuine heat, some firestorm awakening in her.

The shrieking Pyke, up against her, crows blacker, larger than night. And Jocelyne, too, all of them writhing as the flames danced.

Dancing as the flames licked.

("It isn't *about* the dance," Lorraine Miens said in a quiet part of Shiels's brain still able to watch it all unfold. "You *are* the dance. Find out what dance you need to be.)"

This dance. This night. Dream or no dream. After all that had happened, now she was here, moving like an underground river. Her body loosening, finally. Breathing, throbbing, twisting, soaring.

There was no denying it, she had to move with it, she had to stay awake and keep her wits and . . .

In the middle of the flames.

The whole house on fire.

With the crows fanning. Pyke laughed, Jocelyne waved her new wings. . . . They were outside in a moment, the fire was just bigger, they danced around it, and those who could fly rode the updrafts. . . .

Shiels steamed from the inside. The more brightly the old cabin burned, the more the rest of the world disappeared into surrounding darkness until it was possible to believe the world was gone, the cabin had become the sun, they were all whirling around it boiling on the inside, freezing where their backs were turned to the night.

What part of it was dream? What was possible and what

not? This frenzy? Hour after hour? Where did the carcass come from, carried in torn-apart pieces by crows to be set upon? Did Pyke slash it with his beak? Did Jocelyne spear and guzzle her share? Was it a wolf? A deer? Struck by a far-off car in the night and carried here by the murder of crows?

Was it carrion?

How long had it been frozen before being passed through the flames again and again, to feed their feast?

Was this the spell again, Pyke reasserting his power? If Shiels ate her share, would she cross over? Was this the cliff-edge leap that would force folded wings to crash out through the bones of her back?

She had already crossed so many lines. And she was hungry. Pyke tore a strip of flesh. He dangled it, danced with it, teased her, shook it slowly, then quickly, as she lunged, starving for it.

"I am human!" she yelled at him, and her voice was strong, full of flame.

Dream or not, maybe this was exactly where she needed to be: her frozen river, her burning cabin, her endless night.

She seized the flesh finally, gorged herself. Chilly and burned at the same time.

She grabbed more from the beak of a passing crow, fought off others, heard herself laughing.

This was her dance. Her night to feast, without fear, to burn the whole thing down.

XXXI

In the morning she awoke on a battered board not far from where the cabin fire still steamed and hissed. Sunlight trembled on one side of the surrounding hills. The river sounded louder, ever-flowing beneath the ice.

She was cold, stiff, hungry. The twisted head of a moose carcass glared at her through glassy eyes.

Really? A moose?

Yet here it was, gigantic, half-emptied, its flesh and guts spilling into the ashes.

Silence.

Shiels examined herself, and laughed—her arms were still arms, legs still legs. But oh she was sore from yesterday! Her shoulder from the landing, her hands from hanging on to Pyke so long then tearing up those boards, everything aching and stiff from the fitful few hours of cold sleep before a dying fire.

High in a fir tree she spied what seemed to be a pair of ancient handbags hanging together from a limb. Pyke and Jocelyne—they were rousing themselves too, unfolding their wings sleepily. Jocelyne pushed off, stretched out and caught an updraft as if she had been doing it all her life. Pyke sprang after her, and the two circled each other, calling and shrieking.

There were no crows. The white frozen river looked mostly innocent of any debaucheries from the night before. A few glistening black feathers littered the snow. New frost was forming on some of the cinders.

Pyke's security bracelet lay near her feet. How had he pried it open? Had the crows, or Jocelyne, last night—

Pyke and Jocelyne circled, circled, came closer and performed a sort of flypast, swooping low toward Shiels then pulling up, shrieking, waving. She could not join them, not now, never again. She was stuck in this aching body, unfit to be a beast.

She smiled, she cried at the thought of it.

Good-bye, good-bye! the pterodactyls shrieked, and soared away.

Shiels picked up the abandoned security bracelet, clicked it shut. Was it still working? Surely the authorities would find her now, if she hung on to it. It wouldn't be long. Her parents would have haunted the police station all day and night, urging action! Or was she beyond the reach of the signal?

She moved farther along the riverbank. There, by more abandoned shacks, was a snow-covered road. She was wearing her yellow running shoes, her torn mitts, a winter jacket not meant for wilderness.

But this was a road. A thin crust, good footing.

She could stay, she supposed, maybe even coax more heat from the remnants of last night's fire. But it didn't really seem to be an option. As she moved, her body began to forgive her. She started along, whacking her sides to warm herself. She was hungry but she had eaten of last night's half-scorched roadkill moose. (Could crows bring down a moose by themselves? Even ten thousand of them?)

She began to run. It only seemed natural. She straightened herself as Linton had taught her, leaned from her ankles, tried not to overstride. Where was her breathing? (In her belly, down below.)

Her feet felt lighter than usual.

She warmed up rather quickly, considering everything, and all of her began to feel lighter.

She imagined herself suddenly becoming Jocelyne Legault (who had, after all, suddenly become a flying beast), perfectly sure and light of foot, effortless and quick, with stride after efficient stride.

She felt quick. Her eyes seemed . . . stronger. She picked out a tiny movement from all the way across the river and halfway up the hill, far in the distance. Pyke and Jocelyne, just specks now against what was becoming an astonishingly bright blue morning sky.

She could see their fine wings, could sense their hearts thrumming with the delirium of flight.

We know you, they were saying.

She felt again the warmth of clutching Pyke while he had flown her far above the Earth.

Now Pyke and Jocelyne circled higher, getting smaller, until they disappeared behind the sun-blessed hill. The road took a curve then too. When it straightened out again, the flying beasts were gone, swallowed by the sky. Impossible to prove they had ever been there.

She surprised herself. She reared back suddenly and, perhaps channeling Jeremy Jeffreys, hurled the security bracelet as high as she could. It soared, lodged perfectly in an upper tree branch, a startling throw. There it stayed, glowing slightly against the darkness of the fir. Surely it would not be long before a crow stole it off, some new prized possession to be deposited even deeper in the woods.

On, on she ran. It felt good now, this human body of hers, like it was made to move, to travel great distances.

Stride, stride, posture, breathing. Was this a dream? The whole thing? Just this moment, right now, seemed more real than anything could be. A curve coming. Shiels sped up, leaned into it, took it on.

Who was she? her footfalls seemed to be saying.

Who was she now?

Many turns later the road straightened out, she climbed a hill, her stride was holding. Ahead of her she saw a red pickup truck angled into the ditch, the battered hood propped open, an elderly man in a trucker's cap, a heavy coat, and tired boots leaning into the engine. He straightened up at her approach, wiped his face with the back of his hand. He looked hurt. His forehead had a welt on it. "Are you out here—jogging? Really?" he said. "Did you frostbite your nose or something? Looks like you're peeling."

Her nose did feel itchy. She touched it, and a corner of skin came off, purple on the surface. In the reflection from the truck's side mirror she could see the skin beneath was lighter, almost pink.

"Nothing serious," she said. "What's happened to you— are you all right?"

He smiled crookedly. "Been rattled worse in my time, I guess." The truck really did look banged up, the body dented badly, the windshield broken but held together in parts with new-looking tape. "Blame thing. Took the wrong road last night, hit a moose come from nowhere. Bung my head up against the steering wheel. Truck's so old, doesn't even have an air bag. Lucky to be alive, really. Must've been dazed. I swear about a million crows come swarmed me, some of them dastard huge, excuse my language."

"Really?" Shiels said.

"Never seen anything like it! Completely forgot my phone had a camera! Not that I know how to use it. The grandkids are gonna laugh!"

He was tall, snowy-haired. He had a kind grin, some of his teeth. Something about his bearing reminded her of Linton.

"Sometimes strange things happen," Shiels said.

"Need a lift somewhere? I'm just about to give this rig another try. Think I can make it back to Duggan." He lowered the bashed hood, fastened it somewhat closed with a bungee cord.

Where the hell was Duggan? It didn't matter. The guy climbed into his truck, and she stood with her hands on her hips breathing, looking at everything: morning dawning on the hills, a frozen river so white it almost hurt to take it in. He tried the engine. It shrieked, coughed, then turned over and started to purr. Then he threw it into reverse and she jumped out of the way as he wrangled the wreck back onto the road.

"Get in!" he cried, and the mangled passenger-side door swung open all on its own. She climbed up. The seat belt didn't work. She had to hold the door closed. The cold wind blew in through a dozen cracks and gaps.

"I swear one of those crows," the driver said, "had a beak this big!" He abandoned the steering wheel for a moment, stretched his arms as far as they could go. "No one's going to believe me. And I don't know how the bloody moose survived impact and walked into the bush. But I sure couldn't find him in the morning. No tracks—gone without a trace! How'd *you* get here, anyway?"

He had an easy smile, as if used to a gobsmacking world, to telling stories wide and wider.

"I guess I just flew in," she said. "How far to Duggan?"

The drafts were cold, but her body was warm still, her heart full to swelling.

"Not more'n twenty miles. You runnin' the whole way? You some elite athlete or something? Should I know who you are?"

Bump, bump—the truck rattled like it might come apart any moment, but kept on rolling.

"Shiels Krane," she said, and felt herself smiling from the roots of her hair to the arching soles of her yellow shoes.

Author's Note

First of all, my deep thanks to Libba Bray, whose January 2012 lecture at the Vermont College of Fine Arts, in which she briefly mentioned the fascinating nature of the ptero-dactyl boyfriend experience, set me on the path of the cur-rent study. Her throwaway remark lit up a constellation of thoughts and considerations within me. When I told her of my burgeoning interest, she immediately gave me her bless-ing. Libba—I did go for it, as you can see. Many thanks!

Due to the sensitive nature of my research, few of my study subjects agreed to speak on the record, so I am pre-senting this work in its entirety as a "fiction." The charac-ters and events described are not true to life; locations have been obscured, and all names have been changed. The one notable exception, of course, is Professor Lorraine Miens, who declined to be interviewed, citing privacy issues concerning a current student. Her works are well-known and speak for themselves.

Heartfelt thanks to several funding bodies that made the investigation and completion of this work possible: the Canada Council for the Arts, the Ontario Arts Council, the City of Ottawa Arts Funding Program, and the Berton House writer's residency program in Dawson City, Yukon, sponsored by the Writers' Trust of Canada, with additional help from the Dawson City Community Library board and the Klondike Visitors Association. Truly, this financial backing and artistic encouragement have been invaluable over the years it has taken to complete the effort.

I also write with the love and support of an extraordinary family. Without my brother Richard's example and enthusiasm, I would never have pursued writing as a lifelong vocation. My daughters, Gwen and Anna, brother Steve, niece Ashleigh Elson, and sister-in-law Wendy Evans all read early drafts and helped shape the work, as did dear friends Helena Spector, Kate Preston, and Kathy Bergquist. My mother, Suzanne Cumyn, has always read my initial efforts with loving interest and in this case was especially encouraging in her enthusiasm for my ongoing pterodactyl studies. My wife, Suzanne Evans, tenaciously helped me sort through a number of difficult sections with her usual unerring instinct and iron determination. Many thanks as well to my agent, Ellen Levine, for championing this work from the moment she saw it, and to my editor, Caitlyn Dlouhy, whose passion, patience, skills, and insight were invaluable throughout, especially considering the wildness of the undertaking.

Finally, a note of gratitude to paleontologist Mark P. Witton for his scholarly yet accessible work *Pterosaurs*, and to the American Museum of Natural History in New York City for their enlightening exhibit *Pterosaurs: Flight in the Age of Dinosaurs*, both of which were invaluable in helping me access my own inner pterodactyl.

Any inaccuracies in the physiology or psychology of teenage pterodactyl behavior, and all other deficiencies in the work, remain, of course, my responsibility.

Alan Cumyn
Ottawa, April 2015